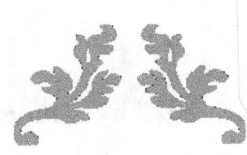

Dream Agents

The Intergalactic Awakening

Warriors of the Cosmos

Written by

Simon Mennell

Disclaimer

This book is a work of speculative fiction. It explores advanced technology, extra-terrestrial life, and futuristic concepts, none of which should be interpreted as scientific fact or predictive certainty. While some elements may draw from real-world theories, the events, characters, and worlds depicted are entirely fictional.

The views and opinions expressed by the characters are their own and do not necessarily reflect those of the author or publisher. This book is not intended to provide scientific, legal, medical, or philosophical advice. Readers seeking factual guidance on any topics mentioned should consult relevant experts.

Neither the author nor the publisher assumes any responsibility for interpretations, actions, or consequences arising from engagement with the content of this book.

DEDICATION

To Ailsa and Rory

In a universe filled with endless possibilities, always dream big and reach for what seems impossible.   You are my greatest dream come true.

TABLE OF CONTENTS

CHAPTER 1

The Fall of Sankat 3

In the dark, silent void of space, at the outer fringe of Rivaxian territory, Sankat 3 stood as a breath-taking oasis—a moon shimmering beneath the radiance of two suns. Nestled within the vibrant twelve-planet Arisara System, this stunning celestial body, nearly the size of Earth, orbited a majestic gas giant that loomed like a titan in the sky.

Swirling bands of turquoise and gold interwove, casting a hypnotic glow over Sankat 3's surface, transforming it into a mesmerizing tableau of life and colour. It was the year R50, cycle 3, on Zylar 15—a time marked by impending change.

As the twin suns lingered high in their slow, stately embrace, they bathed the landscape below in hues beyond imagination. Their golden light pierced the canopies of ancient trees, their twisted trunks forming elegant shapes, while swirls of brown and orange bled into the earth, creating a cathedral of verdant splendour. Below, vibrant flora exploded in a kaleidoscope of colours, each bloom pulsing with life, releasing fragrant waves into the warm air. Giant, antlike creatures with elongated necks rummaged through the fallen foliage, pausing to communicate in bubbling tones as they worked.

Deep turquoise lakes dotted the terrain, their tranquil surfaces glistening in the morning sunshine, reflecting the twin suns with mesmerizing precision. Beneath these waters lurked a myriad of life, gliding effortlessly, blissfully unaware of the world above. Within the crystalline depths of Sankat 3's lakes swim the Haldriane, a wondrous creature embodying the enchantment of this mystical world. Imagine a being with the graceful elegance of the human form, yet cloaked in the magic of the aquatic realm. A strikingly beautiful female visage, her features radiating serene strength—a gentle, knowing smile that seems to hold the secrets of the universe.

Its body, akin to that of a dolphin on Earth, begins just below the shoulders, where two arms extend with effortless fluidity. It glides through the water, blending agility and grace in a mesmerizing display of motion. Its skin glistens like polished opal, casting shimmering reflections as it dances beneath the surface before suddenly leaping across the waves. The slight curvature of its torso highlights its powerful muscles, allowing it to navigate the lakes with astonishing speed—appearing both ethereal and formidable in its domain.

Perhaps most captivating is its hair—an extraordinary spectacle, flowing like seaweed that drifts gracefully in the water. Golden in hue and luminescent, as if kissed by the rays of an otherworldly sun, each strand shimmers with glints of emerald, fading to green at the tips, forming an enchanting halo as it moves. When it swims, its hair billows around it like a mystical veil, evoking the image of a goddess rising from the depths.

The presence of this mystical creature symbolizes the delicate harmony between the land and waters of Sankat 3, embodying the planet's fusion of magic and life. Rivaxian legends tell of them as the sacred guardians of the lakes, protectors of hidden knowledge and ancient wisdom. Those fortunate enough to witness one are often left spellbound.

As it surfaces for a breath, it casts an almost hypnotic aura over its surroundings. It emits melodic sounds, communicating with the lake's other inhabitants, harmonizing in a symphony understood only by the aquatic life of Sankat 3.

In this extraordinary world, the Haldriane serves as a bridge between reality and fantasy—a living reminder of the beauty and mysteries hidden beneath the waters, and an invitation for adventurers to delve into both the lakes and the depths of their own imaginations.

Mountains encircled the lakes, their snow-capped peaks shimmering in a pale blue hue as they stretched toward the skies. Giant parrot-like creatures, with wingspans of at least 20 feet, soared overhead, their calls echoing like the haunting songs of Earth's whales. This was truly a moon like no other.

Nestled within the breathtaking beauty of Sankat 3, the last hope for the Rivaxian species lay hidden behind the fortified walls of the Tanexa V facility—an expansive refuge that mesmerized visitors with its stunning landscapes and tranquil allure. On the surface, it appeared to be a luxurious sanctuary, where intricate gardens flourished in a riot of vibrant colours, each petal kissed by the twin suns. The air was rich with the scent of exotic blooms, their delicate sways orchestrated by the warm, whispering breeze that drifted through them. As the wind drifts through the bushes, it carries a soothing, soft whistle.

Delicate pathways weave through lush, wooded expanses, flanked by towering trees that offer both shade and a profound sense of tranquillity. The gentle rustling of leaves harmonizes with the melodic calls of birdlike creatures, composing a symphony of nature that beckons wanderers to explore the majestic landscape. Sunlight filters through the canopy, scattering intricate patterns across the ground, while secluded glades provide serene retreats, inviting moments of peaceful solitude within this vibrant sanctuary.

Scattered across the gardens, shimmering lakes and tranquil ponds glisten under the sunlight. Elegantly designed fountains punctuate the landscape, sending cascades of water soaring into the sky, where the light catches each droplet, transforming them into radiant rainbows. These fountains infuse the surroundings with an enchanting allure, deepening the serene ambiance that envelops the facility.

In this enchanting utopia, expansive white domes rise gracefully above the landscape, their architectural elegance harmonizing effortlessly with the surrounding natural beauty. Each dome serves as a vibrant hub, housing a variety of amenities and inviting spaces where guests and residents can gather, connect, and unwind amid the splendour of their surroundings.

A monorail glides effortlessly through the expanse, seamlessly transporting passengers from one breathtaking location to another. Its smooth, fluid motion provides a surreal perspective, showcasing the magnificent gardens and shimmering lakes from a vantage point that enhances their grandeur. As the train follows its elevated path, the landscape unfolds like a living tapestry, evoking awe and wonder with every turn.

Beneath this serene exterior lay the true heart of the operation—forty levels deep, buried within the moon's core, the main research and storage facility thrummed with purpose. This underground fortress, where the lifeblood of the Rivaxian people was preserved and studied, housed some of the greatest scientific minds, tirelessly developing new methods to secure their species' survival. Here, temperatures remained at sub-zero levels, delicately sustaining millions of embryos in cryogenic suspension—the last whisper of a future, flickering like a distant star.

The corridors were lined with state-of-the-art equipment, their walls designed to cultivate an atmosphere of calm, fostering creativity and collaboration. Softly illuminated panels cast a soothing glow, while all around, advanced research unfolded—whether in the creation of groundbreaking pharmaceuticals or bioengineering projects seeking to solve the universe's most pressing dilemmas. Yet, despite its magnificence, Sankat 3 was not a place of boundless innovation. It was the final hope of a dying race.

Their home planet faced an unprecedented challenge—an extinction-level event. Though the planet itself remained intact—its buildings unscathed, its infrastructure preserved—the once-thriving world of Rivaxia had been irrevocably altered by the Varak Tri bomb. A catastrophic technological marvel, it was developed by the Nythrix, a highly advanced species known for creating and selling weapons to the highest bidder. The Varks, a ruthless species driven by an unyielding desire for conquest, had acquired this devastating weapon. Designed to deliver maximum destruction without warning or sound, it was a silent spectre of annihilation—insidious and treacherous.

Deployed some 50 years ago from an untraceable ship hovering silently in the upper atmosphere, the weapon detonated with a pulse that rippled outward like waves upon water, extending far beyond the surface of Rivaxia. As it erupted, invisible shockwaves pierced the air, saturating the atmosphere with lethal particles that spiralled downward, enshrouding the entire planet in an ominous veil of despair.

The bomb did not ravage structures or landscapes; instead, it silently infiltrated the air, seeping into the very essence of existence. For months after the attack, its true devastation remained undetectable, its lethal effects lurking beneath the surface. At first, life seemed to go on as usual—families carried on, oblivious to the looming catastrophe. Over time, a grim reality took shape—one that would alter the course of their civilization forever. The Varak Tri had rendered the population irreversibly sterile, their ability to reproduce stolen in an instant. A once-thriving world descended into an abyss of despair, where the laughter of children faded into haunting silence, leaving behind only the echoes of shattered dreams.

As cities remained unscathed, brimming with memories yet empty of future generations, the bitter truth took hold—the Rivaxians were on a slow march toward old age and, ultimately, extinction. Their future had been stolen, severed like threads from a magnificent tapestry, unravelling the fabric of family and community. The spectre of sterility cast its shadow over every aspect of life, suffocating the once-vibrant spirit of their people beneath a heavy shroud of grief.

In the face of this stark reality, they did not waver. From the depths of sorrow, they forged a collective resolve, standing together in defiance of despair. Their hopes turned to Sankat 3, a lush oasis they believed to be safe from Vark attacks—at least, for a time. There, they established Tanexa V, a fortress dedicated to preserving the last embers of their future. They harvested as many eggs as possible from the remaining females, traveling to distant outposts to secure what little remained. More than just a sanctuary for embryos, this facility became a beacon of survival.

A towering species, standing at least eight feet tall, with striking green or deep electric blue eyes and human-like skin tones. Their heads were slightly longer than those of humans, but their mouths, noses, and ears were identical. If not for their imposing height, they could almost pass as human.

Leading this vital endeavour was Professor Zuk Nall, a revered elder in the field of genetics. With an illustrious career spanning both military and medical disciplines, he was renowned across the galaxy for his groundbreaking research. His towering presence, enhanced by a penetrating gaze that conveyed both wisdom and urgency, commanded the respect of his peers. His deep green skin shimmered under the sterile facility lights, reflecting an almost otherworldly glow. With a subtle touch to the implant on the side of his head, he adjusted his eye lens, bringing the floating holographic displays into sharp focus. Intricate genetic sequences and research data flickered before him, demanding his full attention.

Zuk Nall was supported by a small yet highly skilled team of dedicated researchers, each a master in their respective fields. Among them was Dr. Fem Dam, a strikingly intelligent molecular biologist whose keen mind was matched only by her unwavering determination. Her obsidian hair cascaded in waves down her back as she meticulously operated the sequencing machines, analysing samples with a vigilance that reflected her deep commitment to the cause.

Beside her worked Tarek Its, a young bioengineer whose infectious enthusiasm often eased the weight of their work. His jagged auburn hair framed a face etched with determination, and he blended technical prowess with innovative thinking. One striking truth about Taxana V was its absence of youth—there were no young people. Everyone was at least 50 Earth years old, most far older.

As they searched for ways to save their species, an idea emerged—to transport their DNA across the galaxy. Tarek Its was tasked with designing the micro-ships that would serve as vessels for their genetic legacy. He had repurposed the very technology the Vark had used to disperse their bomb, but this time, for an entirely different purpose.

The lab hummed with activity, and amid the steady rhythm of research, Dr. Fem Dam exchanged a smile while conversing with another technician.

"I'm heading back to Rivaxa in two days, and I'm so excited! My brother is getting married. I know a lot of people stopped celebrating weddings once we learned our fate, but it's wonderful that they still want to go through with it. It's a rare moment of happiness for our family—we haven't had a wedding in over 30 years." The technician glanced back and smiled.

"That's great! Let's have dinner tonight to celebrate. My family stopped doing things like this a long time ago." With that, they returned to their work, scanning screens and conducting tests.

Dr. Fem Dam left the lab and walked down the corridor, pressing a series of numbers on a keypad before placing her hand on the glass screen beside it. The door slid open with a swish, and she stepped inside, the familiar scent of ozone and sterilizing solution filling her nostrils. The low hum of the machinery was ever-present—a constant reminder of the monumental task at hand.

The lead technician, Jax, stood before a complex array of shimmering holographic displays, his face etched with an intensity that bordered on obsession. His fingers danced across the console with practiced precision. Around him, three other technicians, their faces illuminated by the ethereal glow of the screens, worked in focused silence. They were all immersed in Project Chronos—a top-secret endeavour to manipulate the very fabric of spacetime. Only a select few within the Rivaxian council knew of its existence—Cha, the Elders, and a handful of trusted individuals. The official purpose—a carefully constructed narrative meant to obscure the true ambition—was the preservation of Rivaxian embryos. The lab, a hidden fortress deep beneath Sankat 3's surface, stood at the heart of a mission that could reshape the fate of civilizations. The very air thrummed with the potential to rewrite time—a power both exhilarating and terrifying.

Zuk Nall walked into the room, his gaze sweeping over those present.

"How much progress did you make yesterday with testing the Temporal Chrono Spectra Modulator (TCSM)?" he asked.

"We're getting pretty close," Dr. Fem Dam replied. "I'd say we're about eighty percent there."

"That's good. It is essential that it works, even though I hope we may never have to use it. Have a good evening—I'm heading back; I'm exhausted," Zuk Nall said, patting Dr. Fem Dam on the back as he walked out the door and into the corridor.

Early the next morning, the lab began filling with people. When Zuk Nall entered, a worried and puzzled expression clouded his face.

"Morning, everyone. Tarek Its, are the ships ready to take on the DNA?" Zuk Nall asked, his voice edged with urgency.

"Yes, they're ready. I've already conducted several test flights—they work perfectly," Tarek Its replied confidently.

"That is excellent news—and likely just in time. I'm sorry to be the bearer of bad news, but I've just received word from Rivaxia. The unthinkable has happened." Zuk Nall paused, his expression grave. "The Vark have finally broken through our last outer defences in the system and are now heading straight for us. They will be here within hours, if not sooner.

"Although we have the orbital shield around the moon, it likely won't hold their attack for more than a day. I've been informed that they are close to acquiring the codes to shut it down. Our primary concern now is to protect the embryos.

"I need you all to begin deleting any files and data that could be used by the Vark. Ships are waiting to evacuate you back to Rivaxia. Please, work quickly—once your files are cleared, board the ships immediately. We have very little time!"

"I'll start deleting the files now," Dr. Fem Dam said.

"No, you need to get on the ships now. I'll take care of that," Zuk Nall insisted.

Dr. Fem Dam looked at him with a slight smile. "No. The future of our species is here. I'm not going to leave just to save myself."

Zuk Nall exhaled sharply. He pulled Dr. Fem Dam into a side room, lowering his voice. "I need you to take all the data we have on the TCSM and get it back to Rivaxia. You and the team working on this must leave immediately. This is not up for debate—you must go as soon as you've downloaded the files."

Dr. Fem Dam nodded, though hesitation flickered in her eyes. "I understand. But I want you to know—I wanted to stay here with all of you, not run away."

"I know that, but your duty is now back on Rivaxia, continuing the research. Otherwise, all of this will have been for nothing. Plus, you have your brother's wedding to attend," Zuk Nall said with a faint smile.

Dr. Fem Dam managed a small smile in return. "How can I think of weddings now?" she murmured.

At that moment, Dr. Aris overheard the tense exchange between Zuk Nall and Dr. Fem Dam, and a cold chill ran through him. Had they been deceived about their true purpose on Sankat 3? The thought gripped him like a vice as he slipped away toward the waiting ships, his heart pounding. Behind him, the Vark loomed ever closer.

Back in the main room, the team was frantic. What felt like mere minutes had stretched into hours. A violent thrum reverberated through the ground, punctuating their urgent conversation. The tremors felt like death creeping closer, each moment amplifying their sense of vulnerability. In the suffocating silence, uneasy glances were exchanged, each expression reflecting the gravity of the moment.

Dr. Fem Dam turned and ran down the corridor. Within minutes, she had secured the data and was boarding the evacuation ship, tears streaming down her face. She knew she would never see Zuk Nall alive again.

"Did the evacuation ships get away?" asked Zuk Nall.

"Yes, they did, sir," came the reply.

"Thank the mighty Cha for that."

Tarek Its looked up; his eyes wide with concern. "They're getting closer, aren't they?" he asked nervously, glancing at Zuk Nall.

"Too close. They are relentless," Zuk Nall replied, steeling himself for what was to come. "But we need to stay focused now more than ever. This facility is built to withstand considerable force, but we'd be fools to underestimate the Vark's determination."

As they got to work, the facility's cutting-edge technology sprang to life. Robotics whirred into action, securing cryogenic chambers and reinforcing critical areas with seamless automation. Holographic maps projected the Vark ships circling above, their positions shifting in real time, while a countdown timer marked the moments until invasion.

As they got to work, the facility's cutting-edge technology sprang to life. Robotics whirred into action, securing cryogenic chambers and reinforcing critical areas with seamless automation. The air inside Tanexa V crackled with tension as Zuk Nall sprinted toward the central command terminal, urgency propelling him forward.

The embryos lay secured beneath an almost impenetrable forcefield, its energy shimmering and flickering like a protective halo. Zuk Nall's twin hearts pounded in his chest as he barked orders to his team. "Set the explosives!" he commanded; his voice resolute despite the swirling anxiety that filled the vast chamber.

"This is our final safeguard—if they breach the forcefield, the embryos must remain protected." The weight of the moment bore down on them all, but Zuk Nall felt it most. They weren't just defending the last remnants of their lineage; they were preserving the very essence of their future.

Tarek Its, ever diligent in his duties, nodded sharply as he worked rapidly at his controls. "The first wave of micro ships is ready to launch now, sir!" he declared, his voice a mixture of excitement and apprehension.

Zuk Nall shifted his focus to another terminal, his fingers dancing over the controls as he activated the screens before him. The holographic display illuminated the vast operations room, revealing a video link with the Cha, the esteemed Rivaxian Nam and their leader. Dressed in Tudor-style robes of kingfisher blue intricately woven with gold thread, a striking medallion of gold and ruby red adorned his forehead, making him appear every bit the regal king of his race.

"We are ready, mighty Cha. Activate the micro wormhole," Zuk Nall said, his voice tinged with urgency as he locked eyes with the Cha on the screen. "Understood. We are forever in your debt for this sacrifice. May the Sacred Nur protect you all," the Cha replied, his gaze burning with fierce intensity.

The screen flickered and went dark as the weight of responsibility settled over Zuk Nall like a heavy mantle. Moments stretched into eternity as anticipation pulsed through the air. Then, without warning, the sensor readings spiked.

"Micro wormhole detected!" someone shouted, their voice a mix of disbelief and exhilaration.

Zuk Nall clenched his fists, channelling his worries into focus.

"Launch the ships now!"

Engines roared to life, arcs of energy trailing in vibrant hues as the ships hurtled toward the yawning darkness of the wormhole.

"This should only take a few moments," Tarek Its said, his voice tight with tension. But as the first ships slipped into the shimmering portal, alarms blared throughout the facility. The Vark had detected the sudden energy surge from the launch. "What is that energy surge?" screamed General Thexis, the imposing leader of the Vark forces, from the command ship hovering high above the moon.

His voice resonated with authority and urgency. Beside the General stood his loyal Pyronyx—an awe-inspiring creature, a true marvel of the Vark world. This wolf-like beast possessed a sleek, armored body that shimmered with iridescent scales in deep crimson and molten gold, embodying the very essence of fire.

Roughly the size of a large goat, it boasts two powerful front legs that anchor it firmly, while a set of four muscular hind legs propels it with incredible speed and agility.

With each movement, a rhythmic clicking emanates from its armored joints, echoing through the air like the ominous patter of distant thunder.

With eyes that shimmer like embers and sharp, elongated fangs, the Pyronyx can unleash formidable blasts of fire and corrosive acid, capable of melting through solid rock. Its connection to its owner runs deep, bound by a telepathic link that transcends worlds, ensuring unwavering loyalty until death.

However, if its master dies, the Pyronyx possesses the rare ability to bond with a new one, forging a fresh connection that preserves its fierce loyalty and untamed spirit. As it prowled the landscape, the very ground trembled beneath its feet—a harbinger of both beauty and dread.

"General, they appear to be launching something, but we can't determine what it is yet!" came the frantic response, thick with tension.

Without hesitation, the general yanked the soldier away from the console and slammed his hands against the controls. "They're launching micro ships—FIRE NOW, YOU INCOMPETENT FOOLS! THEY MUST NOT GET THROUGH THE WORMHOLE!" General Thexis bellowed.

His fleet erupted, plasma guns unleashing a relentless barrage toward the wormhole.

"They hit some ships, sir, but several from the first wave made it through," Tarek Its reported.

The Vark unleashed a relentless barrage of missiles, each streaking toward the surface and hammering the facility. Every explosion sent shockwaves rippling across the landscape, painting it in violent flashes. The sky swarmed with panicked wildlife, while animals on the ground bolted in terror, desperate to escape the onslaught.

Vark soldiers deployed in vast numbers from their ships, descending upon Sankat 3 with the ferocity of storm clouds—armoured, relentless, and ready to claim what they deemed rightfully theirs. Clad in jagged, near-impenetrable black Armor, they moved like an unstoppable force.

Their fully covered heads gave them an almost robotic appearance, yet there was no machinery beneath—only ruthless, battle-hardened warriors. Renowned across the galaxy, they showed no mercy to their enemies.

The Rivaxians fought back fiercely, their advanced technology clashing with brute force in a desperate struggle for survival. The fate of their kind hung in the balance.

Amid the chaos, Zuk Nall's voice cut through the commotion.

"Tarek Its, we need to send the last of the ships now! It's now or never!"

The urgency in his tone sent a surge of determination through the command centre. Time was slipping through their fingers like sand.

Tarek Its reacted instantly. He activated the final launch sequence, his fist slamming against the console as the last ships roared to life.

Meanwhile, Zuk Nall rallied his remaining forces. "All units, focus on the northern flank! We need to create a diversion!"

The Rivaxian warriors advanced with unwavering precision, their powerful frames silhouetted against the chaos of battle. In a breath-taking display of unity and strength, they surged forward, unleashing a relentless barrage of firepower. Their weapons sent shockwaves tearing through the invading Vark lines, carving out a fleeting yet vital window of opportunity for their desperate escape.

The ground shook with ferocious intensity as Vark missiles rained down, scarring the land, toppling trees, and disrupting the delicate balance of life that had long thrived on this moon. Yet, the Rivaxians, driven by the weight of their history and the fragile hope of survival, surged forward, fighting tooth and nail—not just for their embryos, but for the very soul of their race.

With the final launch mere moments away, Zuk Nall cast a fleeting glance skyward, his heart hammering against his ribs. The last remaining micro ships hovered at the wormhole's edge, their fate hanging in the balance.

"Now!" he bellowed, his voice cutting through the chaos.

Engines roared to life as the final fleet surged forward, vanishing into the swirling maw of the micro wormhole. The shimmering portal pulsed once before swallowing them whole.

Across the horizon, explosions ripped through the battlefield, fire and smoke choking the sky. Yet, amid the devastation, Zuk Nall felt it—a surge of hope blazing through the chaos. "We sent them through! Now let's make sure they survive!" he shouted, rallying his forces, their determination burning with the belief that the Rivaxians' legacy would endure.

And with that, they threw everything they had into the fight, a surge of resilience igniting within them. The battle raged on, but it was more than a struggle for survival—it was a testament to their spirit, tempered by adversity and burning defiantly against the encroaching darkness. The fight for Sankat 3 was not just a last stand; it was a battle for their very existence—a fight for a future that would echo beyond the stars.

With that, the wormhole snapped shut. "Yes! Yes!" shouted Tarek Its. "Let's hope they make it to Earth."

The fleeting triumph was shattered by the deafening roar of bombs and laser fire above them. "They're here!" Zuk Nall shouted, the realization striking like a bolt of lightning. The Vark forces had breached their outer defenses and were closing in on the heart of their stronghold. Amid the chaos, the weight of their dire situation made every heartbeat feel like a ticking clock. Urgency etched into his face; Tarek Its forced his way through the turmoil.

"Zuk Nall, I'm going down!" he shouted, determination blazing in his eyes. "Someone has to protect the embryos. Detonate the charges once I'm there."

Zuk Nall shot him a sharp glance, fully grasping the weight of his decision. The forcefield might shield the embryos for now, but if the Vark broke through, there would be no time left. "Hurry!" he urged; his voice tight with desperation as he watched Tarek Its rush toward the lift. Tarek Its nodded, urgency propelling him forward. "With its own energy supply and everything I need; I can hold out for years!"

Without hesitation, Tarek Its stepped into the lift, offering a brief wave, his expression resolute as the doors sealed shut behind him. Zuk Nall watched, knowing this was a farewell—Tarek Its was sacrificing himself to safeguard the last hope of their people.

Tension tightened like a vice as Zuk Nall turned to his team. "Detonate the charges!" he ordered, his voice steady and unyielding. "Lock down the embryos!"

A series of confirmations echoed through the comms, and with that, Zuk Nall felt the floor shudder beneath him as the explosives armed. The countdown began, each second a weight pressing against their resolve.

Alarms blared, their piercing wail reverberating through the chamber as they braced for what came next. The charges were primed to form a protective barrier around the embryos—a cocoon of destruction meant to keep them from falling into Vark hands, no matter the cost.

"Stand by!" Zuk Nall shouted over the wailing sirens, his focus razor-sharp. The air crackled with tension, thick with desperation and urgency. "We just need to hold on a little longer!"

Then, a thunderous series of explosions tore through the facility, shaking its very foundation. The forcefield flickered, struggling against the shockwaves as the blasts sent tremors rippling through the walls. Echoes of chaos rattled their nerves—then, as the dust settled, an eerie silence descended, a fragile calm in the wake of devastation.

Zuk Nall scanned his team, their faces etched with disbelief and reluctant awe.

"Put down your weapons," he said, his voice heavy with solemn finality. "There's nothing more we can do. We surrender. We were never soldiers."

The weight of those words settled over them like a shroud, the bitter taste of defeat sinking deep. Their once-unshakable resolve wavered, cracking beneath the relentless advance of the Vark.

Suddenly, as if conjured by fate, General Threxis strode through the billowing smoke, his formidable presence slicing through the eerie stillness of the aftermath. At his side, his loyal Pyronyx prowled, muscles coiled, ready to strike at the slightest movement from the Rivaxians.

"Who commands here?" he boomed, his voice a deep, resonant force that thundered through the ruined space. The air thickened with tension as General Threxis locked his piercing gaze onto Zuk Nall.

Zuk Nall's twin hearts pounded as he stepped forward, forcing himself to meet the General's intense gaze.

"I am the one in charge," he said, his voice steady despite the turmoil within. "What you've done here is an atrocity. You've tried to erase us, but you're too late. You will fail."

Threxis glared at him, a low growl rumbling from his throat. The deep black eyes of his helmet gleamed with cold scrutiny. Then, without warning, he struck Zuk Nall across the face. But Zuk Nall stood firm, bearing the weight of their struggle, desperation fueling his resolve.

"We have lost so much," he continued, his voice trembling but unwavering. "Those embryos are our last hope. You will not have them."

In that moment, as Zuk Nall stood before one of his civilization's greatest threats, the weight of their history and the fragility of their future pressed down on him. The stakes had never been higher, their fates hanging by a tenuous thread.

"Take them away for interrogation. And shut off those alarms," General Threxis boomed as he dropped into the chair, casually propping his boots on the console.

The escape ships hissed and trembled as they touched down on the designated landing pad, Rivaxia's shimmering heat haze twisting the already surreal landscape. One by one, the pods hissed open, releasing the dazed Rivaxians. Dr. Fem

Dam was the first to emerge, her face lined with exhaustion yet set with determination.

She moved past the waiting medical team without hesitation, her gaze sweeping over the assembled dignitaries. She walked toward the Cha, his commanding presence filling the chamber. His typically stoic expression flickered with something akin to relief as he watched her approach. He extended a hand, his touch unexpectedly gentle.

"Dr. Fem Dam," Cha said, his voice a low rumble that carried through the hushed assembly. "I am relieved you are safe. Zuk Nall's sacrifice, and that of the others, will not be in vain. The Council of Elders has entrusted you with his legacy."

"Project Chronos now falls to you. We have lost much, but our resilience must drive us forward. Your dedication and expertise are vital, and the road ahead will be arduous. But you, Fem, are the one who must lead us through this turbulent time. The fate of our species may rest on your shoulders."

"Dr. Aris, observing the exchange from across the room, noticed Cha's gaze linger on Dr. Fem Dam just a moment longer than necessary. His own expression remained unreadable, but there was a hint of something—an underlying tension, perhaps. A subtle flicker in his gaze as Cha spoke of potential failure, a rare crack in his usual composure."

CHAPTER 2

◦◁◇▷◦

Whispers Across Realms

The year was 1975, and the air at the Kennedy Space Centre in Florida buzzed with excitement and possibility. Under the warm Florida sun, gleaming white buildings stood tall against the endless blue sky—a testament to humanity's ambition to reach beyond the stars.

A steady stream of onlookers, tourists, and scientists moved through the expansive grounds, their lively voices mingling with the hum of engines and the rhythmic buzz of machinery. Families wandered through the exhibits, children pointing skyward in awe at the massive rockets poised for launch, while technicians and engineers hurried past, their minds racing with plans for upcoming missions.

Stars and Stripes flags fluttered in the gentle breeze, and the scent of adventure hung in the air—an intoxicating blend that fuelled the hopes of a nation on the brink of unprecedented achievement. As the world outside buzzed with life, inside a spacious office, the walls were adorned with models of spacecraft and photographs of astronauts who had become national heroes.

At the centre of this hub of ambition sat Lewis Gell III, the head of NASA—an authoritative figure in a sharp suit, his dark hair cut in a precise military style. Leaning over his desk, which was cluttered with blueprints, reports, and mission plans, he sifted through his thoughts, the gleam of determination sharp in his eyes.

Suddenly, he broke the silence that hung in the room like a thick fog. "Who is the greatest mind in the world on sleep and dreams?" he asked, his voice cutting through the stillness.

A soft murmur rippled through his leadership team, each member exchanging knowledge and theories like the volatile reactions of a chemistry experiment. Finally, one bold voice broke the tension.

"Professor Rory Walker, head of the faculty for sleep at Harvard Medical School. He's pioneering ground-breaking research in the field." "Anyone else?" the NASA director asked, scanning the room. No one spoke.

"Very well," he said, the corners of his mouth lifting in a determined smile. "What do we know about the professor? I want you all back in my office in 30 minutes with a summary." Seth Rogers, the brave soul who spoke came back in to provide the background summary.

"Professor Walker is a Harvard graduate and has led the Sleep Disorder Centre at Harvard for 15 years. He is highly regarded by both his colleagues and students for his relaxed yet knowledgeable approach. He's unmarried, his parents have passed away, and he has one brother in California, though they are not close.

He has been published in numerous journals, collaborated with Brigham and Women's Hospital on sleep research, and authored three books on the subject. He is, without a doubt, the leading expert in this field."

Lewis looked across and said, "We need to get him here. It's time to start the program."

As plans swiftly unfolded, a team of professionals boarded their government-issued vehicles, heading toward the private jet waiting on the runway. The rich aroma of fresh coffee filled the cabin as they took off for Cambridge, Massachusetts.

Arriving at Harvard, they navigated the campus, weaving past grand buildings steeped in history. The group entered a lecture hall filled with eager students, their lively discussions and laughter resonating against the walls. Professor Rory Walker, a man in his late fifties, stood at the front, his hands animatedly expressing the intricacies of the human mind, weaving together facts about sleep architecture, the stages of dreams, and the emerging understanding of the subconscious.

As the lecture concluded and students began to disperse, the professor gathered his papers, offering a quick smile to those who lingered, still captivated by his insights. The academic atmosphere buzzed with energy as chairs scraped against the floor and messenger bags rustled, but he remained focused, collecting his notes with the ease of well-practiced routine. Just then, a tall figure—a commanding presence—emerged from the shadows of the now-empty lecture hall. His sharply tailored uniform cut a powerful silhouette against the dim backdrop. Professor Walker, clad in his usual tartan waistcoat and brown corduroy trousers, looked up, curiosity piqued.

"Excuse me, are you Professor Rory Walker?" the commander asked, his voice laced with authority—though he already knew the answer.

"Yes, I am," Rory replied, intrigue threading his tone. "How can I help you? The commander stepped closer, the gravity of the moment settling as he leaned in and whispered into the professor's ear,

"I am here on the authority of the President of the United States. You need to come with me now, sir "Really? The President of the United States? What on earth would he want with me?" Rory asked with a chuckle, his eyebrows lifting in disbelief. He glanced around the empty hall, trying to gauge the seriousness of this unexpected encounter.

"Sir, you'll find out soon. I'm not authorized to discuss this, but I need you to come with me now," the commander replied, his tone firm and business-like. "Now, sir—please. We have a jet waiting on the tarmac." Rory hesitated for a split second, a whirlwind of questions swirling in his mind, but curiosity pushed him forward. What could the President possibly want with him? Surely, he didn't have sleep issues. Rory looked at the commander, tilting his head with a slight smile before saying,

"I'm afraid I can't just drop everything and go with you, even if the President himself requested it. My job, my students—Harvard needs me. It's not that simple. I can't just walk away."

The commander leaned in, locking eyes with Rory. "Don't worry about that Professor, your 6-month sabbatical leave has been granted by the Dean, effective immediately. Here, takes a look for yourself" The commander handing Rory a signed approval document. Rory grabbed the document and gave it a quick glance.

"Okay, I'm not sure how the hell you pulled that off, but I'm intrigued. Before I go anywhere, I need to pack a bag."

"That's already taken care of, Professor. Your bag is in the car—we picked up a few essentials from your apartment." Rory followed the commander out of the lecture hall, his steps cautious as he approached the waiting cars, wondering what lay ahead.

As Rory arrived at the vast complex of NASA, he noticed people all around him, oblivious to the monumental events unfolding before them. He took a moment to absorb his surroundings, feeling the air thrumming with the weight of ambition and discovery that permeated the site. As he was escorted through the bustling halls, the muted chatter of busy personnel and the distant hum of advanced technology filled the air, creating an atmosphere charged with purpose and urgency. Upon reaching the heads office, Rory was greeted by Lewis and two others who stood poised nearby, ready to engage in the unfolding mission.

"Welcome, Professor Walker," Lewis said, extending a hand. "I'm glad you could make it." Rory smiled at Lewis as he shook his hand.

Rory returned the smile as he shook Lewis's hand.

"I didn't exactly have a choice."

Lewis gestured to the first figure, a tall man with sharp features and an analytical demeanour. "This is Seth Hogan, VP of Satellite and Communications." Rory nodded at Seth before Lewis turned to the woman beside him, dressed in a bright red dress and silver-rimmed glasses, her smile warm as she looked at Rory.

"And this is Beth Coulson, head of SETI. She and her team search for little green men in the sky. Please, take a seat." Lewis motioned toward a large, polished conference table.

As Rory settled into his chair, he felt the weight of their gazes, anticipation crackling in the air.

"Given the circumstances, may I ask why you've brought me here—practically against my will? And how the hell did you get the Dean to approve my leave?" Rory asked. "That was easy—he's my cousin, though we don't exactly advertise that," Lewis said with a slight grin.

"What I'm about to tell you is highly classified," Lewis began, his tone shifting the atmosphere in the room. "I had to get clearance from the President of the United States just to brief you on this."

He pulled a document from a folder and slid it across the table toward Rory. "Before I go any further, you need to sign this confidentiality agreement Rory glanced down at the paper, a flush of colour rising to his cheeks as he noted—this was the second time they'd invoked the President's name.

"Wait a minute. I'm just a college lecturer. What could you possibly tell me that warrants something this serious?" He lifted his gaze to Lewis, scepticism sharp in his eyes. "I'm not sure I want to sign this damn thing—it says I could face the death penalty if I breach it."

Lewis studied him intently, his calm demeanour a stark contrast to Rory's rising anxiety. Leaning back in his chair, he crossed his arms.

"I'm afraid, Professor, this isn't up for debate. Sign it, and everything will be revealed. If not, that big guy is going to shoot you," Lewis said with a smile, his tone half-joking.

Still hesitant, but recognizing the gravity of the situation—and his lack of options—Rory took a deep breath. He picked up the document again, scanning it swiftly for details. The harsh penalties detailed in the document sent a chill down his spine, but curiosity pushed him forward. With a nod, he carefully signed it and placed it back on the desk, aware that his fate was now in motion.

"Thank you," Lewis said, his demeanour softening slightly. "I understand it may seem harsh, but that only matters if you talk—and we both know you won't." He paused, gathering his thoughts before revealing what was to come.

"Just over five years ago, we received a communication from a distant planet outside our solar system—through a wormhole. A micro wormhole, to be precise."

The word "wormhole" caught Rory's attention, sparking his fascination.

"Did you say micro wormhole? What is this, Star Trek? What in heaven's name is that?" Rory asked, his expression filled with curiosity.

"We once considered it nothing more than a theoretical concept—essentially, it's a shortcut tunnel connecting two distinct points in space," Lewis explained.

"It sounds like science fiction. But what did the message say?" Rory asked, intrigue colouring his voice as he leaned forward.

Lewis continued, "The communication came from an alien race that has been closely monitoring our progress in space flight. Once we reached a critical milestone, they made contact. The transmission contained a highly detailed set of instructions—precise guidelines on how to respond."

Rory could barely contain his excitement as the weight of the revelation settled over him. His mind raced, grasping the implications of such advanced technology and the doors it could open for humanity's future.

"What kind of information are we talking about? This is incredible!" he pressed; his voice alive with excitement.

"A lot," Lewis emphasized, his eyes gleaming with intensity. "We're talking about space travel, advanced communications, energy systems, and computer programs that push the boundaries of what we thought possible. They've even shared techniques for manipulating particles at the microscopic level. These discoveries could completely transform our capabilities. But there's more."

As Rory listened intently, he noticed Lewis's expression darken, the atmosphere thickening with anticipation. "Our first two-way communication with them actually dates back to the Apollo program. It intensified during the Skylab mission in 1973." The official narrative framed it as a program to showcase human life in space, but the truth was far more significant. Once we established that vital contact, we received an even more profound set of instructions."

As the weight of the moment settled around them, Rory leaned back in his chair, his gaze drifting to the ceiling, captivated by the enormity of what he was about to learn.

"So, the species that sent this communication—who are they? Are they aggressive, peaceful? What do we know?" Rory asked, his curiosity bubbling to the surface once again.

"They call themselves the Rivaxians," Lewis replied, his voice steady but carrying an undercurrent of excitement. "They are an advanced race and have been observing us for decades. About fifty years ago, they began sending micro-ships to Earth, and they have been dormant in orbit until the Rviaxians activated them"

Rory's mind raced. "Micro-ships? What do you mean—are they too small to be seen with the naked eye?"

"Exactly," Beth answered. "These vessels are incredibly small and advanced, so much so that even our best technology couldn't detect them. What they did was remarkable—they downloaded crucial specifications and data directly into NASA's computers. At first, it was basic information, but once we built our first computer using their designs, a floodgate of knowledge opened. It was as if we had unlocked a treasure trove of information. We had to establish a secret budget to develop a facility—one hidden from public knowledge—so we could properly respond to the Rivaxians' outreach."

Rory's excitement mingled with awe. "So, you're telling me that while the world thought we were just experimenting with life in space, we were actually laying the groundwork for interacting with an extra-terrestrial civilization? I still don't understand why I'm here, though."

"Exactly," Lewis said, the weight of the revelations growing heavier. "And we'll explain your key role in all of this. After the initial technology downloads, we realized we needed a more permanent presence on the ground—hence the construction of a specialized facility. It was designed to monitor ongoing interactions, facilitate deeper communications, and develop the technology provided by the Rivaxians." "We repurposed the old West Area Computer Company buildings for this project," Lewis explained. "We'll take you there now and outline your role. Beth, can you arrange the cars?"

Rory stepped out of the car, glancing up at the aged façade of the West Area building before heading inside. They moved down a long, dimly lit corridor. At the end, Beth stopped and pushed open a large, wooden-panelled door, revealing an elevator behind it.

"After you, Rory," Beth said, gesturing toward the elevator.

"Which floor are we going to?" Rory asked.

"Negative 27," she replied as the doors slid shut.

Moments later, the elevator opened, revealing a breath-taking sight. Before Rory stretched a vast chamber lined with advanced computers and screens—far more sophisticated than anything he had seen at NASA's surface facilities. The technology hummed with untapped potential, a realm of innovation waiting to be explored.

As they navigated the maze of intricate machinery, Rory couldn't hold back his curiosity. He bombarded the group with questions—pressing for details about the technology's origins, its inner workings, and the specifics of the alien communication.

"We've kept all of this under wraps to prevent public panic and political fallout," Lewis explained, his tone grave as he gestured toward the array of equipment surrounding them. "Every piece of technology here stems directly from the instructions we received. It's far more advanced than anything the world believes exists. The aliens aren't just observing—they're engaged, and they want to help."

Rory's eyes widened as he absorbed the sight before him—sleek consoles and towering screens mapping out the solar system in breath-taking detail. The sheer scale of their achievements was staggering. This was real science, tangible proof of phenomena he had only ever encountered in textbooks.

Along one wall, a massive screen—towering three stories high—displayed a rotating map of the solar system. The names of planets and moons, many unfamiliar to Rory, glowed in vibrant colours, illuminating the space with an otherworldly brilliance.

"This is the main room," Lewis announced proudly. "This is where you'll lead the team as we push this project forward."

"Lead a team?" Rory echoed, a mix of surprise and elation in his voice. "I'm just a lecturer—what do I know about leading a scientific endeavour of this scale?"

"Well, you're the foremost expert on the study of dreams and consciousness, and that is the key to how all of this works," Beth interjected, her expression earnest. "We believe understanding these elements is crucial to what comes next. This project isn't just about technology—it's about the human mind and its connection to the universe, something the instructions alluded to. There are people out there with abilities beyond those of normal humans."

"But first," Lewis said, "we need to find them!"

CHAPTER 3

The Search Begins

They had now moved into a spacious office in the corner of the main laboratory. "Professor, this is your office—make yourself at home. You'll be spending a lot of time here," Lewis said with a wry smile.

"Please, everyone, just call me Rory. We are all the same here, and I'd prefer we drop the formalities and simply use first names. Call me sceptical, but sending all this amazing technology makes me question why."

They stepped inside and settled around Rory's new desk as Lewis continued.

"So far, it's clear we don't know everything. But that shouldn't stop us from moving forward. What we do know is that the micro-ships orbiting Earth for decades have provided us with more than just advanced technology—they also contained Rivaxian DNA and sequencing data. We would never have been able to achieve this without their technology, and they want us to be aware of that.

Over time, these ships have been releasing their DNA payloads into our atmosphere, which has gradually filtered into the human population. As a result, certain individuals have been born with latent abilities—abilities they are unaware of, as they can only be activated within a special dream state. This has led to the emergence of a unique group we have named the 'Dream Agents.'"

Rory's heart raced as he leaned back in his chair, clasping his hands behind his head, the revelation sending a jolt of astonishment through him. "Dream Agents? What does that mean?"

Lewis took a deep breath, fully aware of the weight of what he was about to reveal. "From what the Rivaxians have told us so far, these individuals possess an extraordinary ability—one unlike anything mankind has ever seen before. They can travel through space, but not in the traditional sense. The Rivaxians have explained that their journeys take place through dreams. They enter an altered state of consciousness and, using the technology sent to us, can manifest in a physical form on distant alien worlds."

"What? You're joking," Rory exclaimed, the concept stretching the boundaries of his understanding. "How is that possible? It sounds like pure fiction."

"I'm sure it does," Lewis acknowledged, a calm smile playing on his lips. "But let us show you—it's easier to understand that way."

With that, he gestured for Rory to follow as they moved deeper into the facility. The air hummed with potential, anticipation tightening in Rory's chest as they passed rows of advanced computers and intricate machinery designed to monitor dream activity and consciousness patterns.

They entered a specialised lab bathed in soft blue light, where scientists worked diligently at consoles displaying a myriad of biometric data and neural readings. At the centre of the room stood a sleek glass enclosure, its rhythmic pulsations mirroring the excitement flowing through the team.

"Rory, this is your main team," Lewis said. "I suggest you get acquainted."

Rory's focus sharpened. "Hi, everyone. Really glad to be here—hopefully, you'll all bring me up to speed on where things stand. First question: have we identified any of the Dream Agents yet?"

"Hello, my name is Dr Rambolt. I've read all your work, and let me say—it's an absolute privilege to work with you. We've yet to identify any Dream Agents and have been awaiting your arrival."

Rory looked around the room, his eyes wide as he bit his lip.

"Then I suggest that becomes our immediate priority," he said, addressing the room. "We need to identify the Dream Agents the Rivaxians claim are already among us."

One of the technicians sprang to his feet. "We've been informed that there are five Dream Agents we must locate. They have no idea who—or what—they are, and it's imperative we find them before the window of opportunity closes."

Lewis nodded, his expression growing serious as he leaned forward.

"Rory, how do you propose we identify these individuals? What criteria should we use?"

Rory ran a hand through his thick grey hair, considering the question. "As a first step, we need access to both medical and mental health records spanning the past several decades. We should look for behavioural patterns—individuals who have reported recurring dream disturbances or psychological anomalies suggesting heightened sensitivity to their subconscious."

"We've attempted that already, without success," Dr Rambolt admitted, his tone flat.

"Are there any specific conditions that might indicate a connection to the Dream Agents?" Lewis asked.

"Yes," Rory replied, his enthusiasm mounting. "Conditions such as sleep apnoea or severe insomnia could indicate heightened dream activity. We need to identify individuals who may have been labelled 'emotionally disturbed' or classified under 'developmental differences.' It's crucial to focus on their unique perception of the world—those with an acute sensitivity to patterns, emotions, and nuances that others often overlook.

"In this context, we must look beyond the obvious. Many individuals, particularly those who have drifted in and out of hospitals, may possess extraordinary insights into the dream realm—an intuitive understanding that could help us unlock mysteries we have yet to grasp."

Dr Rambolt jumped in. "Is there anything else we should use to narrow the search?"

Rory looked at him, then grabbed a pad. "How does this thing work?" he asked a nearby technician. As he began sketching on the pad, he continued,

"Let's focus on those who may seem withdrawn or unconventional—their quiet exteriors often mask a remarkable depth of thought and perception. We're searching for individuals whose unique perspectives could shed light on the uncharted territories of our minds and dreams. Trust your instincts; the most profound Dream Agents may challenge society's preconceived notions of normality."

Beth chimed in, "We should also consider individuals referenced in psychological evaluations or studies—those identified as 'special' or exceptional in some capacity. This could lead us to someone with a stronger link to DNA modification."

Rory nodded, encouraged by their input. "Exactly. Additionally, we should investigate reports of outlier behaviours—people who may not conform to societal norms yet possess vivid imaginations or artistic inclinations that suggest a deeper connection to their subconscious. Artists, writers, and even scientists might exhibit these traits, indicating a potential for exceptional dream activity..."

"I can reach out to our contacts within the health system and educational institutions to obtain the necessary data," Beth suggested, her tone practical. "They may have records we can review without raising too many suspicions."

"That's crucial," Rory agreed. "We must tread carefully to ensure our investigation doesn't cause unnecessary alarm. This information is sensitive, and we don't want to create panic among the population or alert anyone to what we're doing."

Lewis put his hand up. "No need," he said as he walked over to a desk where a man was sitting. "This is Doctor Sean McClean, who has also just joined the team. He will assist with any medical information, as he has complete access to the world's medical records. Don't ask me how, but the

Rivaxian system can tell him what doctors write in their notes."

"Good evening, team," said Sean. "I've already started and have identified twelve potential candidates around the world. We can then reach out, conduct interviews, and gauge their dream experiences in more depth."

"Yes, but we also need to consider how we approach them," Beth stated. "These people will likely be unaware of their gifts or the involvement of the Rivaxians. We must frame our outreach carefully to avoid unsettling them."

"Of course," Rory responded, a plan forming in his mind. "We can present ourselves as researchers studying dream phenomena. This way, we create a safe space for them to share their experiences without revealing the complexities of their situation or the adventure ahead of them."

"Sounds like a plan," Lewis affirmed, glancing over the assembly. "We need to move swiftly. Time is of the essence, and we cannot afford to lose track of the Dream Agents."

With renewed determination, they began outlining leadership roles for the investigation and data gathering. Rory felt invigorated—they were assembling a task force to unravel the mysteries of dreams, consciousness, and the unseen connections woven through their reality.

As they concluded their discussion, Rory looked at his new colleagues—each one filled with the same passion as he was for the task ahead. Still, it was bewildering to think that only a few days ago, he had been lecturing at Harvard, oblivious to any of this. As he sat back in his chair, he reflected on the extraordinary journey they were about to embark on—one that could not only forge links between humanity and the Rivaxians but also unlock the very essence of reality as they understood it.

Rory had always believed that dreams were more than mere information processing by the brain. Yet now, it felt as though his life's work was on the verge of being completely rewritten, reshaping everything he thought he understood about the nature of dreams and consciousness. They stood on the precipice of something monumental—a quest that could redefine not only his career but also the future of civilisation itself.

The task ahead loomed daunting, filled with unknowns that both exhilarated and unsettled him. Together, they would navigate the intricate complexities of human experience, striving to uncover the elusive truth behind the Dream Agents. Yet, a thread of doubt tugged at Rory's mind. What were the Rivaxians' true intentions? Had they shared their knowledge freely, or was there an underlying agenda—one that could alter the course of humanity in ways they had yet to fathom?

The implications of their findings were immense; he knew they had the potential to either revolutionise their understanding of the mind or, conversely, unleash forces beyond their control. This dual edge sharpened Rory's resolve but also grounded him in the reality that the journey ahead could challenge everything he held dear. It was a delicate balance between hope and caution—the thrill of discovery weighed against the risk of misunderstanding what lay hidden within their dreams.

For now, though, he needed some sleep. It had been an exhausting few days. He grabbed his coffee cup and headed to his room.

CHAPTER 4

The First Dream Agent

As activity intensified around the command centre, a wave of urgency electrified the air. Sean McClean, his voice ringing with excitement, shouted across the room, "Professor Walker, I believe I have narrowed down the first potential Dream Agent!"

There was no immediate reaction from Rory, who was deep in conversation with one of his team.

McClean, looking around, suddenly caught Rory's eye. "Rory!" His frantic tone cut through the bustling noise surrounding them.

Rory, momentarily pulled from his thoughts, rushed over to the desk where Sean was intently working, his heart racing with anticipation.

"What have you got?" Rory asked, placing a hand on Sean's shoulder.

Sean gestured emphatically towards the large screen as it whirred to life. A world map filled the display, vibrant colours pulsating across the globe before centring on a flashing light over the Indian city of Bangalore. The screen shifted, revealing a detailed map of Bangalore, its bustling streets unfolding before them.

Moments later, the screen displayed a photograph of a young man, around twenty-seven years old, wearing thick-rimmed glasses that accentuated his bright, inquisitive eyes.

"This is Sumeet Sharma," McClean explained, pointing at the image. "He's an accountant at a company called Chowdary and Associates, based in Bangalore, India. According to his medical records, he has experienced significant issues with dreams and sleep—so much so that his doctor has been administering barbiturates to help him rest."

"Not the best idea, given the risk of addiction," Rory remarked. "Sean, please continue."

"His parents live in New Delhi, and he has an older sister who is married and lives in Bombay with her two children. No history of sleep or dream-related issues has ever been reported by her. That's it—he's a reclusive man with no real friends, just goes to work and keeps to himself."

Rory felt a rush of adrenaline course through him. "OK, thanks for that, Sean. We need to move quickly and bring him here as soon as possible," he said, urgency sharpening his tone. "Get the team ready. We're flying to India."

Within the hour, Rory and a small group of staff boarded a private jet poised on the tarmac, its engines roaring to life as they prepared for take-off. Then, suddenly, they were airborne. The aircraft soared through the clouds, traversing the oceans towards Bangalore. Rory gazed out of the window, his mind racing with the magnitude of what they were about to do—this could be the breakthrough they needed.

A stewardess approached and offered Rory a cup of coffee.

"Thank you," he replied.

"Would you like something to eat, Professor?" she asked with a smile.

"Just bring me a sandwich and an ice-cold Dr Pepper, thank you."

Seated at the main table in the middle of the plane, the team began reviewing the dossiers Sean had prepared before their flight, trying to gather as much information as possible on Sumeet before landing.

"OK, let's get some sleep. It's going to be a long day," Rory told the team.

One by one, they returned to their seats as the cabin dimmed into darkness, the quiet hum of the plane filling the space. The only light remaining was the soft glow of the overhead lamp above Rory. He was too fuelled by adrenaline to even think about sleeping.

As they came in to land at a small airport in Bangalore, the city below unfolded in a chaotic yet mesmerising display—crowds of people on bicycles, a scattering of cars blaring their horns, and the vibrant energy of the streets greeting them like a wild heartbeat. Rory felt his pulse quicken as he stepped off the plane. The air was thick with humidity, laced with the rich aroma of street food and spices, a sensory introduction to the culture surrounding them.

"Let's move!" he ordered, rallying the team as they piled into US military vehicles. Alongside the doctors, ten NASA agents were present—the muscle for this trip, should it be required.

They sped through the bustling streets of Bangalore, weaving between throngs of cyclists, honking cars, and vibrant marketplaces. The city teemed with life, a world brimming with possibility—and somewhere within it, Sumeet Sharma lay waiting.

After navigating the labyrinth of roads and alleys, Rory instructed the team to proceed towards Chowdary's building, where Sumeet worked. As they pulled up to the sleek, modern structure, urgency swirled around them while they quickly devised a plan to approach their target.

Rory stressed the need for discretion. "We can't alert any bystanders or the Indian authorities," he warned, fully aware of the delicate nature of their mission. "We need to take him quietly."

The team moved into action, coordinating with a small group of discreet agents stationed nearby. Before long, they spotted Sumeet stepping out of the office, engrossed in conversation with another man. The two suddenly stopped talking, exchanged a brief farewell, and parted ways. It was now or never.

In a seamless manoeuvre, they moved in swiftly, surrounding him just as he turned to face them.

"What the—" Sumeet's expression flickered with shock as he pushed his glasses back up his nose, confusion flooding his features. Before he could react further, they closed in, subduing him quickly and efficiently.

"Sorry for the abrupt interruption," one of the agents whispered, ensuring Sumeet couldn't call for help. "You're coming with us."

Before he could fully process what was happening, Sumeet was swiftly ushered into a vehicle, driven off through the vibrant throngs of Bangalore—so alive, yet completely unaware of the extraordinary secret stirring beneath its surface.

Upon arrival at their hidden facility, Sumeet was escorted into a secure room filled with a handful of scientists and an array of medical equipment. Rory stood among a group of doctors, waiting for Sumeet to regain his composure, adrenaline still coursing through him.

As Sumeet looked around, his eyes wide and pulse racing, Rory stepped forward. "You're safe now, Sumeet. We mean you no harm," he assured him, his voice calm yet firm. "We need to talk about your dreams. You've been experiencing something unusual, haven't you?"

Sumeet shook his head, his expression a mixture of bewilderment and unease. "What are you talking about? I—I don't know what you mean."

"Please," Rory urged; his tone gentle but insistent. "We have reason to believe you've been having strange dreams for many years now. You've felt different, haven't you? Unusual dreams, experiences you can't quite explain?"

As the team settled into the facility, the tension in the air thickened with anticipation. Rory faced Sumeet, who looked increasingly overwhelmed by the sudden turn of events. The young accountant's wide eyes darted around the room, scanning the sleek medical equipment and the anxious faces of the waiting scientists.

Sumeet rubbed the back of his neck, confusion flickering across his face. "I—I don't know what you're talking about. This is crazy! I'm just an accountant, a nobody! I go to work every day and come home. I live alone—I'm boring. I'm very boring!"

"But you've encountered unusual dreams, haven't you?" Rory pressed, sensing Sumeet's hesitation. "You've felt different from those around you?"

Sumeet stumbled back, clearly unsettled. "I've had dreams, but everyone dreams! Sometimes they're vivid or strange, sure, but... I don't think they're anything special. What do you want from me?"

Rory glanced at his colleagues, knowing they needed more than vague reassurances. "We can't explain everything yet, but the dreams you're experiencing could be connected to something much larger than yourself."

As the doctors closed in, their thoroughness driving their pursuit of clarity, Sumeet's anxiety heightened further. He exchanged glances with the agents, thoughts of escape swirling in his mind. Paranoia crept in, feeding the fear that they had intentions he couldn't fully grasp.

Before Rory could say more, Sumeet abruptly sprang to his feet, his eyes wild.

"No! I need to get out of here!" he shouted, panic propelling him into a sudden sprint towards the open door.

The room erupted into chaos as Rory and the others lunged to intercept him.

"Stop!" Rory called, but Sumeet bolted down the corridor, sprinting towards freedom. In that moment, instinct took over—the urge to flee overpowering reason, fuelled by a creeping paranoia that had begun to take root. He couldn't shake the feeling that they were after him for something— something deeply unsettling.

The agents and doctors surged forward, splitting into teams to corner him. They navigated the labyrinthine halls of the facility, breathless as they shouted commands in an effort to trap the young accountant. Rory pressed on, adrenaline fuelling his pursuit, but age was his enemy against a far younger man, and he was soon gasping for breath. The stakes grew higher with every passing second. They had to reach him before he escaped.

"Sumeet, wait!" Rory called, striving to keep his tone steady. "We just want to help! Please don't make this harder than it needs to be!"

But Sumeet, driven by panic, dashed out of the building and into the bustling streets of Bangalore, slipping through the chaos to evade his pursuers. He was swallowed by the city—horns blaring, vendors calling out, pedestrians lost in their daily routines. A rush of vivid sights and sounds bombarded his senses, momentarily drowning out the shouts behind him.

He crashed into a woman on a bicycle, sending them both tumbling to the ground. Sumeet scrambled to his feet and kept running.

"I'm sorry!" he called back to the woman.

Rory and the agents burst into the street, searching frantically.

"Split up! We need to cover more ground!" Rory commanded, urgency creeping into his voice. He darted into the throng of people, panting as he scanned the crowd for any sign of Sumeet.

As he manoeuvred through the dense sea of bodies, Rory caught glimpses of the accountant weaving through traffic, glancing over his shoulder as though he could feel their eyes lingering on him. The sensation of being hunted intensified, feeding Sumeet's paranoia and propelling him forward at an even greater pace.

"Over there!" one of the agents shouted, pointing to Sumeet as he ducked into an alleyway. The team regrouped and gave chase, sprinting down the narrow path.

Suddenly, they hit a dead end—Sumeet was pressed against a brick wall, cornered.

Rory approached cautiously, raising his hands in a gesture of peace. "Sumeet, please!" he urged. "We're not your enemies. We're trying to help you. Just talk to us!"

Sumeet's breathing was rapid, his eyes darting as he frantically assessed any possible escape routes. "Why should I trust you?" he gasped, exhaustion and fear spilling from his voice. "You've got me trapped! What do you want from me?"

"We want to understand your dreams and what you can do," Rory said, his voice firm yet calm.

The intensity of Rory's words seemed to resonate with Sumeet, his shoulders slackening slightly as fear mingled with intrigue. "Chosen? What do you mean? What are you talking about? How is any of this possible?"

Rory took a cautious step closer, sensing an opening in Sumeet's defences. "We believe your dreams have connected you to something far beyond the ordinary. We really are here to help you make sense of this."

Sumeet's breathing steadied as he processed this new information, his mind racing with questions. "I've had strange dreams, yes—dreams where I felt like I was somewhere else, in worlds that didn't feel like Earth. Sometimes, I just know things I shouldn't. I thought it was just my imagination running wild..."

Rory pressed on, his voice steady. "That's the beginning of our understanding, Sumeet. You might have the ability to navigate realities beyond our comprehension. But we can't help you unless you come with us."

"I... I don't know," Sumeet replied, uncertainty flickering across his face. "What if you're lying? What if this is all just a ruse?"

"There's no ruse," Rory assured him, his tone urgent yet sincere. "We've been studying consciousness for years, and we're on the brink of discovering something extraordinary—something that could affect not just you, but the fate of our entire species. You're part of something far greater than any of us ever imagined."

Sumeet hesitated, glancing towards the alleyway's exit. The weight of his dreams bore down on him, urging him to explore what lay ahead rather than flee. Sensing the shift, Rory offered one final plea.

"Please, Sumeet. Trust us. We can keep you safe, and together, we can unlock your potential. This is your chance to understand the gifts you possess—and the role you are meant to play."

After a few moments of contemplation, Sumeet finally nodded, resignation mingling with curiosity as it flickered across his features.

"Okay," he murmured, his voice barely above a whisper. "I'll go with you. But I still don't completely understand what you need from me. And I'll need to tell my parents—they'll worry."

Relief washed over Rory as he motioned for the agents to lower their guard.

"Thank you, Sumeet. We can send a message to your parents—tell them you've gone away with some friends. We'll explain everything on the way."

With Rory leading the way, they carefully wove through the bustling streets of Bangalore, this time with a Dream Agent in tow. As they navigated the crowded marketplace—alive with people and vibrant stalls—Sumeet glanced around, uncertainty flickering in his eyes as he wondered what this next step would mean for him.

"Where are we going?" he asked, curiosity beginning to edge out his lingering anxiety.

"To our facility at NASA in America," Rory explained. "There, we can conduct more tests and help you better understand your dreams and abilities. It's a secure environment, away from prying eyes."

"I don't even have a passport," Sumeet announced.

"Don't worry about that—we've got it covered," Rory said.

As they reached the waiting vehicles, Rory and the agents closed in around Sumeet, ushering him discreetly into the rear seat. They sped off towards the airport, the adrenaline of departure mingling with the unspoken promise of discovery ahead.

The convoy pulled up beside the plane, and without hesitation, they stepped out and ascended the stairs, boarding swiftly.

"Sumeet, please take a seat," Rory said as he buckled in beside him, turning to offer a reassuring smile.

Sumeet gazed out of the window as the others settled into their seats, trying to process how his life had changed beyond recognition in the last eight hours.

The atmosphere inside the jet was charged with anticipation as Rory, Sumeet, and a small team of specialists took off from Bangalore, soaring into the night sky. Sumeet sat beside Rory, his expression flickering between excitement and apprehension. The roar of the engines pulsed like a heartbeat as the world below receded, leaving only the vast expanse of sky around them.

"I can't believe this is happening," Sumeet said, turning to Rory. "Just hours ago, I was living an ordinary life, and now I'm being whisked away because of dreams I thought were just figments of my imagination."

Rory smiled, sensing the weight of Sumeet's thoughts. "You have experiences that may hold the key to connecting with things we don't yet understand. Together, we might uncover something that transcends our knowledge of consciousness and existence itself. Now, how about a hot drink and something to eat to help you settle?"

As the plane cruised through the night sky, Rory seized the opportunity to probe deeper into Sumeet's experiences. They spoke of his dreams—the sensations of flight and connection—and the vivid images of otherworldly beings. Each recollection painted a picture of a life straddling two realities.

Then, as if to punctuate their conversation, Rory's communicator—the one Lewis had given him before he left NASA—buzzed, shattering the quiet hum of the engines. He glanced at the device, aware that it represented a vital link to the ongoing mission.

"Excuse me, Sumeet, I need to take this." Rory grabbed the communicator quickly, his heart pounding at the prospect of urgent news. Rising from his seat, he strode towards the far end of the plane, ensuring privacy before answering.

"Sean?" he said, immediately recognising his colleague's voice.

"Yes, Rory! We've identified two more potential Dream Agents!" Sean's excited voice crackled through the static.

"One of them might be a challenge—he's in an asylum in Mississippi. Micky T. Jr. has been there for the past four years. According to his profile, he's 38 years old, 6 foot 3, with blonde hair. The other is Kerra Springfield—she's a trader on the New York Stock Exchange, single, living in Manhattan. She also has a history of drug use, primarily cocaine."

"Excellent work, Sean!" Rory exclaimed, sensing the mission was gathering momentum. "Once we land with Sumeet, we'll set off to pick them up."

"How did he take you coming for him?" Sean asked.

"I'll explain when we meet in person. Let's just say it was eventful, but he seems calmer now."

Settling into an empty seat at the front of the plane, Rory resumed his conversation with Sean.

"Micky T's case could be delicate, given his circumstances. What do you know about him?"

"Micky is unmarried and lived with his mother until she passed away about six years ago. Since then, he has drifted from one dead-end job to another, until he was sent to prison for six months for assault, shortly after her death. He is known for his vivid dreams, often displaying patterns resonating with interstellar imagery. Unfortunately, his mental health diagnosis has left him all but forgotten in the institution," Sean informed Rory.

"As for Kerra, she's also single, works long hours, and has a known affinity for drugs—having spent time in rehab on multiple occasions. Her dream reports indicate she has experienced unusual phenomena as well. They say she sometimes appears distant and distracted during trading hours, which could explain her reliance on coke."

Rory considered the implications of each case.

"We'll need to plan our approach carefully. Extracting Micky from the asylum will require tact, and we must ensure that Kerra feels safe and is willing to cooperate when the time comes."

"Absolutely," Sean agreed. "I suggest we deploy a small team to extract Micky. We could create a diversion to make his exit easier."

Rory glanced down the plane at Sumeet before responding,

"My concern with that approach is that it could raise alarms, and we need to avoid drawing unwanted attention. Perhaps a transfer would be a better option? Do we have anyone experienced in this kind of extraction, especially given the logistical challenges?"

Lewis jumped onto the line.

"Yes, we have a unit available. Brian Fowler is in charge, and he'll arrange a transfer for Micky. I'll speak to him so they're ready to move for both Micky and Kerra as soon as possible."

"Good. I'll stay with Sumeet at NASA when we get back to make sure he remains calm. See you soon," Rory said before ending the call.

As he walked back to his seat, Rory cast a glance at Sumeet, his expression a mix of concern and wonder.

"What is that contraption you were speaking into? I've never seen anything like it before," Sumeet asked, his brow furrowed in confusion.

"Oh, this is a simple communicator we use at NASA," Rory replied, holding it up for Sumeet to see. "You're about to witness far more impressive things."

"What about me?" Sumeet asked hesitantly. "What role do I play in all this?"

"You'll be integral to the mission. Others will be joining soon—Micky and Kerra are next. Once we arrive at NASA, you'll meet more of my team. For now, you should get some rest," Rory said, his tone reassuring, reinforcing his belief in Sumeet's abilities.

"Once everyone is assembled at NASA, we'll run further tests and fully brief you on what it all means."

Sumeet nodded, absorbing the weight of his newfound identity.

"I understand. I just want to make sense of all this."

As they soared through the clouds, anticipation hung thick in the air—the journey was only just beginning.

CHAPTER 5

The quest for Dream Agents

B y now, the plane had landed at NASA's air base, where a convoy of cars awaited just off the runway, their blue lights flashing in a show of authority.

"Let's go," Rory said to Sumeet. "There's a group of people in white coats waiting, and we have far more sophisticated equipment here than we did in India. Don't be afraid of them—they just wear those coats to look important," he added with a playful smile.

Sumeet walked alongside Rory and the others into the building and stepped into the lift. This was no ordinary lab—it was an advanced sanctuary, bathed in the soft glow of dim blue lights. Holographic screens hovered effortlessly in mid-air, their ever-shifting forms displaying streams of complex data. A group of specialists stood ready to receive them.

"Good morning, Sumeet. My name is Dr Campbell, and I head this specialist sleep-monitoring team under Rory's leadership. If you'd kindly follow me down this corridor, we've prepared a dedicated room to monitor your brain activity," Dr Campbell said, striding ahead with quiet confidence.

As they stepped inside, the medical team sprang into action. With swift precision, they set up the sophisticated equipment required for the assessment—arrays of sensor probes designed to monitor brainwave activity hovered above sleek, modular workstations. Sumeet stood hesitantly at the centre of the room, taking in the advanced surroundings, the air filled with the rhythmic beeping of machines and the soft glow of holographic displays.

"If you could lie down on this examination bed, we need to position a few sensors around your head. I assure you, it won't hurt," one of the technicians reassured him while carefully adjusting a series of delicate probes, each shimmering with a faint light to indicate its readiness.

"Let's begin with some basic assessments," Dr. Campbell continued, stepping forward with an electronic pad that glinted under the dim lighting. "These sensors will allow us to monitor your brainwave activity in real-time and provide insight into your neurological patterns." Sumeet, though nervous, felt a faint thrill at being part of such groundbreaking research.

"Wow, what's that?" Sumeet asked, intrigued by the device.

"Oh, just a basic notepad that lets me record as we go—it's seamlessly integrated with the main system," Dr. Campbell explained. "Right, we'll start with some initial tests to assess your physiological responses and see if we can identify any unique markers or patterns."

"This place is full of technology I've never seen or even heard of before. Where has it all come from?" Sumeet asked, staring at Rory with a startled expression.

"Sumeet, this is NASA—we put men on the moon. We have all kinds of technology here," Dr. Campbell said with a wry smile.

Rory stood nearby, ready to offer support while keeping a close watch on Sumeet's reactions. The young man held a mixture of apprehension and intrigue as the medical team calmly and gently explained the process.

As more sensors were attached to Sumeet, he closed his eyes, trying to focus despite the whirlwind of sensations. The fear of the unknown flickered in his chest, but a voice deep within urged him to embrace this journey—to uncover the true extent of his abilities.

"Prepare for the dream analysis," Rory instructed, double-checking the equipment's calibration. This was uncharted territory, and he felt a deep responsibility to guide Sumeet as they ventured into his experiences.

"Alright, Sumeet," Rory said, keeping his composure. "We're going to administer an injection that will induce a dream-like sleep state. Unlike conventional dream analysis, we'll be able to communicate with you throughout the process and, hopefully, help you recall what you've seen in your dreams. Just relax, focus on your dreams, and when you're ready, describe your experiences in as much detail as possible."

Sumeet took a deep breath, feeling the sensors pressed against his temples and the snug embrace of the equipment around his body. Slowly, he closed his eyes, his gaze lingering on Rory before he drifted off.

"I'll do my best," he murmured, his voice slow and slightly slurred, the uncertainty clear as he tried to piece his thoughts together. "It's difficult to recall everything clearly—my memories come in fragments."

"Just let your mind flow," Rory encouraged softly. "You might be surprised by what you can visualise and recall. Start with the most vivid dream."

Sumeet nodded, closing his eyes once more as he turned his focus inward. The chaos of earlier events faded, giving way to a dreamlike haze of swirling colours and sensations.

"In one of my dreams," he began, his voice growing steadier, "I was standing on a beach—but not like any beach I've ever seen. The sand was fine and golden, and the sky was awash with colours I can't quite describe—deep purples and rich blues, intertwining like waves."

He paused, letting the warmth of the sunlight sink into his skin as he immersed himself in the memory.

"The waves were gentle, yet they carried a soft, humming sound—almost like music. I felt… connected, as if the ocean itself was speaking to me. I remember looking out at the horizon and seeing this massive light, almost as if there were two suns. It was bright yet soothing, drawing me in."

Rory watched closely, captivated by Sumeet's description.

"That sounds beautiful," he said encouragingly. "What happened next?"

A faint sheen of sweat glistened on Sumeet's forehead as he concentrated, striving to recall the details of his experience.

"I walked towards the water, and with each step, I felt a strange energy surging through me—like an electric current pulsing through my body. It was both exhilarating and terrifying. Then, suddenly, I was lifted off the ground, soaring above the shoreline. It felt as though I was truly flying, surrounded by enormous birds that resembled vibrant parrots swooping around me. But they weren't like any parrots found on Earth—these creatures were immense, and their calls sounded as though they were coming from underwater."

"Flying?" Rory interjected, his fingers tapping swiftly on the pad as he made notes. "Did you feel any sense of control in that moment?" He looked up, curiosity etched across his face, eager to grasp the depth of Sumeet's experience.

"Yes, but it also felt as if I was being guided," Sumeet continued, his voice alight with excitement and bewilderment. "I soared over a vast expanse of trees and mountains—more vibrant than anything I'd ever seen in a dream before. Then, everything began to shift."

"Shift?" Rory prompted, his intrigue deepening.

"Yeah. I was lifted into this grand hall—like a palace made of light. There were beings there—figures that felt both familiar and foreign—but I couldn't make out their features distinctly. They seemed tall, but that was all I could discern. They didn't speak; instead, it felt as if we were sharing thoughts or emotions."

The room fell silent, each member of the medical team captivated by Sumeet's narration. Rory leaned in slightly, his eyes alight with curiosity. "What did they show you?"

Sumeet hesitated before speaking carefully. "I saw images— stars, planets, and strange landscapes. An overwhelming sense of purpose washed over me as I took them in. I felt connected to something far greater than myself."

He drew another deep breath, the memories rushing back with startling clarity. "But then, it all faded. I felt myself being pulled back—dragged into reality. When I woke, I was confused and… alone."

Rory nodded, absorbing the information. "Do you dream about this place often? Or have you started experiencing other dreams that feel just as profound?"

Sumeet opened his eyes and sat up as the nurse handed him a glass of water. "Almost every night now," he admitted, running a hand through his hair, sweat glistening on his forehead.

"Alright, let's try again," Rory said as Sumeet lay back down and drifted off once more.

"Carry on, Sumeet," Rory murmured, settling into the chair beside the bed.

"Each time, I return to that palace. Sometimes, the beings are there—other times, they're not."

"This is fascinating, Sumeet," Rory replied, absorbing the details. "It seems your subconscious is guiding you towards understanding, perhaps urging you to recall more of those connections."

Just then, one of the doctors glanced at the monitors, her eyes widening slightly.

"We're seeing significant fluctuations in his brainwave activity," she announced, a mix of excitement and concern in her voice. "It appears the dream analysis is triggering something. We need to monitor his physiological responses closely."

Rory turned back to Sumeet. "If you can, focus on those dreams—on the energy you felt. Perhaps you can channel that emotion into a deeper understanding of your experience. It may help us uncover the key information we need."

Sumeet nodded, determination flickering through the vulnerability of his earlier panic. "I just... I feel like I'm waking up from something I never even realised I was a part of. It's all so overwhelming."

"I understand this may feel overwhelming, especially given that you were unaware of any of this just a few days ago you were going about your normal life in India. Try to relax— you are here now, and we are committed to helping you understand what all of this means. Please, continue," said Rory.

As the moment deepened, Sumeet continued unveiling fragments of his experiences, his voice quickening with each recollection. Rory could sense the path unfolding before them, leading into the heart of something far greater than he had anticipated. Each dream Sumeet recounted revealed an intricate web of connections between the two worlds, weaving together threads of knowledge, power, and the Rivaxian influence that had touched him so profoundly.

"Can you describe more about your interactions with these beings?" Rory encouraged, leaning in closer, intrigued by the young man's unfolding story. "Did they communicate any messages or intentions to you?"

Sweat was now dripping down the side of Sumeet's head as he sent his thoughts racing back through the fog of dreams.

"As I said before, they don't speak in words; not like we do. It's something more profound—an exchange of feelings and thoughts. It felt as if they were trying to convey a sense of urgency, as if they needed me to understand the importance of our connection. I remember one specific dream; they showed me a vision of a collapsing world—like something was being destroyed."

Rory's mind raced at the implications. "A collapsing world? Do you know what it's called?"

"No, I don't, and now I'm really tired," Sumeet replied.

"Alright, we'll pause here for now. Sumeet, get some rest, and we'll continue this discussion in the morning. Dan will escort you back to your room," Rory said, placing a reassuring hand on Sumeet's back.

A technician approached Sumeet and gently removed the wires attached to his head. "Alright, Sumeet, all done. Come with me, and I'll show you to your room," Dan said, his voice calm and reassuring.

The next morning, Rory walked into Sumeet's room, a steaming cup of coffee in hand.

"I thought you might need this. How are you feeling?"

Sumeet rubbed his eyes and turned to Rory, who was leaning casually against the bedroom wall. "I'm okay. That was the best night's sleep I've had in a long time—I didn't even dream."

Rory grabbed a chair and pulled it closer to Sumeet's bed. Now sitting upright and sipping his coffee, Sumeet felt a weight lift from him, as though the revelations of the previous day had freed him from some shrouded truth.

"Sumeet, what I'm about to tell you may come as a shock. Try not to be afraid—it will make far more sense now that we've started analysing your dreams," Rory said, his tone serious.

"Alright, lay it on me. Nothing can shock me now—I've seen what you lot have," Sumeet replied, determination brimming in his voice.

Rory met Sumeet's gaze and offered a reassuring smile.

"In 1971, an alien race called the Rivaxians made contact with us. They were the ones who provided much of the advanced technology you've encountered since your arrival. We believe some of them have been reaching out to you through your dreams."

"Why would they do that?" Sumeet asked, glancing back at Rory while taking another sip of coffee.

"Well, we're still piecing together the puzzle," Rory said. "But you have unique abilities that distinguish you—skills most others don't possess. Here, we refer to you as a Dream Agent."

"Dream Agent? That sounds pretty cool," Sumeet said, now energised. He sprang up from his bed and began pacing the room, the weight of his new identity igniting a thrill within him.

"Sumeet, please, sit down," Rory urged, concern flickering in his eyes

At that, Sumeet returned to the bed, sitting beside Rory, his attention laser-focused as he clung to every word. The truth was unfolding before him like the first light of dawn, and he felt as if he were finally embarking on the journey he was destined to take.

"So, are you ready to conduct a few more tests?" Rory asked.

"Sure, let's go for it! Let me grab a quick shower and change—I'll literally be five minutes. My friends won't believe this; I'm so cool now!

"Sumeet, you can't tell a soul about any of this. Do you understand?"

Sumeet looked at Rory and nodded.

"That's a real shame. It would've been so cool."

"Now, take your time with that shower. Amy's waiting outside to take you to the lab. I'll see you down there."

With that, Rory walked out of the room, the door gliding shut behind him.

Sumeet entered the lab, looking refreshed and ready for the next round of tests.

Once again, the technicians connected him to the various monitors.

"All set," one of them said to Rory.

Rory pulled his chair closer to the bed where Sumeet was lying.

"Alright, Sumeet, let's pick up from yesterday. You mentioned a world collapsing, but you didn't know who it belonged to. Now that you know the alien race that contacted us is called the Rivaxians, could it have been them?"

"I don't know. As I said, the world was collapsing—not in a physical sense, but as if it simply couldn't survive. There was an overwhelming sense of fear and panic in my dream…"

"Did they show you any evidence of if they feared another race, or species even?" asked Rory.

Sumeet shook his head, his uncertainty evident. "It was all hazy. But I definitely felt fear—a deep, resonant fear. A sense of dread, as if things were falling apart and I was somehow connected to it."

Rory took a moment to process this chilling revelation. He glanced at the doctors, who were scribbling notes furiously, their expressions intense as they absorbed the information.

"This is significant. I think this is the key to everything," Rory said thoughtfully. "It sounds like the Rivaxians may be reaching out to you—in their time of need. We need to truly understand what is happening. I strongly believe this holds the answer to why they contacted us."

"Yes, Sumeet, it's as if they're trying to warn you," one of the doctors interjected, adjusting the monitoring equipment. "Perhaps you, as a Dream Agent, are not just connected to your own human experience but to a far greater cosmic struggle."

Sumeet looked increasingly troubled, the weight of the situation pressing down on him. "But I still don't understand—why me? What do they want from me? From us?"

Rory stepped in, his voice calm yet firm.

"This is a rare gift, Sumeet—a connection to the Rivaxians that could be crucial in understanding their plight and, ultimately, in forging a bond between our civilizations. As I said yesterday, we don't have all the answers yet, but you're helping us unravel much of what we don't know. Once the other Dream Agents arrive, hopefully, everything will become clearer."

As Rory spoke, a flurry of activity erupted in the lab. Monitors flickered to life, displaying sharp spikes in Sumeet's brainwave patterns as he delved deeper into his recollections. The team sprang into action, documenting the moment with precision and urgency.

CHAPTER 6

The Extraction

The black SUVs glided to a silent stop outside the bleak facility in Mississippi, its faded bricks and cold, unwelcoming façade a stark testament to years of neglect. The building loomed ominously against the overcast sky, its dim, flickering lights barely piercing the gloom of the cracked driveway—a place where hope was an afterthought and no visitor would enter willingly. A palpable tension hung in the air as a small, crack team of agents emerged, their keen eyes sweeping the desolate surroundings for any sign of danger.

Dr. Vincent, a sharply dressed man exuding confidence, adjusted his tie before striding purposefully towards the entrance. Beside him, a nurse walked in step, her composed expression laced with unspoken worry, as if she could sense the oppressive bleakness that clung to the air.

As they stepped through the entrance and into the building, the fluorescent lights overhead flickered ominously, casting harsh, erratic shadows against sterile white walls that felt more like a prison than a place of healing. Ceiling fans turned sluggishly, looking as though they had seen better days, whilst mosquitoes hovered near the lights. The air inside was thick with an unsettling quiet, broken only by the low hum of life struggling to persist in a place seemingly designed to suppress it. Stark institutional décor and peeling paint bore the heavy weight of forgotten souls, while the faint scent of antiseptic did little to mask the underlying misery.

Outside, a few other agents lingered, concealed in the shadows, each one armed and alert for any unforeseen escalation. They understood the significance of this place— a facility where mental health patients were often cast away, their stories lost to time and stigma. The air was thick with unspoken fears, foreshadowing the grim secrets buried within these walls.

As Vincent approached the front desk, a UV insect trap emitted a sharp zap as an unfortunate insect met its end. He nodded to the receptionist, flashing a practiced smile.

"Hello, my name is Dr. Vincent. I'm here to transfer one of your patients—Micky T Jr."

The receptionist glanced up, a cigarette dangling from her lips, her face void of emotion. Without a word, she turned to a filing cabinet behind the desk and retrieved a file labelled Micky T Jr.

"I'll need to speak to the doctor in charge," she said, her voice rough and husky, as if years of smoking had burned the softness from it. She picked up the phone and dialled for assistance.

"Of course," Vincent replied smoothly; his expression unwavering as he waited for her to finish the call. The minutes dragged on, each second stretching the tension taut, but he remained composed, mentally preparing for the conversation ahead.

Suddenly, a weary-looking doctor emerged from an adjacent room, he exhaled slowly, his shoulders drooping slightly as if he had been pulled from deep thought.

"Doctor Vincent, I presume?" he said, extending a hand. "I understand you're here to discuss a patient. Please, come into my office and take a seat."

"Yes, that's correct," Vincent replied firmly, shaking the doctor's hand and meeting his gaze. "I've been authorised to transfer Micky T Jr. We believe it's in his best interest to receive specialised treatment elsewhere."

The doctor's expression hardened slightly, scepticism flickering beneath his professional demeanour.

"Oh, really? That's interesting," he said with a puzzled look on his face features tightening slightly "I appreciate your intentions, but I must inform you that we cannot move Micky due to his condition. He's unstable and has exhibited highly aggressive behaviour. Transferring him without a proper assessment could be dangerous."

Vincent held his gaze, unwavering.

"With all due respect, as I've already stated, I am a doctor, this is my nurse, and I have a presidential order granting me the authority to transfer him. This isn't a request—it's not open to negotiation."

The doctor hesitated, eyeing Vincent warily.

"I'll need to see the documentation, of course, but I must warn you—Micky is not easily managed."

With a resolute nod, Vincent produced the presidential authorization, sliding it across the desk. The doctor scanned the document, his frown deepening as the reality of the situation settled in.

"Impressive. You must have powerful connections, but I can't imagine why you'd want Micky. Even with this document, I can't allow you to take him without ensuring all protocols are followed. We have procedures in place for a reason," the doctor said, a note of defiance in his voice as he cast a wary glance towards the hallway.

"Very well," Vincent replied, weighing his options. "Take me to Micky, and I'll assess his readiness for transfer myself."

The doctor sighed, knowing he had little choice. "Fine. Follow me."

The two men, accompanied by the nurse, navigated the labyrinthine corridors of the facility. Distant shouts from distressed patients echoed through the halls until they reached a reinforced door marked Holding Cell. The doctor unlocked the door and pushed it open, stepping aside to let them in.

Instantly, they were engulfed in a cacophony of noise. Micky T Jr. was bound to the wall, thrashing violently against his restraints, his eyes wide with panic. His voice was hoarse with desperation as he struggled.

"Let me out! You can't keep me here! I know the truth!" Micky shouted.

Vincent surveyed the scene, taking in Micky's distressed state.

"You see, Doctor Vincent," the doctor said, turning towards him, "he's clearly unstable. This isn't safe for anyone.

"Why the hell is he tied to the wall? Is this some sort of medieval torture chamber? No wonder he's distressed. We are taking him now," Vincent said sternly, fixing the doctor with a hard stare.

The doctor glanced apprehensively at Micky, who continued to shout incoherent phrases, his words laced with furious cries about dreams and visions that tormented him in the night.

"Okay, we'll need to sedate him for the transfer," the doctor finally conceded, recognising the futility of resisting further.

Vincent nodded in agreement. "Get him ready for the transfer. There is no way I'm leaving him here. You should be ashamed of using such methods—I should report you to the authorities. But lucky for you, I don't have the time."

As the nurse prepared the sedative, Rory's earlier revelations about the significance of Sumeet and the Dream Agents echoed in Vincent's mind. If Micky was indeed one of them, we need to get him to NASA.

The nurse stepped forward with a syringe, her hands steady, though her expression bore the weight of the moment.

"This will help calm him down," she said gently, carefully moving closer to Micky while ensuring he posed no threat.

"No! Don't!" Micky shouted, panicking as the needle glinted under the harsh lights. "You don't understand! I'm connected to them! I know things! I need to help!"

Micky cried out, his voice laced with desperation as he strained against his restraints. The fear in his eyes reflected a deep understanding of something profound—something Rory and the others sought to uncover.

"They need me!" he shouted again, panic radiating from him as the nurse approached. "You can't take me away! I'm not crazy! I can reach them! I have to reach them!"

Vincent exchanged glances with the doctor, who seemed torn between his clinical duty and the urgency of their mission.

"You see? He's completely insane. I told you this from the start," the asylum doctor said.

"We're not here to hurt you, Micky," Vincent said firmly, his voice steady in an attempt to assert calm. "We need you to come with us, but you have to relax. The sedation is for your own safety."

The nurse moved with care, kneeling to Micky's level as she prepared the syringe. "Please, try to breathe," she urged, her voice soothing yet firm. "This will help you feel better."

As the needle neared his skin, panic clouded Micky's thoughts.

"No, please! I'm connected! You don't understand what I've seen!" He thrashed in a desperate struggle, fuelled by the frenzy of his dreams and the unshakable belief that he was meant for something greater.

Then, in an instant, an image flared in his mind—the vast, glowing landscapes he had traversed, the beings who spoke without words, and the Rivaxians guiding him through the ether.

"I have to go back!" he shouted, desperation mingling with the realisation that time was slipping away.

Vincent saw the raw urgency in Micky's eyes and leaned in, his voice steady yet measured.

"We know you're afraid, Micky, but we have a plan," he said, his tone firm but reassuring. "We understand that you're connected—that's exactly why we need you. Help us awaken those connections. We're not your enemies. Trust us; we want to understand what you know."

With a swift, practiced motion, the nurse pressed the needle into Micky's arm, delivering the sedative. Almost instantly, his thrashing subsided, the drug's effects seeping into his system as his body slackened.

"You... don't understand..." he murmured, his voice fading, eyelids growing heavy.

"Good job," the nurse murmured, her voice soft against the hum of fluorescent lights and the tension thick in the air. "You'll feel much better soon."

Vincent stepped forward, his concern evident but his resolve unshaken. "Let's get him prepped for transfer and into the vehicles."

The team moved swiftly, unfastening Micky's restraints and easing him onto a gurney before securing him in place. As they wheeled him out of the holding cell, both Vincent and the nurse felt urgency pulse through them. This was a turning point—a critical step towards uncovering the truth about the Dream Agents and fulfilling their mission.

The air crackled with tension as they navigated the facility, their pace quickening towards the exit.

When they reached the black SUVs idling nearby, Micky's unconscious form was carefully secured in the back. The team piled in, Vincent taking the front seat as the engines rumbled to life.

As they sped away, Vincent cast a glance over his shoulder at Micky, who lay motionless yet exposed—oblivious to the extraordinary journey ahead. The plan was simple: get him to NASA, where they could monitor him and begin unlocking the gifts he had yet to comprehend.

Minutes later, the convoy pulled onto a private airstrip, where a waiting jet stood primed for take-off. The crew moved swiftly, unloading Micky and transferring him onto the aircraft, readying for departure.

As they settled in, a ripple of excitement and anxiety coursed through Vincent. This was more than just collecting Dream Agents—it was about restoring hope and forging connections that stretched across worlds.

Once the plane was airborne, a hush fell over the cabin. Agents and medical staff busied themselves with preparations, each aware that their mission was only just beginning.

Upon arrival at NASA, technicians swiftly unloaded Micky from the plane and transferred him into an ambulance. Meanwhile, Vincent readied himself for the next phase of the mission. His orders were clear: fly to New York and retrieve Kerra Springfield, the third identified Dream Agent.

The captain's voice crackled through the intercom.

"We are now refuelled and preparing for departure to New York."

As the jet engines roared to life, Vincent settled into his seat, mentally bracing himself for the challenge ahead.

The plane lifted off smoothly, slicing through the clouds and ascending into the open sky. Moments later, the pilot's voice returned over the intercom, steady and professional.

"Flight time to Teterboro Airport is approximately two and a half hours. We have clear skies ahead, so I'll check in with you again just before landing."

Vincent gazed out of the window, his hand resting thoughtfully beneath his chin as he surveyed the vast expanse of sky, the weight of the unknown pressing in around him.

"Let's hope she's still in that area," he murmured to the nurse beside him, a hint of apprehension in his voice.

A moment later, the stewardess approached and handed him a cup of coffee.

"You look like you need this," she said with a warm smile.

"Thank you, I really do," he replied, returning her smile as he placed the cup on the table in front of him.

With a determined flick, he activated his communicator, pulling up the latest data on Kerra. The screen glowed, displaying vital information that confirmed her whereabouts, bringing a fleeting sense of relief.

"Yes, she's still at The Velvet Poodle, a bar on 64th Street near Lexington Avenue," he reported, glancing at the team gathered around him, worry etched on their faces.

Vincent shifted his focus to strategizing their approach to the unpredictable situation ahead. After a smooth flight, they descended through the clouds, landing at Teterboro Airport without incident. The team wasted no time, swiftly jumping into the waiting cars and speeding towards the looming shadows of the city.

As they manoeuvred through the bustling traffic of Manhattan, a light drizzle began to fall, glistening like tiny diamonds against the car windows. The rhythmic patter echoed the tension mounting within them.

"We need to be swift," he instructed the driver, his tone firm. "The longer we wait, the greater the chance she'll slip away."

Arriving at The Velvet Poodle, the lively ambience of the bar stood in stark contrast to the urgency pressing down upon them like a thick fog. Laughter and chatter spilled from the entrance, creating an atmosphere that felt almost surreal given the gravity of their mission. Stepping out of the car, they quickly approached the doorway, ready to confront whatever unknowns lay ahead.

Inside, the dimly lit room echoed with the sounds of clinking glasses and lively conversation, but one sight stole Vincent's focus immediately—Kerra, slumped at the bar, a half-empty drink in hand. Her usual vibrant energy was dulled, and it was evident she had indulged far too much. A faint dusting of white powder around her nostrils confirmed her vulnerable state, lost in a haze of alcohol and drugs, oblivious to the chaos surrounding her.

"Kerra!" Vincent called as he approached her. He needed to get her outside, away from the throng of people and the intoxicating atmosphere that surrounded them. "We need to talk. It's important."

She turned slowly, her expression unfocused as she blinked at him, struggling to process his presence.

"Who are you?" she mumbled, irritation threading through her slurred speech. "I'm not interested. Go away."

Before Vincent could respond, a rough-looking man stepped between them, his protective instincts flaring. "Back off, mate! She doesn't want to talk to you," he growled, his glare sharp as a knife.

"I'm her brother," Vincent asserted swiftly, thinking on his feet. "Who are you?"

The man's aggressive demeanour faltered slightly at Vincent's claim. After a tense moment, he pulled back, his protective stance softening with uncertainty. "Fine. I'm just looking out for her," he muttered, stepping away.

"Thank you. I appreciate that," Vincent said, relieved as the confrontation dissolved. He turned back to Kerra, whose focus wavered between clarity and confusion. "Kerra, you need to come with us. You've had enough to drink tonight."

"So, you're my brother? Funny that—I don't have one," she slurred, her voice thick with intoxication.

A flicker of resistance crossed her face. "I'm fine here," she protested weakly, lifting her glass for another sip.

"No, you're not," Vincent said firmly, concern threading through his voice. "You've had too much to drink. Let's get out of here—it's time to leave." He reached out to steady her, noting how unsteady she was on her feet.

Reluctantly, Kerra rose, swaying slightly as she stumbled towards the exit. Vincent stayed close, alert for any potential interference.

Behind them, the barman hurried over, swiftly wiping away the white powder from the counter as his gaze flicked towards the door.

Once outside, the cool evening air struck her face like a splash of cold water. She blinked rapidly, struggling to shake off the haze.

As they reached the waiting car, Vincent helped her inside, his instincts on high alert. The urgency of their mission pulsed through him as he cast a final glance back at the bar, acutely aware of how narrowly they had avoided further confrontation.

As the vehicle sped down the street towards the airport, Vincent glanced at Kerra, who sat slumped against the door, her eyes half-closed.

"She's completely out of it. There's no point trying to talk to her now. Let's get her to NASA—the team can take it from there," he remarked to the driver, shaking his head with a mix of regret and frustration.

"If Micky and Kerra are the ones we collected today to help save the Rivaxians... heaven help them—they're going to need it."

After the flight, they finally arrived at the NASA complex. Exiting the cars, they made their way towards the West Area Computer Building and down the corridors. Vincent pushed Kerra in a wheelchair into the lift, mindful of her condition as they hurried inside.

The medical team was already standing by, ready to assess her. Vincent turned to Rory, who was waiting for them, concern etched across his face.

"What happened?" Rory asked, taking in the sight of Kerra, slumped in the wheelchair.

"Let's just say she was pretty loaded by the time we found her," Vincent replied, shaking his head. "She'll need to sleep this off—she's no use to us tonight. Take her to her room."

The next morning, Rory entered Kerra's room, offering her a large mug of coffee. "Here, hopefully this helps. I've got you some aspirin as well," he said gently.

Kerra blinked up at him, confusion and vulnerability etched across her face.

"I don't even know what's happening," she murmured, her voice weary. "Where am I? Why am I here? What do you want from me?"

Rory, sensing her trepidation, spoke softly to reassure her.

"What I'm about to say might freak you out a little more than you already are, but please hear me out. You're here because your unique dream experiences are crucial to our understanding. You've noticed how unusual your dreams are, haven't you?"

Kerra looked at Rory, then glanced away at the wall, her defences rising. "How on earth do you know what I dream about?" she retorted sharply. "You have no idea what my dreams have done to me over the years."

Rory offered a reassuring smile. "I know this isn't easy, and being brought here so suddenly must feel overwhelming."

"Too right it is," Kerra snapped. "Who the hell are you people?"

"You're in Florida—NASA, to be precise," Rory said gently. "Kerra, you're not alone in this. There are others like you who experience similar dreams. I'd like you to meet someone who might help you understand them better. When you're ready, they'll take you down to the lab."

He gestured towards the bathroom door. "Oh, and by the way, there's a wardrobe over there with clothes for you. They should fit, so help yourself—they're yours."

With that, Rory turned and left the room, heading back to the lab.

Entering the lab, Rory joined Beth and Vincent in the boardroom. As Vincent poured himself a fresh cup of coffee, he looked up. "How is she this morning?" he asked.

Rory paused, glancing at the ceiling before meeting Vincent's gaze. "You know, I've been thinking all night. What if the Rivaxians have got this wrong? Of the three people we've identified so far, only one seems competent and free of issues. What the hell are we doing? This facility's costing a fortune, and all we have is chaos."

Just then, Lewis strolled in, grabbing a coffee with his usual cheerful demeanour. "Morning, team! What's happening with our Dream Agents today?" he asked brightly, oblivious to the tension in the room.

Rory leaned against the boardroom table, doubt clouding his expression. "Honestly, I'm concerned. We're pouring resources into this, but if we can't find the right individuals—or even understand what the Rivaxians are truly after—we might be missing the mark entirely."

Beth, absorbing the weight of Rory's concerns, nodded thoughtfully. "We need to focus on understanding the bigger picture. This isn't just about identifying Dream Agents—it's about grasping the connection between their dreams and the alien technology."

Lewis sipped his coffee, considering their words. "Rory, remember, breakthroughs have come from chaos before. It's the nature of innovation."

Rory sighed, glancing at Lewis, whose optimism remained unwavering.

"I get what you're saying, Lewis. It's just frustrating. We need clarity—and soon. Kerra and the others might be the key, but we can't stumble blindly."

Lewis, unperturbed, replied, "Let's concentrate on today's results. Each step brings us closer to understanding. And her meeting another Dream Agent could open doors for all of us."

Meanwhile, back in her room, Kerra contemplated Rory's words, feeling a strange mix of apprehension and curiosity. She dressed quickly, drawn not only by the allure of answers but also by the sense of belonging to something larger.

As she made her way to the lab, the air seemed charged with anticipation, the mysteries of her dreams holding new promise under the strange guidance of the Rivaxians.

Kerra now stood outside the boardroom, waiting. Rory gestured for her to enter.

"Good morning, Kerra. I'm Lewis Gell, the Head of NASA, and I'm really pleased to meet you. Please, have a seat."

Vincent looked across at her. "Good morning, Kerra. How are you feeling this morning?"

"Much better, thank you," came the reply.

Beth then walked over and introduced herself.

"Okay then, we're all here—with one exception," said Rory.

As Kerra sat in the boardroom, nervously tapping her fingers on the table, the door swung open, and a young man stepped in with a warm, approachable smile.

"Hello, my name is Sumeet Sharma, and I believe you must be Kerra," he said, pronouncing her name with an endearing lilt that immediately put her at ease. Kerra nodded, offering a tentative smile as Sumeet took a seat across from her. Keen to break the ice, he launched into a discussion about the remarkable technology he had encountered and the enigmatic Rivaxians who had bestowed it upon them. As their conversation unfolded, Sumeet described the tests he had undergone, relayed his vivid dreams, and shared his growing comprehension of their alien benefactors. His candour and insight gave Kerra a broader perspective, helping her piece together the fragments of the unfolding mystery around them. In Sumeet, she discovered an unexpected ally—someone who, like herself, was navigating the uncertain terrain of dreams and otherworldly connections.

"Okay, you two, are you ready for more tests today?" Rory asked as he stood up from the table.

Kerra and Sumeet exchanged a glance before nodding.

"All right, then. Come with me, and I'll get you set up," said one of the technicians, leading them out of the room.

Vincent turned to Rory. "We'll need to guide her gently through her recollections. The sedative should help calm her racing thoughts, allowing us to probe her memories without overwhelming her. But we must tread carefully—

uncovering those memories may take time. I'm also concerned about the effects of the drugs and alcohol she has consumed over the years."

"Now that she has met Sumeet, and they seem to have hit it off, I'm sure she'll be fine," said Rory. "We want her to feel safe as she navigates these experiences. I can be present during the initial discussions."

As he walked down to the inner lab, where the tests were being administered, Rory knew they needed to bring Micky into the group quickly.

"I want to bring Micky into tomorrow's session. He will have had time to adjust by then. How is he doing, Doctor Rambolt, since he arrived?"

"The first-round tests yesterday were astonishing. His brain activity placed him well beyond Sumeet's level, and I expect he may even surpass Kerra's—but we'll see today. Honestly, it's as if a massive weight has been lifted off him. He's already pushing himself as hard as he can."

"Great, then he's definitely in tomorrow's session," Rory said with a broad smile.

Once the arrangements were complete, they gently guided Kerra into a new, softer space illuminated by warm lighting. Cushioned seating and calming décor enveloped her, while two large beds positioned side by side created an inviting atmosphere designed to ease her anxieties.

"As she settled onto the bed, Rory approached and sat across from her.

"Kerra, can you hear me?" he asked gently, his voice low and soothing.

She nodded slowly, her focus wavering as the sedative took hold.

"I'm here," she murmured, blinking as if trying to reorient herself.

"Take a deep breath," Rory said softly. "You're in a safe space, and we're here to help you." He watched as her body relaxed further. "Can you tell me about your dreams? Anything unusual you've experienced?"

"Kerra's gaze shifted as she momentarily drifted away, lost in thought. Fighting through the fog of the sedative, she began to share fragments of vivid memories.

"I dream of a place... a world of vivid colours, unfamiliar yet mesmerising. Sometimes, I'm in a forest with silver trees, and there's this feeling of flight—like I'm soaring over everything."

Rory listened intently, aware of the significance of every detail.

"And do you see anyone in your dreams? Any beings you don't recognise?"

Kerra hesitated, slightly flustered. "There are figures... shadows watching me. They don't speak, but... I feel connected to them. It's comforting, yet terrifying."

"As she spoke, Rory sensed a shift—a deep-seated connection between the memories she was recalling and what lay ahead. They would need to piece together these fragments into a cohesive understanding before moving forward.

"Thank you for sharing that with me, Kerra," Rory said, his voice warm and reassuring. "We're here to help you embrace this, and together, we may find the clarity we seek."

Kerra's eyes softened as she continued speaking, her earlier unease gradually melting away. "Sometimes, it feels like I'm being called... as if there's a purpose behind my dreams. I always wake up with a sense of longing, as though I've left something important behind."

"Exactly," Rory replied, eager to connect the dots. "That sense of longing may be your subconscious trying to communicate something vital. We need to delve deeper into these feelings as we explore your dreams further."

Nearby, Dr Campbell observed Kerra's reactions, catching Rory's attention.

"Rory, once we complete the assessment, we must integrate our findings with Sumeet's. The patterns in their dreams may reveal latent connections to the Rivaxians."

"Rory nodded thoughtfully, recognising the potential unfolding in their collaboration. "Yes, we should analyse both Sumeet's and Kerra's experiences. We must also ensure Mickey is included, particularly as his insights appear clearer than any we've encountered before. If their dreams reveal similarities, it may offer a deeper understanding of their origins and the motivations behind the Rivaxians' influence. This knowledge could prove invaluable in shaping our future interactions."

"Beth interjected, "We must also consider the immediate next steps for Sumeet, Kerra, and Mickey T. It is crucial that they receive ongoing support throughout their journeys and remain protected from any external forces that could interfere with their latent abilities."

"Agreed," Rory said, turning to Kerra. "Once we have gathered sufficient information, we will ensure that you both understand your role and the significance of what lies within you. You are not alone in this—we will face any challenges together."

"In that moment, a sense of unity settled over the group. Rory felt the growing determination among them; they were forging a path towards understanding and discovery—one that could not only reshape their own bewildering experiences through dreams but also influence the future of humanity, and perhaps even the Rivaxians.

As evening descended upon the facility, Rory and the team continued their discussions with Kerra, reassuring her that she was safe and surrounded by experts ready to help her interpret her experiences. Each new revelation added to their understanding, further unveiling the intricate connections between Sumeet, Mickey T, and Kerra."

"Hours passed, yet the work remained crucial. With each layer they uncovered, Rory began to recognise emerging patterns—a framework for the larger movement that would take shape once they established contact with the remaining Dream Agents.

Following the intense session with Kerra, Vincent reconvened with Rory at the main control centre. "Our priority now is finding the remaining Dream Agents," he said, his voice resolute. "From this foundation, we can construct a broader strategy."

"Absolutely. I need a clear understanding of what we're dealing with," Rory replied. "We've identified Sumeet, Kerra, and Mickey, but it's vital that we obtain information on the remaining potential Dream Agents as soon as possible."

CHAPTER 7

The Search for the Last Two Agents

As dawn broke over the facility, the first light filtered through the old windows of the West Area Computing offices. Deep underground, anticipation crackled in the air as they prepared to embark on the next phase of their mission—tracking down the remaining Dream Agents. With three agents now identified, Rory felt a growing urgency to complete the team and press forward. They needed the final pieces of the puzzle.

"Alright, team, settle down—we've got work to do," Rory said. "Sean, over to you."

"Sean stood at the head of the glass table. With the press of a button, the surface lit up, revealing maps and the faces of the two remaining Dream Agents.

"We have two final Dream Agents to locate. First on the list is Buddy Spencer, a B-movie film star based in California. An interesting character—he presents himself as a

Hollywood success, but the reality of his career, and indeed his bank account, suggests otherwise. He's a textbook case of someone living beyond their means. He has appeared in a handful of minor films and magazine spreads, having initially started out as a model—likely how he transitioned into acting."

"We need to arrange a meeting with him. The plan is to lure him in under the guise of discussing a brand-new blockbuster film project—something that should definitely appeal to someone like him."

Lewis nodded, leaning over the table to examine the details.

"We need to make sure he believes this is a legitimate opportunity. It's crucial that we don't raise any suspicions about our true intentions just yet. We can tell him the film set is located within the NASA site—pitch it as a space film. Once he's here, we'll reveal the real reason for his involvement. Let's give that a little more thought."

"And what about the final agent?" Rory asked, noting the apprehension etched across the faces around the table. A heavy silence settled over the room before Sean finally spoke.

"Lord Barnes," Sean replied, his voice low as he scanned the data on his tablet. "He's currently in the UK, residing in Sussex. The problem is, he's something of an enigma—distantly connected to the British royal family and protected by a substantial security detail. And that's not even the most intriguing part. The files indicate he served in the Marines before working for British intelligence, though the details are heavily redacted—suggesting a less-than-honourable departure. Approaching him will be a significant challenge, but we might be able to exploit his ego—if we can make him feel he's part of something truly momentous."

Rory considered the complexity of tracking down a member of royalty, aware that their usual tactics would need to evolve to meet an entirely different level of scrutiny.

"We'll need a meticulous plan for Lord Barnes. Perhaps we can leverage intelligence resources to gain deeper insight into his daily routine and security protocols. If his abilities are indeed connected to the Rivaxians, we must proceed with the utmost caution."

Beth spoke up, her dedication unmistakable in her tone.

"We need to track his movements carefully and pinpoint a moment when he's most accessible. I have an ex-boyfriend at the FBI—I could take him out for dinner and see if he has any intel on Lord Barnes."

"That's a solid lead, but be careful—we can't risk the FBI catching wind of what we're doing," Lewis cautioned. "For now, let's keep our attention on Buddy. Time is against us, and we need to secure him before Hollywood tempts him with an actual project."

Rory nodded. "Vincent, would you mind taking the lead on reaching out to Buddy's representatives?"

"Of course, no problem. I'll also coordinate with the transportation team to secure a flight."

As they finalised their plans, the atmosphere in the room shifted, charged with the anticipation of the discoveries ahead. With the jet prepped for departure to Burbank-Glendale, California, Vincent ascended the steps and boarded, fully aware that these would likely be the most challenging agents to recruit.

Hours later, as the team arrived in Burbank, they were met with bright sunshine and the unmistakable glamour of

Hollywood. Without delay, they made their way to Buddy Spencer's agent's office on Sunset Boulevard, where their meeting with the actor was set to take place.

"Stay focused," Vincent reminded the team as they neared the building. "Our goal is to make this pitch so compelling that Buddy has no choice but to join us."

Inside, they were greeted by impeccably polished staff and the fast-paced buzz of the talent agency. After a brief wait, they were ushered into a sleek, well-appointed conference room—where Buddy Spencer lounged casually, exuding effortless charisma. His thick, perfectly styled hair and athletic physique framed a grin that seemed to light up the room.

"Gentlemen, what brings you to my neck of the woods?" Buddy asked, his expression laced with bemusement.

"We have an exciting proposition for you, Mr Spencer," Vincent began, keeping his voice steady. "We're considering you for a leading role in a groundbreaking sci-fi blockbuster. It's a project that could redefine cinematic experiences and push the boundaries of modern filmmaking."

Buddy raised an eyebrow, intrigued but clearly weighing the offer. "Oh? I must admit, that's a bold claim. What makes this project so special?"

"Without revealing too much," Vincent said, his tone cautious, "I can assure you it involves cutting-edge technology and concepts that transcend traditional narratives. This isn't just another film—it's an opportunity to be part of something truly historic. We intend to film the entire production on location at NASA in Florida to enhance its authenticity."

As they pitched the project, Vincent and his colleagues subtly gauged Buddy's reactions, reading his body language and expressions. The conversation flowed smoothly, and Vincent felt a growing sense of confidence. If they played their cards right, they might just convince the star to join their ranks.

After several minutes of discussion, Danny, one of the senior team members, stepped in, reinforcing the project's significance and its potential to push the boundaries of filmmaking.

Finally, Buddy leaned back in his chair, a thoughtful frown crossing his face.

"Sounds exhilarating," he said, a grin finally breaking through. "Alright, I'm intrigued. But let's not beat around the bush—how much?"

He leaned forward, his gaze fixed on Vincent.

Vincent, suppressing a sigh of relief, scribbled a figure onto a slip of paper and handed it to Buddy. The actor's eyes widened before he wordlessly passed the note to his agent. A barely perceptible nod and a knowing wink—the silent agreement was sealed.

"When do you need me on set?" Buddy asked.

"Immediately," Vincent replied, the lie heavy on his tongue. "Here's your ticket to Florida. Someone will meet you at the airport."

A surge of relief washed over him—the hardest part was done. But as he considered what lay ahead, he knew the real challenge had only just begun. Lord Barnes was next, and with him came a new, unpredictable narrative.

They departed, leaving Buddy elated. "Holy shit, did you see that figure?!" he exclaimed, grinning as he slapped a high five with his agent. The contrast between them was striking—his agent, impeccably dressed in a tailored suit and an expensive watch, while Buddy lounged in worn jeans and a faded t-shirt.

Buddy climbed into his battered Mustang; the cracked leather seats a familiar comfort against the sting of his recent failures. The iron gates of his agent's Bel Air estate swung open—a testament to the agent's success and a stark contrast to Buddy's dwindling fortunes. The long driveway, lined with manicured lawns and towering trees, stretched before him—a landscape of opulence he could only dream of.

He didn't stop at the main house. Instead, he veered down a barely visible side road, heading towards a secluded cabin nestled deep within the woods—his temporary refuge, a quiet reminder of his current reality. Gathering a bag and a change of clothes, he hailed a cab to the airport, the weight of uncertainty still heavy on his shoulders. Yet, for the first time in a long while, he allowed himself to believe that his luck had finally changed.

As Vincent and the team boarded their jet, he activated his communicator to update Rory on the situation with Buddy— and the fact that he'd fabricated a figure to get him on the plane to Florida.

"Rory, I had to make up a number to get Buddy over to NASA. Once he's inside the facility, you'll need to tell him the truth. He's likely to be furious when he finds out."

"It's fine," Rory replied. "Once he knows the truth, I doubt he'll care about some fictional movie deal. This is the biggest role Buddy will ever play. I'll handle it—you just focus on bringing in Lord Barnes."

With that, the plane's engines roared to life, and soon they were once again climbing through the clouds, leaving behind the sun-soaked splendour of California for the rolling green countryside of Sussex.

The cabin buzzed with a quiet tension as the team reviewed their approach to Lord Barnes. This time, the stakes were undeniably higher.

"We need to be at our absolute best—this isn't some Hollywood star whose ego we can easily manipulate," Vincent cautioned. "We're dealing with a member of the royal family, albeit a distant one. This mission demands the utmost discretion."

Vincent reconnected with Rory over the communicator, discussing possible approaches to the problem.

"I suggest you present yourselves as researchers studying dreams and their impact on human potential," Rory said. "From what we know, his background suggests he's had some unusual experiences of his own. Our hope is that he'll be open to the conversation—curious enough to want to explore it further."

As the plane soared over the ocean, their discussions continued. Rory couldn't shake the feeling that this was their biggest challenge yet—but it was still possible to get him into the NASA facility.

After what felt like mere moments—but was in fact hours—the pilot announced their descent into London. They touched down at Biggin Hill Airport, a small airfield on the outskirts of the city, chosen to avoid drawing too much attention. A waiting transport swiftly took them towards Sussex.

The drive through the countryside was picturesque, with rolling hills dotted with sheep and grand estates. But

Vincent's mind remained fixed on the task ahead, indifferent to England's scenic charm. At last, they arrived at a grand estate, its manicured gardens framing a stately building that exuded both history and prestige.

"We have a brief window for this meeting," Vincent reminded them as they stepped out of the vehicle. "Stay sharp—Lord Barnes may have considerable security, and any misstep could put everything we're working towards at risk."

As they neared the grand oak doors, Vincent took a steadying breath, the weight of expectation pressing down on him. He knew they were piecing together a destiny that could alter the course of their mission. He pressed the doorbell to the right of the imposing entrance and glanced around the open parkland as they waited—everything was still, almost unnervingly so. Moments later, the door swung open, revealing a butler standing in a lavish foyer adorned with rich décor and antique furnishings—an elegant tribute to a noble heritage.

"We have an audience with Lord Barnes," Vincent said, his tone measured as he stepped forward.

The butler gave a curt nod and ushered them into a tastefully furnished sitting room. There, they waited in tense silence, the weight of expectation hanging in the air. Vincent could feel the anticipation mounting, each passing second bringing them closer to an encounter that could alter their future.

When Lord Barnes finally entered, he was every inch the aristocrat—tall and distinguished, despite being only in his early thirties, yet possessing an air of authority that commanded respect. His immaculate attire and sharp features hinted at both wisdom and experience, though his expression remained unreadable as he assessed the group. He had the look of an MI6 agent.

"Good afternoon," he said, his voice smooth and inviting, yet laced with caution. "What brings you to my estate?"

"Thank you for seeing us, Lord Barnes," Vincent said, stepping forward to introduce the team. "We're researchers investigating the connection between consciousness, dreams, and a potentially extraordinary phenomenon that could have global implications."

"That's quite the intriguing introduction—though rather vague, wouldn't you say?" Barnes remarked, arching an inquisitive eyebrow as he retrieved a cigarette from a box on the desk. "What exactly are you suggesting?"

Vincent stepped a little closer, carefully selecting his next words. "This may sound unusual, but we have reason to believe you've had unique experiences related to dreams— experiences that connect you to a much larger initiative we're undertaking. We'd like to discuss the implications of these experiences, particularly in relation to an ongoing situation involving an extraterrestrial race."

Barnes regarded Vincent intently, the corner of his mouth twitching around his cigarette as he weighed the audacity of the claim. "Extraterrestrial, you say. You do realise how utterly preposterous that sounds? Tell me—has Charlie put you up to this?"

"No, we are entirely serious. Please, hear us out," Vincent urged, realising he needed to tread carefully to prevent Barnes from dismissing them outright.

"I understand this sounds far-fetched—perhaps even absurd—but I assure you, we mean no alarm. We need to learn more about your experiences, as they may prove critical in understanding the implications of what we've uncovered regarding a species and their connection to humanity."

A heavy silence settled over the room as Lord Barnes studied them, his expression unreadable as he weighed their sincerity against the sheer implausibility of their claims.

"Very well," he conceded, a flicker of curiosity glinting in his eyes. "You have my attention. But tread carefully—such extraordinary claims are not to be taken lightly."

Vincent inclined his head, fully aware of Barnes' scrutiny. "We understand, and we appreciate the opportunity to elaborate. This isn't mere speculation; we have tangible evidence and experiences that could reveal a connection— not only within your dreams but on a universal scale."

With a slow nod, Lord Barnes gestured for them to sit in the sitting room, which was decorated with plush furnishings and art that spoke of a rich history. Vincent and the others settled in, keenly aware of the significance of the moment.

"Now, let's get to the point," Barnes said, his voice steady and commanding. "What exactly do you want from me, and why do you believe I'm involved in this grand narrative?"

Vincent took a breath. "We believe you may have encountered dreams or experiences tied to an altered state of consciousness—something that could allow you to interact with other realms or beings. We're searching for individuals who've had similar dreams, dreams about distant planets. If I may be candid, Lord Barnes, we've been contacted by an alien race through NASA."

Lord Barnes leaned back, processing the information. "So, hang on a moment, Mr. Vincent. You're telling me a species from another planet has contacted you and mentioned me?" Barnes said with a chuckle. "Isn't it a bit early in the day for drinking? You speak of dreams, modifications, and civilizations that apparently watch over us," he added, scepticism colouring his words. "How can I know your story is credible?"

"We have documented cases of unique dream occurrences from multiple individuals," Vincent interjected. "They're at NASA, helping us understand their dreams and what they mean."

At the mention of others, Barnes' interest seemed to sharpen. "And you believe I'm like these people? That I share their dreams and gifts? How do you know this?"

"Based on patterns we've observed in dream data, we've identified you as a potential Dream Agent—this is the term we use for people like you, Lord Barnes," Vincent explained. "The aliens have been monitoring individuals who exhibit signs of heightened sensitivity and connectivity, and we believe you're one of them. We want to learn more about your experiences and explore what you might remember about them."

Barnes stared at them for a long moment, contemplation crossing his features. "And if I decide to cooperate, what's in it for me?"

"Knowledge," Vincent replied earnestly. "Knowledge about yourself, your dreams, and the broader role you might play—not only in your own life but perhaps in the fate of both our world and the aliens. Together, we can uncover the potential that lies dormant within you. This is a chance to understand your abilities—and perhaps even a greater mission."

"Interesting…" Barnes replied, a fleeting smile tugging at the corners of his lips. "But I will not take blind steps into this obscurity without some assurances. If I agree to my involvement, I want to know exactly what happens next."

"Of course," Vincent responded. "We will thoroughly explain how the project operates, what your participation will entail, and we will always prioritize your safety and autonomy. You can withdraw at any time should you choose."

Barnes considered their offer, leaning in with a newfound gleam in his eye.

"Do these aliens have a name?" Barnes asked, looking directly at Vincent.

"Yes, they're called Rivaxians," Vincent replied.

"Very well. I am prepared to hear you out further on these matters. My dreams and experiences have puzzled me for years—if your claims hold any merit, we may be on the brink of unveiling something truly remarkable. Therefore, you can all call me Bertie."

Feeling the atmosphere shift in their favour, Vincent nodded in understanding and gratitude. "Thank you, Lord Barnes— I mean, Bertie. The journey of discovery begins here, and together we may illuminate paths not just for you, but for all Dream Agents."

As their conversation continued, Vincent felt a massive sense of relief, realising that all five Dream Agents were now beginning to weave together. Each agent represented a vital piece of a grander puzzle, and with their combined efforts, they could stitch together the fragments of their experiences, unravelling the mystery behind the Rivaxian contact and unlocking a future filled with possibility.

Upon concluding the discussion, Vincent knew they needed to act swiftly to secure the last Dream Agent before any threats could arise.

"So, Bertie, let's head off to NASA, where the team and the other Dream Agents are waiting. We have a plane ready at Biggin Hill. Can you pack a bag, and we'll wait?"

"Smithers, can you pack a bag for me?"

"How long will you be gone, Sir?" asked the butler.

Bertie looked across at Vincent, as if seeking the answer.

"I'd suggest at least a few weeks," replied Vincent.

"You heard the man. Let's get started," said Bertie. "I'm going to NASA."

CHAPTER 8

Unravelling the Dreams

As the first light of dawn crept across the vast NASA site, Dr. Campbell stepped into the conference room deep beneath the bustling campus, where his team had already gathered. The atmosphere buzzed with anticipation, an electric undercurrent pulsing through the air as everyone prepared for a day dedicated to understanding their newly assembled Dream Agents. Lewis and Beth were at the forefront, poring over notes and diagrams, their excitement at the realisation that this was finally happening evident in their expressions.

Rory sat at his desk, organising the notes and discussions surrounding their mission, preparing to head into the conference room for the meeting when Buddy Spencer walked in, an amused expression fixed on his face.

"Hey, Rory! Where's this big film deal I was promised?" Buddy asked, leaning casually against the doorframe, his charisma undeniably infectious.

Rory's smile faded into a more serious expression as he met Buddy's eager gaze.

"Buddy, take a seat for a moment. I'm afraid there's no film deal," he said, the gravity of his words settling between them. "However, there's something far bigger at stake. Come with me, and we'll explain everything."

Buddy's smile faltered slightly at the unexpected turn, curiosity gleaming in his eyes. "Alright," he replied, straightening up and following Rory as he led the way out of the office. "What's really going on, and will I get paid for it?"

As they walked down the corridor and into the conference room, Rory felt the weight of responsibility pressing on him, knowing he was about to unveil the extraordinary circumstances that linked Buddy and the other Dream Agents to a greater destiny. He opened the door to the main meeting room, where the rest of the team was gathered, including Sumeet, Micky T, and Kerra, who were engaged in animated discussion.

"Everyone, I'd like you to meet Buddy Spencer," Rory said, gesturing for him to step forward. "Buddy, this is our team, and today we're not discussing a film; we're embarking on a mission to connect with you and understand the extraordinary gifts you possess."

As the buzz of conversation in the room began to subside, Rory cleared his throat, aware that the time had come to brief the newly formed team on the gravity of their mission.

"It's time I brief you," he said, his voice steady. "When you walk into those labs, you'll see a team operating equipment that may seem foreign to you—something out of a sci-fi film, almost. It's unlike anything you've ever encountered." With that, Sumeet piped up, "It really is, I couldn't believe it!"

Rory's gaze swept across the expectant faces in the room, absorbing their intrigue. "I expect you're wondering how all this came about."

Before he could elaborate further, Micky T Jr. interjected with a smirk, "Well, you are NASA, so who knows what the little green men have given you."

A ripple of laughter passed through the group, but Rory kept a serious expression as he glanced back at Micky. "Funny you mention little green men," he replied, a spark of intensity in his eyes. "We have been contacted by a species from another world—one that has aided us with this advanced technology, and they helped us find you."

As Rory informing the team of the name,

Gasps of surprise rippled through the room, and the gravity of Rory's words settled over them.

"Yes, that's correct. They are called the Rivaxians, and they have a unique connection with each of you," Rory replied. He then took a moment to let this revelation sink in.

"The technology you'll see is a result of their influence and guidance during our communications. It's why we're here— to understand your experiences and to forge a bridge between worlds."

"Okay, this is getting very interesting, but I'm also scared to death," Kerra said, her interest in the conversation visibly piqued.

"But first, let's go around the table so everyone can give their name, background, and what they do," Rory suggested. "I'll go first: Rory Walker, I head up the Dream Agent unit."

"Lewis Gell, I head up NASA."

"Dr Campbell, sleep specialist."

Sumeet cleared his throat and stood, a new sense of purpose filling the space.

"My name is Sumeet Sharma. I'm an accountant from India, and I've been experiencing strange dreams that connect me to other realms. I feel like there's something more for me to uncover." He stepped back, glancing around the room as the others nodded in acknowledgment.

"Micky T Jr. here," Micky said, standing up and gesturing with a broad smile. "I'm a musician from Mississippi, but I've been stuck in an asylum for the past few years because of my out-of-control dreams. They kept saying I'm insane, but maybe they just didn't understand what I was going through! Since I arrived here a few days ago, I've never felt better. These guys really know what they're talking about, and bro, it's like Star Trek in there—woooooohoooooo!"

"Kerra Springfield," she introduced herself, her confident demeanour evident. "I work at the stock exchange in New York, and lately, my dreams have become intense and surreal. It's as though I have a connection to something alien, and while I'm excited, I'm also unsure about what all this means."

Finally, Buddy chimed in, his voice carrying a charismatic air. "And I'm Buddy Spencer, your friendly neighbourhood film star," he said with a grin, once again lightening the mood. "I came here thinking I was about to star in some big blockbuster, but now it seems I might be part of something... well, cosmic. I'm ready to see where this goes!"

Suddenly, the heavy wooden door creaked open, revealing Lord Barnes stepping into the conference room.

Rory moved forward, eager to welcome him into the fold. "Lord Barnes, thank you for joining us. Everyone here has been introduced, but I'd like to give you a moment to introduce yourself."

"Thank you, Rory," Barnes replied, nodding slightly as he addressed the group. "As you may know, my name is Lord Barnes, but I go by Bertie among friends, and I consider all of you part of that group. I reside in Sussex and, I suppose, might be seen as somewhat of an outsider to this extraordinary gathering. However, I've sensed something transformative in my dreams that I hope aligns with what you all have shared."

As Rory listened, he noticed the way the other Dream Agents regarded Barnes—there was something enigmatic about him, a subtle frisson of intrigue that hinted at depths yet to be explored.

"Dreams have long puzzled me," Barnes continued, his voice rich with thoughtfulness. "Lately, I've found myself navigating vast, swirling landscapes during my nocturnal reveries, filled with figures who seem to beckon me toward a destiny I cannot yet grasp. It's both exhilarating and unsettling."

"All of your experiences may hold the key to understanding the Rivaxian influence in our dreams, and it seems you all share strikingly similar experiences in your dream states," Rory said, encouraging Barnes to elaborate. "As we embark on this journey together, we hope to learn from each other and uncover the full extent of your abilities."

A wave of acceptance washed over the room as the Dream Agents recognized that Lord Barnes, with his unique insights and background, was not merely a participant but also an invaluable member of their quest.

"What do you expect from me, then?" Barnes asked, crossing his arms as he surveyed the group. His expression was sharp, mirroring the gravity of their mission.

"Your perspective as a member of the royal family, coupled with your experiences in the realm of dreams, could provide insights we cannot acquire elsewhere. Your background might offer a unique context to this situation," Rory explained. "Moreover, you understand the complexities of public identity and the far-reaching implications our discoveries may have on society."

Barnes considered this, a faint smile tugging at the corners of his mouth. "I see. I am accustomed to being scrutinized by the public eye; it is, after all, the burden that comes with privilege. I am willing to share my experiences if it helps unlock these mysteries."

At that, Buddy jumped up, grinning widely. "Forget all that, you're James Bond, my friend! We've got James Bond on our team, guys!" He looked around at the other Dream Agents, his excitement contagious.

As Rory welcomed Barnes into their circle, the disparate threads of their capabilities, experiences, and lives were weaving together into something greater. Each Dream Agent brought a unique perspective: Sumeet with his insights into data and numbers, Kerra with her sharp understanding of finance and its connections, Micky with his raw creative energy, and now Barnes, with the depth of his elite background. Rory glanced at Buddy and thought to himself, We will soon discover what your true talents—and the others'—really are.

Rory knew they had the makings of an extraordinary team. "Now, sit tight in here for about thirty minutes, and I'll introduce you to the broader team shortly. There are coffee and doughnuts over there."

Rory, Lewis, and Dr. Campbell walked down the corridor to the large boardroom. "Good morning, everyone," Rory greeted, taking his place at the head of the sleek conference table. The walls were lined with state-of-the-art screens, ready to display their findings. As they went around the room, each member contributed valuable insights. "Sumeet reported an intriguing mix of dream experiences, with recurring themes of flight and exploration," Beth noted, scrolling through her tablet with focused intensity. "We suspect he has a deeper connection to his dreams than he initially realised."

Dr. Campbell added, "Kerra's dreams show significantly enhanced emotional responses, suggesting she's tapping into something psychic that we don't fully understand yet. However, her recent substance use complicates her case. We need to keep a close eye on her mental state as we proceed with her testing."

"Clearly, we have potential issues with both Micky and Kerra," Rory acknowledged, nodding as he considered the implications. "I'd like you all to conduct a deeper analysis alongside their psychological assessments. We must ensure we understand any barriers to their memories and dream functions. Let's get to work."

The team moved purposefully towards the bustling lab adjacent to the conference room. The space was bathed in deep blue lighting, lending an air of mystery that heightened the sense of discovery. Panels displaying data floated in the air, while holographic displays provided real-time information about the physiological states of the Dream Agents.

Doctors and researchers scurried about with tablet-like computers, exchanging ideas and showing notes. As Rory entered the lab, he was greeted by the sight of an intricate dance of technology and intellect—an atmosphere that buzzed with curiosity and quiet determination.

One doctor in particular, Dr. Mallory, stood out as he used an innovative device attached to his finger. With a gentle touch, he summoned a screen that materialized in front of him, displaying intricate blueprints and analyses.

"Here's the latest data on Micky and Kerra," he said, gesturing towards the visual representations of their vital statistics. "We're monitoring their neural activity closely during the testing phases."

"Excellent," Rory replied, nodding in approval as he observed the screens. "Let's begin with the neuroimaging scans. We need to understand their brainwave patterns, particularly when they're under the influence of their dreams."

As the team worked seamlessly to prepare the equipment, Rory signalled to one of the technicians to bring in the Dream Agents. Within moments, they entered the lab. Bertie looked around, his eyes widening.

"Wow, I never expected to see anything like this."

"This is an extraordinary opportunity for all of you," Rory said, glancing at Sumeet, Buddy, Bertie, and Kerra. Micky stood nearby, still blinking away the remnants of sedation.

"Let's transition into the neuroimaging scans. This will allow us to better understand your dream states and how they might relate to your experiences and any potential latent abilities," Rory said, pointing the way.

The room hummed softly with the sound of machinery as the team prepared the equipment. Rory motioned for the Dream Agents to lie back in the pods, each designed for the scans and outfitted with a network of sensors. The setup was intricate, creating a sense of high-tech sophistication paired with an intimate atmosphere—an environment that invited vulnerability.

As the agents reclined, Rory reassured them. "These scans will help us visualize your brainwave activity and how it correlates with your dreams. There's nothing dangerous about this process; we're simply seeking to understand what happens in your mind while you dream."

Sumeet closed his eyes and took a deep breath, trying to centre himself. "It feels like something is waking up inside me," he admitted. "I'm ready to go again and discover what all of this means."

"Great," Rory replied, instilling confidence into Sumeet's resolve. "Just relax and let your mind drift. We'll handle the rest."

As the scans began, deep blue lighting reflected off the sleek surfaces, casting a soft glow throughout the lab. Panels displaying real-time data hovered in the air above each Dream Agent, flashing with readings that would soon unveil the mysteries of their subconscious to the assembled scientists.

Dr. Mallory monitored the readings carefully, issuing commands to the team running the tests. "Here we go," he announced, tapping his tablet-like device. "Initiating scans now."

The machinery hummed to life, and the room fell silent, broken only by the electronic beeping and soft clicking of the equipment. Rory kept a close watch, sensing the energy in the air shift as the scans delved deeper into the minds of the Dream Agents.

After a few moments of stillness, the monitors flickered to life, displaying fluctuating graphs and vibrant patterns that represented each agent's neural activity. Rory and the team leaned in, studying the data that streamed across the screens.

Sumeet's brainwaves appeared as dynamic waves, reflecting a mix of rapid eye movement and deep activity—consistent with the reports of vivid dreaming he had shared.

"Look at these peaks," Dr. Mallory observed, gesturing to Sumeet's readings. "He's clearly experiencing heightened cognitive states. This is remarkable!"

"It's significant," Rory said, a surge of excitement rising within him. "It suggests a deep level of engagement with his dreams, potentially reflecting a strong connection to whatever the Rivaxians intended."

Next, they turned their attention to Kerra, who was also undergoing scans. Her readings displayed sharp spikes and dips, indicative of her emotional struggles during her dream cycles.

"Unresolved feelings," Rory murmured. "She may be wrestling with conflicting interpretations of her dream experiences that we'll need to address."

As the medical team began analysing the brain readings from Lord Barnes and Buddy, Rory observed their reactions intently. The screens flared to life with vibrant colour patterns, reflecting the dramatic fluctuations in each Dream Agent's neural activity.

For Bertie, the data showed clear peaks of heightened brainwave activity, particularly during the REM sleep phase. "He's experiencing a rich variety of dreams," one of the doctors remarked, pointing to the graph that displayed a symphony of vivid spikes and dips. "These readings suggest his mind is deeply engaged, likely linking emotions with vivid imagery, much like what we saw with Sumeet. It appears he has a talent for navigating between worlds within his dreams."

As Rory processed the data, the screen shifted to display the brain readings of Buddy Spencer. The patterns were strikingly similar to those of Sumeet and Bertie, showing bursts of creativity alongside emotional intensity, which suggested a deep connection to the subconscious. "Look at these fluctuations," another doctor remarked. "Buddy's dreams seem to reflect a blend of personal experiences tied to his identity as a film star. He may be channelling his creativity and imagination in ways that could be related to the larger narrative we're investigating."

Both readings indicated an innate ability to access deeper layers of consciousness, implying that each Dream Agent could tap into realms beyond ordinary experience. The shared patterns of exceptional brain activity across all three agents highlighted a compelling connection, suggesting they were likely experiencing profound ties to the same network of dreams—a network possibly woven by the influence of the Rivaxians.

As Rory reviewed the findings, a surge of excitement washed over him. The emerging connections pointed toward the potential for collaborative exploration and the possibility that these Dream Agents held invaluable knowledge waiting to be unlocked. "This is incredible," he said, addressing the team. "These readings reinforce our understanding that they are not only connected through their altered DNA but also through their shared experiences in dreams. If we can unravel the meaning behind these experiences, we could uncover the keys to fulfilling the Rivaxian mission."

With the data laid out before them, it became clear that their efforts needed to focus on unifying these unique individuals. Each Dream Agent brought a distinct perspective on consciousness, and together, they would embark on a journey to uncover the hidden truths that might ultimately bridge the divide between humanity and the mysterious Rivaxians.

Finally, as Micky's scan progressed, the data that emerged immediately captured everyone's attention. His readings were chaotic—an erratic mix of patterns revealing tumultuous mental activity. The team observed alarmingly high fluctuations, with moments of distress interspersed by brief lulls of calm.

"His distress signals are higher than the others," Dr. Mallory said, his concern evident. "It could be linked to his time in the asylum, the strain of his psychological condition."

Rory nodded slowly, the gravity of the situation weighing on him. These agents were venturing through uncharted territory, and some were struggling to maintain their footing. "We must approach him with care," he emphasized. "Understanding Micky's struggles is vital to helping him regain stability."

As the imaging sessions wrapped up, the Dream Agents were helped into a sitting position. They appeared slightly dazed, yet curious about the process they had just experienced.

"How was it?" Rory asked, his gaze shifting across each face, searching for signs of any breakthroughs.

Sumeet shrugged, a mixture of excitement and apprehension in his expression. "It was strange but interesting. I saw flashes of the dreams while I was hooked up. It felt almost like dreaming while awake."

Kerra nodded, offering her thoughts. "I don't quite know how to explain it, but it felt as though I could sense a connection to something greater. It was real, almost tangible."

Dr. Campbell stepped forward, his expression one of encouragement. "This data provides us with a solid foundation to build from. We now have a clearer understanding of each of your experiences, and it's crucial that we build on this knowledge as we move forward."

Bertie piped up, "For the first time, I saw the other Dream Agents in my dream. We were all in the same place."

"Same for me!" Micky shouted. "We were all in the same place."

"Thank you for participating," Rory added, a swell of gratitude rising within him for their courage amidst the uncertainty. "Your willingness to engage in this process is vital to our mission. Each of you brings unique insights that connect you to the Rivaxian influence, and we are on the brink of something momentous as we work together."

A contemplative silence settled in the room, punctuated by the rhythmic beeping of the monitoring equipment as the team processed the magnitude of their undertaking. It was clear that each Dream Agent had experienced profound shifts, and the key to unlocking their full potential seemed just beyond the horizon of understanding.

As they broke for the evening, Rory turned to Lewis and said, "

For the first time, they were truly making progress. The team was connected in ways that went beyond our current understanding. They were embarking on a rare and extraordinary adventure—an opportunity not only to discover the dimensions of the universe but also to explore the depths of the human mind.

Outside, night had fallen, the world growing quieter as stars began to shimmer in the sky. "Now, folks, I'd like you all to get some rest. It's been a long day for you all—and for us. Thank you, everyone, for your efforts today."

The next day would bring new challenges and deepen their collective understanding of the Dream Agents. As the possibilities unfolded, Rory felt an invigorating rush of purpose flow through him—he was ready to embrace the journey ahead, eager to explore the realms of dreams and the gaps that could bridge their civilizations.

CHAPTER 9

A New Dawn

ory jolted awake, the remnants of sleep clinging to him as urgent shouts shattered the fog of slumber. Dr. Kim, one of his team members, burst into his quarters, breathless with excitement.

"Rory! Get up! We've had further contact—come and see!"

His heart pounding, Rory grabbed his dressing gown and dashed from the room, driven by a mixture of confusion and curiosity. He stepped out of the lift, the corridor's cold air a stark contrast to the lingering warmth of his bed. As he neared the main lab, he spotted a group of doctors huddled around a large screen, their faces a blend of anticipation and unease.

"Rory, we've had another contact from the Rivaxians—this time, it's a major message!" one of the doctors called out, urgency thick in the air.

As Rory stepped closer, Lewis emerged, his face a blend of exhilaration and gravity. He, too, wore a dressing gown, evidence that he'd been roused from sleep. "This could change everything. Hopefully, we'll find out what comes next," he said, gesturing for Rory to focus on the screen.

On the display, an image flickered into view, revealing a towering figure—one of the Rivaxians. The being stood nearly nine feet tall, its broad head and deep blue eyes seeming to pierce through the very fabric of reality. Dressed in garments reminiscent of Earth's Tudor era, it exuded an elegance that was both captivating and imposing.

"I'm ready," Rory said, drawing a steady breath as he braced himself for what lay ahead.

With a decisive press of a button, the doctor activated the playback, and the Rivaxian's voice filled the lab—deep, resonant, and otherworldly.

"Greetings, Earth friends. I am Cha, the Rivaxian Nam— what you would call a King. We have observed Earth for fifty of your years, and now we know you have discovered five Dream Agents."

Rory felt the weight of those words. They had made contact with the very beings who had set their extraordinary journey into motion.

"What I am about to tell you goes far beyond our initial contact, where we shared technological data. Now, we must reveal what we need from you."

The room fell silent, tension crackling in the air as Cha continued.

"You have now located five of the individuals connected to us—the Dream Agents, as you call them. They are of great significance to our world; in fact, they are our only hope for salvation. Very soon, a micro ship positioned above your atmosphere will transmit additional data. This will provide the means for the Dream Agents to travel to our world and assist us."

Rory's heart pounded at the implications as he exchanged a glance with Lewis.

"We are a peaceful species, but we face extinction due to a devastating bomb detonated by our aggressive enemy, the Vark. The explosion rendered our population sterile, unable to reproduce," Cha explained.

The sombre weight of his words settled over the room, deepening the gravity of their plight.

"This technology allows the Dream Agents to transport themselves in their sleep, rematerializing here on our planet, Rivaxia. When they arrive, they take on their true form—whole, coherent, and fully aware. Their physical bodies remain with you on Earth, while their essence—what you might think of as their soul—travels through a micro-wormhole."

Cha took a deep breath before continuing. "Their mission is crucial: they must help us recover what remains of the five million frozen embryos currently secured on Sankat 3, a moon at the edge of our solar system. This remote location was chosen for its secrecy, but it is now under the watchful eye of the Vark, who seek to eradicate our race by destroying these embryos.

"Although the embryos are secure for now, it is only a matter of time before the Vark breach the defences and seize or annihilate them. They have already taken control of the moon and slaughtered many of our people—those who dedicated their lives to saving our species."

He paused, letting the gravity of the situation settle. "The Dream Agents are transported through a micro wormhole— a precise and highly advanced technology that enables them to traverse the vast distances between our worlds almost instantaneously. This ability is our greatest hope for securing the future of our species, but we must act before it is too late.

"I understand this is a great deal to process, and at a pace we had not wished to impose. But we are in grave danger. We need human help."

The revelation hit Rory with staggering force, the weight of their responsibility settling over him.

"You are our only hope," Cha concluded, his words carrying a gravity that tightened around Rory's chest like a vice.

"I can't believe it," Rory murmured, still processing the enormity of it all. "We have the ability to help them—but we need to fully grasp this technology first."

The team sprang into action, absorbing every detail of Cha's message. Lewis turned to Rory, his expression expectant.

"This is where your leadership becomes crucial. We must prepare to guide the Dream Agents through this process, but first, we need to analyse the data from the incoming micro ship."

"Let's establish our analysis protocols," Rory instructed, determination surging through him. "Every step must be precise and secure—especially for the Dream Agents. Their lives, and the future of the Rivaxians, depend on our understanding of this process."

As the team mobilised to prepare for the imminent communication from the micro ship, Rory considered the best way to relay this information to the Dream Agents.

As anticipation crackled through the air, the team gathered around the vast central console in the lab, awaiting the incoming data from the micro ship hovering above Earth. The atmosphere thrummed with excitement; their eyes locked onto the screens lining the walls—reminiscent of a command centre from a sci-fi film.

Suddenly, the long-awaited alert chimed, and bursts of activity flared across the monitors. Data streamed in real-time, cascading in a frenzied torrent as the system processed the enormous download. Numbers and codes spiralled across the screens like a digital waterfall, while colourful graphs emerged, revealing intricate layers of shared knowledge.

A technician shouted, snapping everyone's attention to a particular monitor.

"This data dump is enormous—bigger than anything we've ever seen on Earth!" His voice quivered with both astonishment and exhilaration as the team collectively gasped at the torrent of information cascading before them.

Rory felt a surge of adrenaline as the enormity of the moment hit him.

"Get a readout on what we're receiving!" he commanded, his heart pounding. "We need to understand exactly what this data contains. It could be crucial to our comprehension of the Rivaxians and their technology."

"Wait a second—there's something else here. Something is translating the data as it arrives. It's artificial intelligence, but far more advanced than anything we've ever seen. It's calculating in split seconds—truly astounding," said Beth.

As the data continued to flow, the team worked in unison, with extractors and analysts delving into the depths of the newly accessed information. The first graphs revealed foundational technological designs—energy systems, communication protocols, space charts, and revolutionary methods for space travel that functioned seamlessly at speeds previously thought impossible.

"Look at this!" Beth exclaimed, pointing to an intricate layout that had just appeared on the largest screen. "It's a design for an energy generator that harnesses cosmic energy using principles we'd never have conceived of without their guidance!"

Rory stepped closer, transfixed by the blueprints spiralling in mesmerising patterns. "If we can decipher and implement these designs, they could revolutionise our capabilities."

The excitement in the room was electrifying, but it was swiftly interrupted by another announcement from the technician at the keyboard.

"We're also receiving biological data! It looks like they've transmitted genetic information about their DNA modifications!"

Gasps rippled through the group as they turned their attention to the screens, eager to grasp the implications of this newly acquired genetic knowledge. The displays filled with intricate mappings and sequences—illustrations of Rivaxian DNA interwoven with notes and annotations detailing its potential impact on human genetics.

"This is ground-breaking," exclaimed Doctor Kelsey, one of the bioengineers, as she analysed the sequences. "This could explain how the DNA they dispersed among us formed such powerful connections. It's almost liked a playbook for deciphering the modifications!"

Rory nodded vigorously; his excitement contagious. "This could help us develop algorithms to filter for the Dream Agents! We can analyse the human modifications and how they resonate with the Rivaxian genetic structure. If we identify the key indicators, we might gain deeper insight into their unique abilities." He ran his hands through his hair, grinning in disbelief at the data before him.

As the data continued to stream, Rory sensed the energy in the lab shift from excitement to focused determination. They had been granted an unprecedented opportunity to unlock the secrets of an extra-terrestrial civilisation and bridge the gap between their worlds. The knowledge they were acquiring was vital—not just for understanding the Dream Agents, but for ensuring the survival of the Rivaxians themselves.

As they began sifting through the torrent of information, Rory felt the weight of responsibility settle heavily on his shoulders.

"As we analyse this data, let's stay focused—our ultimate goal is to assist if possible, but above all, we must safeguard the Dream Agents."

"Yes! Let's break it down," Lewis said, stepping forward to help organise their thoughts amidst the whirlwind of incoming data. "We can categorise our findings into three main areas: technology transfer, genetic modification, and dream dynamics. Our priority must be to focus on the most critical information for analysis."

"Absolutely," Rory agreed, enthusiasm sparking in his eyes. "Let's establish a timeline to review each section thoroughly. If we can identify key patterns in the genetic data, we may be able to assist them as they explore their identities as Dream Agents. At this stage, it's safe to assume that each will have different outcomes."

In that moment, within the softly illuminated sanctuary of their lab, Rory realised they stood on the precipice of uncovering not just the mysteries surrounding the Dream Agents, but the very essence of what it meant to be human in a universe brimming with infinite possibilities. Each discovery drew them closer to bridging worlds, forging new pathways of understanding that could unite them in ways once thought impossible. The magnitude of their mission crystallised—this symbiotic relationship held the power to reshape humanity's future, and they had a front-row seat to history in the making.

"Let's focus on the genetic data first," Rory declared, his gaze fixed on the information projected across the screens. "We need to isolate the sections related to the Dream Agents, particularly any markers indicating modifications linked to dream activity."

The team sprang into action, each member diving into their designated role. The atmosphere crackled with energy—voices overlapping in discussion, fingers racing across keyboards, and notes hastily scribbled. Their collective excitement fuelled a seamless rhythm of collaboration, driving them forward with unrelenting momentum.

Meanwhile, the screens displayed a vast array of genetic sequences, shifting in rhythmic patterns—streams of data that held the potential to answer the Rivaxians' most pressing questions.

"Look at this," one of the researchers said, eyes fixed on a particular sequence. "These markers align almost perfectly with what we've observed in Sumeet and Kerra's readings. If we can map these patterns, we might be able to identify others who share similar traits."

"Exactly," Rory said, stepping closer to the screens. "Let's compile the data we've gathered from Sumeet and Kerra and overlay it with the incoming genetic modifications. I want to examine any psychological correlations as well."

As the analysis continued, an uneasy thought gnawed at Rory—had the Rivaxians told them everything? He walked over to Lewis.

"Can you step into my office for a moment? We need to talk." As they entered, Rory picked up the coffee pot. "Want some?" he asked.

"Yes, please. It's going to be a long day." Rory handed the cup to Lewis before settling behind his desk. "In all this excitement, we've forgotten that we need to explain everything to the Dream Agents—they might not even be interested."

Lewis was about to respond when, suddenly, the office door burst open. Sumeet, Kerra, Micky, Bertie, and Buddy rushed inside, their expressions a mix of exhilaration and urgency.

"Rory! You won't believe what just happened!" Sumeet exclaimed, his voice breathless. The others echoed his urgency, their voices overlapping in a chaotic mix of excitement.

"What's going on?" Rory asked, astonished. "What happened? One at a time, please."

"We all just received messages in our dreams!" Kerra interjected, her eyes wide with disbelief. "At the exact same moment, the Rivaxians communicated with each of us directly! They showed us images—visions of connections— and told us it was time to unite!"

Rory's heart pounded as he processed the news.

"You all had the same dream? At the same time?" He glanced around the room, the implications sinking in.

"Yes! They even explained how vital our roles are in this mission—the mighty Cha came to me in my dream!" Mickey declared.

A wave of relief washed over Rory.

"At least I don't have to worry about communication issues anymore; the Rivaxians are making direct contact in real time!" He masked his unease at this sudden shift in the process.

"They made it clear—they need our help immediately," Buddy chimed in, his enthusiasm infectious. "We have to prepare for what's coming next."

Rory felt the excitement build as he marvelled at the synchronicity of the Dream Agents.

"We can push this forward faster now. We know what they want us to do—we have to go to Rivaxia," Micky said.

"This change everything! With the Rivaxians communicating directly, we can coordinate at an entirely new level. Their involvement could speed up our timeline significantly," Rory said to Lewis.

"Exactly!" Sumeet added, his excitement matching Rory's. "They're reaching out to guide us, giving us the information, we need to track down the remaining Dream Agents. I could feel the urgency in their presence during the dream—the need to prepare is critical."

Rory looked at Lewis. "Now, hold on a moment. I appreciate the excitement, but we need to take this in carefully. We have to fully understand what is being asked of you."

"Don't worry," Micky said, glancing at the others. "They've already told us—we're going to their world."

CHAPTER 10

Bridging Worlds

In the days following direct communication from Cha, the Rivaxian leader, the atmosphere within the facility shifted. The urgency to construct transport for the Dream Agents had never been greater. Engineers and scientists flooded into the facility with newfound determination, clutching coffee cups and chattering in animated groups. They knew the success of their mission depended on their ability to translate technology from another world— technology that would become the vessels for the Dream Agents' extraordinary journeys.

In the state-of-the-art underground labs, bathed in a mesmerising blue glow, the intricate shimmer of holographic screens and cutting-edge technology created an electrifying atmosphere, pulsing with anticipation and innovation. Rory gathered the team, ready to launch the building process.

"Alright, everyone, settle down, please. Lewis would like to start with a few words," he began, addressing the assembled engineers and lead scientists, their expressions alight with focus and excitement.

"Today marks a pivotal moment in our project. We have gathered some of our finest engineers—many of you played key roles in Mercury and Apollo—so it's an honour to have you all contributing to this vital mission. Your task is to build the pods that will enable the Dream Agents to travel into the Rivaxian realm via micro-wormholes.

We must move swiftly, yet meticulously, ensuring that no steps in the assembly are overlooked. With that, I'll now hand things over to Rory."

Each team member exchanged lively glances; their eagerness palpable as Rory continued.

"These pods are designed to interface directly with the agents' neural pathways. According to the data from the Rivaxians, they should provide a seamless transition as the agents drift into their dreaming states."

One of the engineers, Max, chimed in, his mind racing with ideas.

"If we design the pod interiors to prioritise comfort and security—imagine shapeshifting materials moulding around the user inside—it could minimise anxiety during transport, as well as regulate air circulation."

"Good point—make sure you carefully review the specs on that. The Rivaxians may not care for comfort the way humans do," Rory replied, nodding appreciatively. A ripple of laughter went around the room. "We want the agents to feel at ease, as though they're slipping into sleep at home. Moving on, the interface outline indicates that nodes will attach directly to their heads, allowing us to monitor their brain activity and modulate the connection with the micro-wormhole as they dream."

In another corner of the lab, several scientists were already deep in discussion over the technical details.

"What kind of material are we using for the nodes? They need to be lightweight yet durable enough to ensure accurate readings," Alice, a lead researcher, noted as she scribbled ideas on a whiteboard. "They appear to be made of an aluminium-based material," she added.

Meanwhile, another group was reviewing data on a tablet.

"This design they've sent looks like molecular technology," suggested one of the engineers.

"No," another countered, "this is far smaller than that. It's nanotechnology—adaptable, precise, and capable of providing an accurate connection to real-time brain activity. Once they drift into a dream state, the nano-probes align directly with the micro-ships above."

Rory smiled, encouraging the brainstorming to continue.

"This goes beyond anything we currently understand—or have even imagined," he said. The conversation among the engineers and scientists flowed freely, ideas ricocheting as they dissected every function the pods would require. They pored over the materials and composites provided by the Rivaxians.

"How do we manufacture some of these components without raising suspicion?" one of the engineers asked.

"Don't worry about that—we've got a specialist facility handling it off-site. They should have the parts here within a few days," said Lewis. "You just focus on building the damn things and making sure they work."

While the engineers began assembling the components already at hand, Rory took time to prepare for the briefing with the Dream Agents. The operational aspects of this new technology needed to be crystal clear; he wanted to ensure they fully understood how the pods would function within the broader scope of their mission.

Rory assembled everyone in the main briefing room. The space glowed softly with the hum of technology, holographic screens displaying designs and simulations of the pods under construction. The Dream Agents took their seats, their expressions a mixture of eagerness and apprehension for what lay ahead.

"Thank you all for coming," Rory began, his gaze sweeping over Sumeet, Kerra, Micky, Bertie, and Buddy. Their eyes shone with curious anticipation.

"You've been working together as a team for the past few weeks, and I couldn't be more delighted with how you've come together—it's truly impressive. As you know, we stand on the brink of something ground-breaking: pods that will allow you to travel through space to the Rivaxian realm while you dream. I want to walk you through how this process works so that you feel fully prepared as we move forward."

He gestured towards a screen displaying a 3D rendering of the pod.

"Inside these pods, nodes will gently attach to your heads, monitoring your brain activity and relaying crucial data to the main system as you sleep. This ensures the transport process remains both safe and effective."

As Rory spoke, he observed the Dream Agents absorbing every word, their expressions a blend of intrigue and apprehension.

"The concept is straightforward: as you dream, the pods will synchronise with the micro ships, which serve as conduits, guiding you through the micro wormhole activated by the Rivaxians. If everything goes to plan, you'll wake up on Rivaxia."

"Hold on," Buddy interjected, his tone edged with apprehension. "So, we're just meant to fall asleep and hope for the best?"

"Not quite," Rory interjected swiftly. "You'll be under constant monitoring, and the Rivaxians will be there to guide you as you awaken in their realm. The goal is to prepare you for the role they need you to fulfil. We believe your abilities can help restore balance to their civilisation. According to them, once you arrive, you'll gain skills and talents far beyond anything you could develop on Earth—abilities beyond human comprehension."

"Sounds pretty surreal," Micky mused, scratching his head. "I spent years in an asylum, and who would've thought? Turns out everything I said back then was true. I'd love to shove this right down that doctor's throat! But hey, if I'm dreaming, I might as well dream big."

"Exactly," Rory said with a reassuring smile. "You don't have to face this alone. We'll guide you every step of the way. You'll be surrounded by experts who understand both the technology and the potential within your dreams. Our team will support each of you throughout this process, ensuring your safety and clarity at every stage. And of course, you have the Rivaxians—remember, they've been preparing for this for fifty years!"

Vincent stared at Micky, barely able to believe the transformation. Just days ago, Micky had been in a hospital, yet now it was as if the weight of his past struggles had vanished entirely."

"The atmosphere began to shift as Rory's words sank in, the nervous tension in the room giving way to a growing sense of purpose. A shared understanding settled among the Dream Agents—this mission was not just about their personal journeys but a collective responsibility to the Rivaxians and, ultimately, the fate of two worlds.

'Remember, the task ahead is not something we take lightly,' Rory continued, his voice steady with conviction. 'The stakes are high, and while you may feel trepidation, trust in your connections. You may uncover abilities and insights you never knew existed within you. Now, get some rest and be back here at 09:00 a.m. on Thursday.'"

"The Dream Agents left the main room, dispersing in different directions—except for Kerra and Bertie. Meanwhile, Rory returned to the assembly lab, where the building work had settled into a steady rhythm.

Bertie stood up and turned to Kerra. 'Fancy a cup of coffee?' he asked. She nodded silently. The air between them was thick with tension as they contemplated the imminent journey to Rivaxia."

"I can't shake the feeling that, even though we've all had the same dreams, we're stepping into the unknown," Kerra admitted, her voice low and tinged with apprehension. "The reports coming in don't paint a clear picture. What if we can't handle whatever we find there?"

Bertie, ever the optimist despite the weight of the mission, gave a measured nod.

"Every mission carries risks, Kerra. But think about what Rivaxia represents—an entire world brimming with possibilities. We'll have the chance to explore, to adapt, to develop new strategies. It could be exhilarating. And if what they say is true, we're part Rivaxian ourselves... which means they're our people too."

Kerra sighed, her mind racing with concerns.

"Exciting, sure—but what if there are local factions? If their culture is as intricate as we've heard, navigating it could be treacherous."

Bertie waved a hand dismissively, a small smile creeping onto his lips.

"True, but we've no reason to think that—and besides, we're trained. Remember, unpredictability is part of the allure. It's a chance to learn from them—and maybe even gain allies." The conversation shifted as they speculated about Rivaxia's environment, picturing the vibrant landscapes they had only seen in their dreams. With the mission looming ahead, their excitement and apprehension simmered beneath the surface—a testament to the challenges they were ready to face together.

"As their discussion continued, the flickering overhead lights cast shifting shadows across the room, deepening the weight of their mission. Kerra leaned back, arms crossed, her gaze fixed on the fluctuating data on her tablet."

"What if we unintentionally offend someone in their hierarchy? Perceptions can shift in an instant, and one wrong word might spark a conflict we can't control."

Bertie, sensing her mounting anxiety, responded with quiet reassurance.

"We've all been dreaming of this for years. To me, the Rivaxians are like family—some even closer than those on Earth."

"You're right. They do feel like family," Kerra admitted softly.

After a brief silence, Kerra drew a deep breath, the weight of their responsibility settling heavily on her shoulders.

"I want to be ready for anything. Rivaxia isn't just a place on a map; it's a realm of possibilities—and dangers."

Bertie arched an eyebrow, his expression both grave and reassuring.

"Exactly. Our fears only prove how much this matters to us. And it's that passion that will carry us forward. Together, we'll face whatever Rivaxia has in store."

The intensity of the moment lingered, fueling a shared determination between them. As they concluded their conversation, their camaraderie strengthened—no matter the uncertainties, they were prepared to embrace the journey ahead.

Back in the assembly lab, as Rory finished speaking, the engineers and scientists working on the pods returned to the briefing room, announcing that the first prototype would be ready on Wednesday, just two days away, for initial testing.

After two intense days in the assembly lab, followed by brief tests, the Dream Agents were back in the Boardroom as instructed.

Rory walked in. "Morning, folks. Would you like to come and see how your pods are coming along?" he asked the Dream Agents.

"I, for one, certainly would," said Bertie. "What about you lot?"

They all nodded in agreement.

With that, they stood and followed Rory down the corridor.

"Alright, everyone, try not to get too close—it's very busy in here. But feel free to ask any questions," Rory said.

They stepped into the assembly area, where the pods were being put together. The team gathered around as a pod was rolled in—a sleek, futuristic model with smooth contours and soft blue ambient lights pulsating along its edges.

"Welcome to your new transport!" one of the engineers announced, proudly presenting the pod. "This is where you'll connect with the Rivaxians during your dreams."

The Dream Agents stepped forward, curiosity sparkling in their eyes as they examined the pod's design and features. Rory gestured for them to take note of the control panels and input screens, which would interface directly with their dream states.

"You'll enter through this canopy door here," Rory explained. "Inside, the chamber contains nodes that will attach to your heads, allowing the technology to read your brainwaves and ensure a smooth transport. It's designed for maximum comfort, and while you relax, the systems will handle the rest.

Sumeet spoke up, looking intrigued. "What about our dreams? How will the technology understand what we're experiencing?"

"Excellent question," Rory replied. "The nodes will not only monitor your brain activity but also generate a data stream that captures the nuances of your dreams as they unfold. This allows us to analyse any patterns that emerge during transport and ensure the experience is both safe and beneficial when you reach Rivaxia."

"Will it hurt?" Kerra asked, an edge of concern in her voice.

"Not at all," Rory assured her. "You might feel a slight tingling as the nodes engage with your brain's energy, but nothing more than that. This process is designed to enhance your natural abilities, not hinder them. Plus, we administer sedatives to ensure you remain deep in your dreams."

Rory glanced around at each member of the team before continuing. "There's something I need you all to consider and discuss amongst yourselves. You'll have two days to think about it and come to me with your answer."

"We need a guinea pig—someone to test this first. I don't want to put you all through it at once. I need to understand what's on the other side and ensure that it works. This is something for you to decide as a group—we won't select someone for you."

The team exchanged glances.

"But wait," Buddy said, frowning. "I thought you said this was safe."

Rory glanced back at him. "Nothing is one hundred per cent safe, Buddy."

"I'll do it," said Sumeet. "I was the first one here—I should be the first to test it. It's only fair."

"Any comments?" Rory asked.

The team exchanged glances before nodding in agreement with Sumeet.

"Alright then, we have our test pilot. Go and get plenty of rest, Sumeet—it's going to be an exciting few days for all of us," Rory said with a nod.

CHAPTER 11

⊙⟨◇⟩⊙

The Test Flight

A s the team stood in the bright, blue-lit lab, the excitement in the air was electric. They were on the brink of conducting the first test run of their newly constructed pods, and Sumeet Sharma had volunteered to be the first Dream Agent to undergo the process.

Rory felt a mixture of trepidation and exhilaration as he prepared for this monumental moment.

"Today, we will conduct a test flight," he announced, drawing the team's attention. "Sumeet will be transported to the Rivaxians as part of this initial run. This is a critical step in understanding how the Dream Agents can communicate with them directly."

The atmosphere thickened with anticipation as the engineers and medical staff conducted their final system checks. The steady hum of machines filled the space, while holographic screens displayed vital statistics, monitoring Sumeet's heart rate and brainwave activity.

Sumeet stepped forward, his expression a blend of excitement and nervousness.

"I'm ready. Let's see what this can do," he said, a determined spark igniting in his eyes.

Rory offered a reassuring smile.

"You're embarking on a significant journey, Sumeet. Just relax and focus on the connection you felt in your earlier dreams. We'll be monitoring you closely and keeping the lines of communication open."

With that, the technicians moved in, attaching the nodes to Sumeet's temples. A nurse then stepped forward and gently took hold of his arm.

"This needle will ensure your body receives the necessary nutrients to keep you fit and healthy while you sleep. The second needle administers the sedative to ensure you enter a deep sleep."

As Sumeet lay waiting in the pod, Rory and the team moved into position around the control centre, anticipation radiating throughout the room. The door sealed around Sumeet, and the soft glow of the ambient lights enveloped him, creating an atmosphere of tranquillity.

"We're all with you on this test, Sumeet!" said Micky. "You're one lucky son of a bitch to go first—say hi to that Cha guy for me," he added, grinning as he glanced at the other Dream Agents.

"Activating the pod now," called out a technician, his fingers dancing over the console as he initiated the sequence. Within moments, Sumeet had drifted into sleep, entering the dream phase.

"We'll establish the connection with the micro-wormhole," said Burges, the Chief Technician.

The pod hummed to life, and Rory watched intently as the feedback began streaming in. Lights flickered, the soft whirring escalated momentarily, then settled into a steady rhythm—an indication that synchronization was taking place.

"Neural connectivity established," a technician announced, their voice crackling through the system. "We're ready to initiate the transport."

"Let's do this," Rory urged, his heart thumping in rhythm with the anticipation that filled the room. "Engage the transfer."

With a final press of the button, the pod activated, sending a soft glow of energy that enveloped Sumeet. The room erupted in a cascade of data streaming across the screens as Sumeet's readings fluctuated, signalling that he was entering an altered state of consciousness.

A moment later, the screens flashed, displaying Sumeet's brainwaves responding positively to the stimuli.

"All systems are functioning as expected," Beth said, her eyes wide with excitement as she monitored the readings. "He's successfully entering the dream state."

As the pod pulsed with energy, Rory scanned the various screens around the room. They were on the brink of something extraordinary—watching to see if Sumeet could connect with the Rivaxians as intended. Minutes stretched into what felt like lifetimes as the lab held its collective breath. Tension and anticipation thickened in the air, coalescing into a singular, electrified moment. Rory could only hope for success.

Then, with a sudden hum and a soft flash, the pod's lights flickered. Sumeet's readings surged into perfect synchronisation, sending a wave of excitement rippling through the room.

"Connection established!" a voice rang out, electrified with jubilation, echoing off the walls.

The team watched intently as data streamed across the monitors. Rory glanced at the clock, then turned to Lewis.

"He's been under for three hours now," he said.

"Let's take that as a positive for now," Lewis replied.

Then, suddenly, the pod door slid open, and Rory rushed forward. Sumeet sat up, his face awash with wonder. He blinked, adjusting to the transition back to reality, an invigorated energy radiating from him.

"I saw them!" Sumeet exclaimed, his voice brimming with awe. "I was there, and it felt exactly like being here, talking with you. The Rivaxians! They were there, welcoming me, and they wanted to convey something. It was unbelievable!

"It's such a strange feeling—you're shooting through the stars, and then suddenly, you feel a tingle. And then you're there, actually there, as a whole person. It's really me in their world!"

Rory felt a surge of elation flood through him.

"That's fantastic news! Tell us everything you experienced. But first, we need the medical team to check you over. Once that's complete, we can talk. It's critical that we understand the connection and prepare for future transportations."

Sumeet took a moment to gather his thoughts as the doctors checked his vital signs and brain readouts.

"He's okay—good to go," said the doctor.

Moving to a chair to steady himself, Sumeet asked, "How long was I there? It felt like four days."

"Interesting," Rory mused. "You were only there for a few hours—three, in fact," he said, glancing at the clock. "This suggests that time moves faster in their realm."

Sumeet was still visibly reeling from the experience.

"There was a space filled with light—vast beyond comprehension. I felt their warmth and acceptance, as if I truly belonged. They showed me glimpses of their world—cities built from luminous materials; skies painted in colours I've never seen. But then, there were buildings and people I had seen in my previous dreams. It didn't feel alien to me; it felt normal."

"Sounds remarkable," Rory said, accepting that the Rivaxians had spent years preparing the Dream Agents within their dreams.

"We need to document this. The insight you provide could be crucial as we prepare to bring in the other Dream Agents."

Buddy walked over to Sumeet and smiled.

"Sumeet, you're the first person to travel outside our galaxy—you sure to have plenty of admirers now, son."

Sumeet looked at him, his expression a mix of fear and confusion.

"Really?"

"You sure are," Buddy said as he walked over and sat back down in his chair.

Rory knew they were forging a new connection across the barriers of imagination and reality.

"As you all know, no one outside this project can know what is happening here. I'm sure I don't need to remind you how delicate this situation is."

"Sorry, Sumeet, I guess those admirers will have to wait," Buddy said, laughing.

"Okay, team, the doctors and I need some time to speak with Sumeet alone. We'll bring everyone back together shortly to share more information."

Sumeet stood at the centre of the lab, wrapped in the echoes of his recent experience, the wonder in his eyes igniting a contagious enthusiasm within the team.

"They showed me their world," he began, his voice brimming with awe. "It was breath-taking. Rivaxia—it's so different from Earth, filled with landscapes that feel alive."

"What did you see?" Rory asked, drawn in by the intensity of Sumeet's expression.

"The sky was a shifting blend of colours I can't quite explain—like a sunset, but more vibrant. The trees were tall and glowing, their leaves shimmering in hues of blue and green, pulsing gently as if they had their own heartbeat. As I walked among them, I realised the ground beneath my feet was humming with energy."

Sumeet's voice grew more animated as he recounted the details.

"The Rivaxians themselves... they're remarkable beings. They stand about nine feet tall, their heads slightly rounder than ours. Their skin has a silvery texture, reflecting light in a way that makes them seem almost ethereal. They move with a graceful fluidity, as if they're in tune with the energy of their surroundings."

"Did they speak?" Rory asked, leaning in closer.

"Yes! They communicate verbally—not through thoughts, as you all initially suspected. Their speech is melodious, rich with inflection and warmth. I was apprehensive at first, but their voices had a soothing quality that put me at ease. They welcomed me like an old friend, and I could feel their kindness radiating, even through the strange atmosphere of their world."

"Did they share any specific messages with you?" Vincent asked, his interest piqued.

"Yes," Sumeet replied, his expression turning momentarily serious. "They reiterated the message from the Cha—they have been monitoring us for decades, acknowledging our progress and struggles. Their mission is to assist us technologically, but they need us to fully comprehend what it means to be a Dream Agent. They believe our connection is paramount."

Rory absorbed this information. The Rivaxians were not only ready to assist but eager to share their knowledge and experiences with humanity. "This is incredible, Sumeet. Your encounters could be the key to bridging understanding between our two civilizations."

"Exactly," Sumeet said, his resolve strengthening alongside Rory's. "They conveyed how deeply intertwined our fates are, especially with the looming challenges they face. They're reaching out to us for assistance—not just for their survival, but for ours as well. They want the Dream Agents to travel to their world and help save their species. The most astonishing part is that once we are in their realm, we will gain additional abilities, but they need us there to teach us how to use them."

As the team continued discussing the implications of Sumeet's revelations, the connection between the two worlds became increasingly clear.

"We need to share this with the other Dream Agents," Rory insisted. "We have a powerful message to convey—one that underscores how critical their roles will be in the upcoming journey. I'll arrange a meeting in the morning. You should get some rest now, Sumeet. Tomorrow is going to be a long day."

As the Dream Agents gathered in the boardroom, chatting amongst themselves and sipping coffee, Rory and Sumeet entered, their expressions a mix of excitement and wonder.

"How was it, big fella?" Buddy asked, his eyes gleaming with curiosity. "Were there any good-looking girls there?"

"It was truly amazing," Sumeet replied, still struggling to fully grasp the extraordinary experiences he had just encountered. His mind raced back to the vibrant landscapes of Rivaxia, a world where reality melded with the surreal. He vividly recalled the sprawling crystalline forests that sparkled under a double sun, the iridescent rivers that flowed with liquid light, and the breathtaking vistas that seemed to defy the laws of nature.

"But the best bit," Sumeet continued, his enthusiasm infectious, "Is that when you're on Rivaxia, you gain enhanced powers."

"What powers?" Bertie interjected, leaning forward, intrigued.

"Superpowers," Sumeet said, his eyes widening as he spoke. "But they'll explain everything when we get there."

With that, a buzz of excitement rippled through the group.

"What the heck, folks, we're like the main characters from a comic book!" Micky T shouted, his imagination running wild with possibilities.

Sumeet looked back at him, a bemused smile playing on his lips.

"Not quite," he replied, shaking his head. "But we do have a few things there, that aren't available on Earth." He gestured, and the room seemed to shimmer, offering a glimpse of the wonders awaiting them.

The agents exchanged glances, the gravity of their mission settling in. A blend of apprehension and exhilaration swept through them, each one envisioning the ultimate adventure that awaited. They were no longer merely dream agents; they were on the cusp of becoming pioneers in a realm where the ordinary collided with the extraordinary.

With this milestone firmly behind them, Rory and the team readied themselves to transition into the next phase. They organised the data on Sumeet's experiences, documenting the specifics of the Rivaxians, their culture, and the abilities of the Dream Agents.

"Okay, Dream Agents, we'll do a full transfer in two days. Get some rest."

As the main room emptied and they began walking back to their rooms, Kerra glanced across at Mickey.

"Do you fancy a walk?" Her voice was barely above a whisper, a hesitant smile playing on her lips. The sterile, brightly lit corridor of the NASA facility seemed to close in on her, the relentless hum of advanced technology a constant reminder of the mission ahead. She looked at Mickey, his usual boundless energy subdued by a quiet intensity that mirrored her own. The weight of their impending journey to Rivaxia hung heavily in the air, a blend of excitement and apprehension swirling within her. It had been a gruelling few weeks, testing their abilities, endurance, and friendship to the limit. Yet, amidst the relentless pressure, something new had begun to bloom.

Micky's eyes lit up at her invitation, his usual ebullience returning.

"Sure," he replied, his voice a low chuckle that seemed to ease the tension between them. "Fresh air might be just what we need."

As they stepped into the lift and ascended to the ground level, the cacophony of alarms and urgent conversations fading into the distance, a quiet settled between them. The crisp evening air of Florida, a stark contrast to the sterile environment of the facility, washed over them. In the stillness between rigorous training sessions and late-night briefings, a bond had formed—one far deeper than simple camaraderie. They walked in comfortable silence for a while, lost in their thoughts.

As they strolled along the moonlit path, the conversation drifted to their preparations for the trip to Rivaxia. Kerra confided in Micky about her anxieties, the weight of the responsibility, and the uncertainty of the mission. He listened intently, his empathy and unwavering support offering comfort against her fears. A shared glance, a moment of unspoken understanding amidst the quiet, and a gentle touch on her arm brought them closer. The moon cast long shadows as they walked, the landscape providing a welcome respite from the technological heart of the facility where they had spent weeks training. In the hush of the night, under the calming glow of the moon, an unspoken awareness of their growing connection blossomed—a testament to the strength of their bond, forged not in romance, but in the crucible of shared danger and the imminent adventure awaiting them in a distant galaxy. The looming journey to Rivaxia had somehow led them both to discover an unexpected safe harbour in each other.

"Micky, there's something you need to know about me—my past," Kerra said, looking at him.

"Honey, no one can have a crazier past than me, so don't worry. I don't care," he replied, smiling at her.

They walked back into the building and entered the lift. The heavy blast door hissed shut, plunging them into the sterile, dimly lit confines of their underground quarters. The constant hum of the facility's advanced technology pressed in—a stark reminder of the immense responsibility they carried and the perilous journey to Rivaxia that loomed ahead.

As they walked down the corridor and reached Kerra's room, she stopped and turned to Micky, a hesitant smile playing on her lips. The sterile corridor felt claustrophobic, amplifying her anxiety. She glanced at Micky, his usual ebullience muted and replaced by a quiet intensity that mirrored her own.

"It's... it's been a long day," she began, her voice barely a whisper. "All this training, the simulations... it's taking its toll. Come inside for a few minutes."

Micky's eyes met hers, his usual boundless energy subdued by the shared weight of their impending mission. He reached out, his fingers lightly brushing hers as they walked inside.

"I know," he replied softly, his voice a low murmur that acknowledged the unspoken anxieties hanging between them. "I feel it too. It's not just the physical training; it's the... the uncertainty." He paused, his gaze drifting toward her bed, the sterile medical equipment a jarring contrast to the intimacy beginning to bloom between them. "We're both carrying a lot. We're going to face incredible challenges." He paused again, then added, "And it's not just the Rivaxians. There's the Vark, the embryos…"

He stopped, his voice trailing off. He looked at Kerra's tired face and then continued, "Maybe… maybe some quiet time would help. Just to… ground ourselves before it all kicks off."

As they walked towards her bed, the silence between them weighed heavily, filled with a blend of shared fear and budding affection. The sterile nature of their surroundings heightened their vulnerability, while the looming journey to Rivaxia served as a stark reminder of the uncertainty ahead. Then, Kerra paused. She turned to Micky, her voice little more than a breath, the words lingering between them, fragile and exposed.

"Stay with me tonight," she whispered, "I don't want to be alone."

The unspoken longing for comfort and connection echoed in the quiet intimacy of that shared moment. Micky's eyes mirrored the silent emotions that reflected her own heart. He nodded, his smile soft and understanding, and, with a shared glance, they kissed before falling back onto the bed, seeking solace and the fragile promise of what might lie ahead.

CHAPTER 12

A New World Awaits

The clatter of cutlery against ceramic plates echoed through the cavernous NASA cafeteria, a stark contrast to the hushed anticipation that lingered in the air. The Dream Agents, along with several support staff, gathered for their final breakfast before the transfer to Rivaxia. Sumeet, ever the optimist, entertained the table with stories of his previous trip, his vivid descriptions of Rivaxia's shimmering landscapes painting a scene of both wonder and unease.

Kerra, typically reserved, listened intently, her eyes occasionally meeting Micky's across the table—a silent acknowledgment of the shared anxiety pulsing beneath their carefully maintained professional distance. Bertie, ever the pragmatist, discussed the technical aspects of the pods, while Buddy, his usual boundless energy somewhat tempered by the gravity of the occasion, nervously checked his equipment. Rory, observing them all, felt a surge of both pride and anxiety. These individuals, united by an extraordinary mission, were about to embark on a journey that could alter their lives—and possibly the fate of entire civilizations.

"So, does anyone have any last-minute anxieties?" Rory asked, his voice an attempt to dispel the tension. A ripple of nervous laughter passed around the table, a blend of jokes and genuine unease.

Sumeet chuckled. "I'm ready to go back—let's get this over with." He stole a glance at Kerra. Micky, despite the lightness in his tone, let out a nervous laugh. Kerra's eyes, usually sharp and focused, now held a softness and hesitation as she met Micky's gaze. Their brief connection—a silent acknowledgment of the profound changes and uncertain future ahead—was enough to remind Rory why they had been brought together.

"Okay then, let's get to the lab," Rory said as they all stood and walked out of the canteen.

The entire team of Dream Agents gathered in the sleek, high-tech chamber, surrounded by their shimmering pods—each one a marvel of advanced engineering. Nervous energy crackled in the air as they prepared for the transfer to

Rivaxia, each member lost in thought, contemplating the adventure that lay ahead. Sumeet, whose experience lingered in the back of their minds, offered a reassuring nod.

"Okay, everyone! It's time to finalise the checks," Rory announced, his voice cutting through the tension that thickened the room. They moved to their respective pods, each encased in a translucent shell that pulsed with soft light, evoking both comfort and apprehension.

The Dream Agents eased into the pods, their smooth, contoured surfaces a welcome contrast to the sterile lab environment. Technicians moved with practised precision, affixing a network of delicate sensors to the agents' temples, the cool points of contact sending a brief shiver across their skin. The hum of the machinery deepened as the technicians secured the neural interface, ensuring a seamless connection between the agents' minds and the sophisticated pod systems.

Before them, a vast array of monitors displayed intricate graphs and visualisations, the screens pulsing with data as the final checks progressed. Two slender needles, nearly imperceptible against their skin, slid into each agent's arm— one dispensing a precisely calibrated dose of a dream-inducing serum, the other delivering a nutrient-rich solution to sustain their bodies throughout the transfer.

Nurses and technicians meticulously inspected the connections, their expressions a fusion of professional focus and barely contained anticipation. The lab pulsed with energy—an electrifying mix of excitement and apprehension—as the countdown to transport to Rivaxia commenced. The Dream Agents closed their eyes, a surge of anticipation and trepidation coursing through them. The cutting-edge technology encasing them stood in stark contrast to the world they were about to enter.

As the pod lids descended, sealing the agents within their cocoons, the doors locked with a definitive click. A countdown flickered across the monitors lining the walls, each digit pulsing like a heartbeat. The tension in the room thickened with every passing second as the numbers dropped, and the agents exchanged glances, silently urging one another forward.

"Three… two… one…"

A sudden, piercing alarm shattered the silence, sending a jolt of panic through the group.

"What's happening?" Buddy shouted; his voice edged with alarm. The monitors flared red, isolating a single pod in their frantic glow.

"It's Bertie's pod! There's a glitch!" Rory exclaimed. "Don't panic—we can reset it."

"No problem," Bertie interjected, his voice steady despite the blaring alarm. "I'm sure it's just a minor issue," he added, blending confidence with hope.

They watched as the staff hurried around Bertie's pod, swiftly analysing the problem. Within moments, the alarm fell silent, and the pod's lights returned to a steady glow.

"Are you still good to go?" Rory asked, his concern evident.

"Yes, I'm good to go," Bertie replied with unwavering confidence.

Lewis chimed in, "Let's hope that's our only glitch for this trip," he said, exchanging a glance with Rory.

With the issue resolved, the countdown resumed. The tension eased slightly, replaced by a surge of determination.

"Let's do this!" Buddy shouted, adrenaline surging through him.

"All pods are ready," Burges, the Chief Technician, confirmed as he cast a final glance at Lewis and Rory. The countdown restarted from ten, anticipation thick in the air.

"Three... two... one... Transfer!" Rory called out.

A dazzling light engulfed them, swirling colours flooding their vision as they felt themselves being pulled through space.

For a brief moment, the dream agents experienced weightlessness—then, solid ground met their feet. One by one, they emerged in full form, stepping out of the brilliance and into a vast open expanse, where magnificent flora stretched before them and a sky blazed with breathtaking hues.

In front of them stood the Rivaxian delegation—tall figures draped in elaborate, Tudor-like garments that shimmered under the glow of their twin suns.

"Welcome, Dream Agents of Earth, to Rivaxia!" boomed the lead Rivaxian, his voice deep and resonant with warmth.

"We are honoured to have you here." He paused, his gaze sweeping over them. "I am Naguan, a senior minister of Rivaxia. Your journey is not without purpose—we wish to share with you the wonders of our planet."

With a graceful gesture, the delegation led them to a grand chamber, its towering walls adorned with intricate artefacts and exquisite artworks—each piece a testament to Rivaxia's rich and storied history.

The first days on Rivaxia were a kaleidoscope of wonder. The Dream Agents, their senses heightened by the planet's unique energy, ventured through landscapes unlike anything they had ever imagined. Luminescent caves pulsed with an ethereal glow, their crystalline structures humming with a low, resonant frequency that thrummed through their very bones. Colossal formations, shimmering with an inner light, rose from the landscape like sentient giants, their surfaces rippling with patterns that shifted and danced with the wind. In sun-drenched meadows, flora of impossible colours and shapes swayed gently, their petals unfurling in a mesmerising display. Every step was a revelation, every breath a deeper connection to this alien realm. The Rivaxians, their movements graceful and fluid, guided them through it all, their demeanour calm and reassuring. Yet, even amid the splendour, something felt amiss.

In the evenings, gathered around fires that pulsed with a soft, ethereal glow, the Rivaxians revealed their astonishing abilities. Some moved with impossible speed, their figures blurring as they darted effortlessly through the air. Others could see through solid objects, their gaze piercing walls and uncovering hidden chambers. They shared their technology—far beyond human comprehension—demonstrating how to harness the energy that permeated their world.

One of the Rivaxians stood before the Dream Agents, the firelight casting flickering shadows across his face. "Once, many of our people possessed these enhanced skills. Now, what you see before you are all that remains. It is you, the Dream Agents, who now hold these abilities—and you are the ones who can help us."

Yet, it was in the quiet moments, in the shared glances and subdued conversations, that the Dream Agents began to notice something unsettling. Though Rivaxian society was welcoming and advanced, there were no children. The population appeared to consist almost entirely of mature adults, their faces etched with a wisdom that suggested lifetimes of experience. The absence of children, the almost unnatural maturity of everyone they encountered, cast a shadow beneath the wonder, stirring an unease they could not ignore.

The Dream Agents stood before the Cha, the leader of this vanishing world. They had known the Rivaxians had lost the ability to reproduce, but over the past few days, the stark absence of children had become painfully clear. What had once been a vibrant, alien landscape now concealed a darker, more urgent truth.

"We have shared our world with you so that you may understand the significance of who we are," he began, his voice low and grave. "But now, we face a dire challenge—a threat that could erase our species entirely." The weight of his words, coupled with the stark reality of the children's absence, struck the group like a blow. The Dream Agents, once captivated by the wonders of this world, now felt the crushing gravity of their predicament. They were no longer mere visitors; they had become vital players in a desperate struggle for survival.

"Our existence is under siege by the Vark—formidable warriors who have seized control of Sankat 3, our moon and research centre at the farthest reaches of our solar system. They have taken possession of vital embryos—essential to the survival of our species. We need your help to retrieve them."

A ripple of confusion spread through the group, quickly overshadowed by the grim realisation of the stakes they now faced.

"What exactly are the Vark?" Kerra asked, prompting the Rivaxians to elaborate.

Naguan's expression darkened as he spoke of the Vark—a ruthless and formidable warrior race.

"They stand over six feet tall, clad in heavy black body armour that is nearly impervious to conventional attacks. Their heads are shielded by spiked helmets, concealing their eyes and amplifying their menacing presence. Each Vark wields advanced weaponry infused with cutting-edge technology, capable of unleashing devastating destruction upon their foes," he explained, his voice edged with urgency. "But the Vark are not merely skilled warriors; they are relentless in their pursuit of dominance and masterful strategists on their own terrain. With their vast numbers and fierce territorial instincts, they pose a grave threat to any who dare challenge them."

The room fell silent, each agent absorbing the gravity of the mission before them.

Naguan pressed on. "Retrieving the embryos will not only reclaim a vital part of our future but also prevent the Vark from exploiting them to further their ambitions."

Sumeet spoke up, his voice measured. "What exactly are the embryos used for? I can only assume they hold extraordinary significance."

"Indeed," Naguan affirmed. "They are the key to the next generation of our species. They carry genetic enhancements that refine our abilities and harmonise with the unique energies of Rivaxia. But above all, they are our future. Without them, our people will perish."

Bertie rose to his feet and met Naguan's gaze.

"What's our plan? How do we reach Sankat 3 undetected? And more importantly—if the Vark are as terrifying as you describe, what can five humans possibly do?"

Naguan stood, forcing a smile.

"You are Dream Agents. You have witnessed the power we hold within ourselves—though only a few possess such talents. Now, it is time to show you what you are capable of. Remember, we provided your DNA. Here, on Rivaxia and within this realm, you share our abilities. In fact, yours may surpass even ours."

A Rivaxian walked in, dressed in what appeared to be a military uniform.

"Hello, my name is General Kraw. I will provide you with advanced stealth technology and guidance to navigate the Vark territories. You will undergo training to master your newfound abilities and learn to work together to overcome the challenges ahead. Teamwork will be essential."

Kerra leaned forward, a puzzled expression crossing her face.

"What's the timeline for this mission? We need to be prepared."

"The Vark are likely to strengthen their defences once they catch wind of our plans," the General warned. "We need you to act swiftly. We suggest setting out as soon as you feel ready—preferably within the next few days."

Buddy nodded enthusiastically. "A month or so ago, I never imagined I'd be here—I was hoping for a new movie role. But for the first time in my life, I feel a real connection to something. I know I speak for all of us when I say we'll train hard and be ready for whatever they throw at us. We've got each other's backs."

With the mission outlined and the stakes laid bare, the atmosphere shifted from one of wonder to urgency. The agents understood they were no longer mere visitors to Rivaxia; they were now essential players in a battle to defend the world that had welcomed them. The weight of responsibility settled upon them, igniting a fierce determination to rise to the challenge.

The days that followed were a whirlwind of preparation. The Rivaxians provided advanced simulations and rigorous training sessions, meticulously designed to refine their emerging skills and sharpen their tactical readiness. Each day unfolded with a relentless focus on mastery, setting the stage for the trials ahead.

Sumeet, now proficient in manipulating energy, devoted himself to perfecting his ability to conjure protective shields that shimmered like liquid glass. The sight was mesmerising, yet the journey was fraught with challenges. During an especially demanding session, he misjudged the energy needed to sustain his shield, resulting in a dramatic failure as it shattered spectacularly, leaving him momentarily dazed. Yet, this setback proved invaluable—a stark reminder of the precision and restraint required in battle.

Meanwhile, Bertie threw himself into training with unbridled enthusiasm, darting through meticulously designed obstacle courses that pushed his speed and agility to the limit. His natural gift for movement astonished even the seasoned Rivaxians. Yet, even he encountered setbacks; during a high-speed manoeuvre, he mis stepped and crashed to the ground. Rather than dishearten him, the fall became a lesson in balance and caution, reinforcing that raw speed must be tempered with awareness.

Under the keen supervision of their Rivaxian trainers, the Dream Agents explored new ways to perceive their surroundings. As they refined their ability to identify structural weaknesses in objects, they faced a frustrating setback when Micky mistakenly assessed a solid wall as a weak point, leading to a failed exercise. However, this miscalculation proved invaluable, sharpening his instincts and teaching him to see beyond surface appearances.

Kerra, fiercely determined to enhance her physical strength, tapped into the natural energy that pulsed through Rivaxia. In the intensity of her training, she mastered techniques to harness this power, allowing her to lift weights that had once seemed insurmountable.

Buddy, ever the spirited strategist, honed his skills in tactical manoeuvres that emphasised teamwork and communication. He thrived on the exhilarating rhythm of team drills, drawing energy from the coordinated efforts of his peers.

"Remember, Dream Agents," said General Kraw, "you all possess the same range of powers. It is your responsibility as a group to wield them wisely."

As their training intensified, the agents' bond grew stronger. They learned to trust one another's instincts, channelling their powers as a unified force. Their camaraderie flourished through shared laughter and cheers during gruelling sessions, and each evening, they gathered to exchange strategies and debate hypothetical scenarios. These discussions sparked creativity and innovation, leading to the formation of intricate plans that would prove invaluable in their upcoming mission.

Amidst the laughter and shared stories, the agents forged an unbreakable connection, recognising how their strengths complemented one another. They were no longer just individuals—they were a team, prepared to face whatever threats awaited them in Sankat 3 and beyond. Each training session not only sharpened their skills but also strengthened their resolve, steeling them for the urgency of their mission. As the final days of preparation approached, a tangible sense of unity and determination filled the air, driving them towards the challenges that lay ahead.

"Let's review what we've learned so far," Micky suggested, having naturally stepped into the role of leader. He turned to address each member. "We need to optimise our strengths to function as a cohesive unit. With Sumeet's ability to manipulate wind, he can create distractions or shields when necessary."

Bertie stepped forward; determination evident in his voice. "I've been focusing on speed training. I can dart in and out quickly and scout ahead for intel on Vark positions."

"Great!" Buddy chimed in, his voice brimming with enthusiasm. "I'm ready to put my strategic, and strength skills to the test. I proved I could lift those heavy crates during training, but now I want to see how that translates to real combat. Plus, I've been practising my defensive moves."

Kerra nodded in agreement. "I've been refining my agility, too. With my newfound strength, I'm ready to face any challenge."

Micky, taking charge of the discussion, glanced around at his teammates. "This is fantastic, team. I'm proud of each of you. But we won't truly know how we measure up until we're tested in battle. I swear on my mama's grace, that description of the Vark nearly made my heart jump clean outta my chest." His levity sparked a wave of laughter, breaking the tension.

"Thank goodness you said that—I felt the same," Sumeet added with a chuckle, picking up a rock and tossing it into a nearby pond.

"Alright, here's the plan," Micky announced, his leadership instincts shining through. "Let's run a quick training exercise to put everything to the test. We don't have much time, and getting accustomed to our powers in this environment will give us the edge we need."

They settled into a nearby clearing, dust swirling beneath their feet as they prepared to train. Sumeet summoned a gentle breeze, demonstrating his wind manipulation. "Watch how I can shift the air to form a barrier." He crafted a swirling shield that shimmered against the dull backdrop of Sankat 3.

"I can create a distraction!" Buddy shouted, grinning as he effortlessly hoisted a boulder and hurled it aside. The crash echoed through the desolate landscape. "Did that get their attention?"

"Just enough to practise stealth!" Kerra called back, weaving swiftly between boulders, her agility on full display as she navigated the debris.

Bertie seized the moment, darting into the clearing and back again in a blur, wind whipping around them. "See? I can get from one end to the other in the blink of an eye!" he said, beaming.

As they trained and their skills sharpened, Micky honed his vision. "I can see a few hundred feet ahead," he called out, pointing towards a cluster of rocks. "I think I spot Vark watchtowers in the distance. They're watching us."

Their training sessions became a fusion of strategy and skill-building as they worked to synchronise their abilities. The more they practised, the more at ease they felt in this unforgiving landscape.

"Alright, let's regroup," Micky said, calling them back after an intense session. "We've made solid progress, but we can't rely on our powers alone. We need strategy."

As their days of rigorous training drew to a close, the agents gathered for a final briefing, the air thick with anticipation. Their time as mere visitors in Rivaxia had ended; now, they were vital players in the battle to protect the world that had welcomed them. The Rivaxians had made it clear—the challenges ahead would push their skills and resolve to the limit.

They advanced towards the sleek spacecraft in the distance—a marvel of engineering that gleamed beneath Rivaxia's twin suns. Its aerodynamic contours promised exceptional speed and agility. Excitement and apprehension flickered across their faces as they neared.

"It's incredible," Bertie murmured to Sumeet. "We've trained so hard today, yet I don't feel tired at all."

"Yes, it's a strange sensation, isn't it? I suppose since our real bodies are asleep, we don't feel tired." Sumeet chuckled as they walked towards the spacecraft's entrance.

"Remember, you carry the trust of our people," Naguan said, his voice heavy with hope. "Your courage can change our fate—we believe in you. This is Tang," he added, gesturing towards a tall, muscular Rivaxian standing on the platform at the rear of the spacecraft. "He will be joining you on this journey. He knows Sankat 3 well and will be your guide."

With that, the Dream Agents turned and made their way towards the spacecraft. Buddy was the first to break from the group, practically vibrating with energy as he dashed ahead.

Without hesitation, he leapt into the pilot's seat, a mixture of exhilaration and mischief lighting up his face. As he gripped the controls, it was clear he was utterly enthralled by the prospect of flying.

"Buddy! What the hell are you doing? Surely Tang should be flying us there?" Kerra's voice, sharp with concern and disbelief, cut through the tense silence of the cockpit. The sight of Buddy—his face alight with reckless enthusiasm, hunched over the intricate controls of the Rivaxian spacecraft—sent a wave of anxiety crashing over her. She had hoped he would show restraint, but his impulsive actions stood in stark contrast to her carefully calculated nature.

"I don't know how," Buddy admitted, his grin wide and uncontainable, "but I just know I can fly this thing!" His fingers danced across the console as dim lights flared to life and displays flickered erratically. The low hum of the engines swelled into a deep, resonant thrum, sending a shiver down Kerra's spine. The air crackled with nervous energy; the sharp tang of ozone from the atmosphere recyclers mingled with the weight of anticipation, thick and electric.

"Seriously, Buddy, this isn't a game!" Kerra protested, unease creeping into her voice as she eyed the unfamiliar array of controls. "We could be in serious trouble if—"

Before she could finish, Sumeet, leaning casually against the spacecraft's entrance, let out a low chuckle.

"You actually think you can pilot a Rivaxian spacecraft without any training?" he teased, amusement and disbelief laced in his tone.

Buddy waved a dismissive hand, his confidence teetering on arrogance.

"Come on, Sumeet! I've seen people do it before, well on TV. How hard can it be?" He recalled one of his dreams where he was flying this spacecraft—clearly the countless hours spent absorbing knowledge, attuning himself to the ship's responses, its intuitive flight patterns. Although he had never piloted a real vessel, a strange sense of understanding, a deep connection to the craft, pulsed within him. His fingers, sharp with energy and precision, traced the sequences he had mastered in the simulations. "Just give me a moment!" he urged, determination flaring within him.

The console flared to life, sensors and readouts pulsing with energy, responding eagerly to his touch. The ship shuddered, the powerful thrum of the engines now a tangible force, the reality of their journey setting in with breath-taking clarity.

"Sumeet, take a seat next to me and plot the coordinates."

With that, Sumeet jumped into the seat beside Buddy and began entering data.

Kerra, her concern unwavering, crossed her arms.

"This isn't just a joyride, boys. We have a mission! What if—"

Bertie, sensing the tension, stepped forward and placed a reassuring hand on Kerra's shoulder.

"Take a seat, Kerra. They know what they're doing—trust me." He flashed a playful grin, recognising the infectious energy propelling Buddy forward—a mix of recklessness and unwavering confidence.

Buddy, his focus unshaken, finally announced,

"Sit back and relax, folks. Captain Buddy's gonna give you a smooth ride to Sankat 3."

A shared sense of awe and nervous excitement settled over the group, their earlier anxieties swiftly dissolving. Kerra let out a shaky laugh.

"Holy crap," she whispered. "How the hell did we get ourselves into this?"

Sumeet, ever the optimist, replied,

"Relax. We're Dream Agents, after all." He glanced at Tang for approval.

"You certainly are," Tang affirmed.

The ship roared to life, its systems humming with energy.

"Engaging destination protocol," Sumeet confirmed, scanning the controls. The ship lifted off, gliding smoothly into the vast sky above Rivaxia.

Below them, the landscape unfolded—a breathtaking expanse of colours, textures, and life. A stark reminder of what they were fighting for. With each passing moment, they drew closer to Sankat 3 and the challenges ahead.

"Let's make this count," Micky said, gripping his knees tightly as he glanced back at his team. The weight of their mission pressed upon them, but the air crackled with the electricity of possibility.

Together, they would confront the Vark and fight for the future of Rivaxia. They were ready to embrace their roles as heroes.

The ship proceeded towards Sankat 3.

"Folks, we'll be there in 18 hours. I suggest you relax for now," Sumeet said to the team.

CHAPTER 13

The Race for Existence

We're hidden behind Surin-2, the second moon," Tang's voice, calm yet urgent, cut through the tense silence of the cockpit. "Engage the cloak, and we'll land on Sankat 3." A low hum followed his command as the ship's cloaking field activated, rendering them effectively invisible to the Vark's sensors. "The Vark haven't been able to repair the forcefield we had, so this should be easier than I thought. Set these coordinates," Tang continued, tracing a point on the navigation console, deep within a vast, shadowed crater. "They won't see us land there, and we'll have a far better chance of infiltrating the Vark stronghold undetected."

The ship, now cloaked, moved in near silence, the only sound the steady rhythm of its life support systems. As they descended, the breathtaking beauty of Sankat 3 unfolded beneath them—a striking contrast to the barren wasteland they had expected. Snow-capped mountains, their peaks glistening under the twin suns, rose in quiet majesty, their slopes cradling crystal-clear lakes that shimmered with vibrant hues. The scene was hauntingly exquisite, a masterpiece of nature scarred by the Vark's ruthless assault. Bomb craters pockmarked the once-pristine surface, and charred remnants of flora lay strewn like tragic echoes of lost life. The lakes, once mirrors of untouched splendour, now reflected the devastation around them—a cruel juxtaposition that spoke to the ferocity of the conflict. This was a world of stark beauty and brutal destruction, and the Dream Agents felt the weight of its suffering settle upon them.

"Brace yourselves!" Buddy shouted, gripping the control panel as the ship lurched through a pocket of turbulence. The jolt rippled through their bodies, but they quickly steadied themselves. The ship dipped and swayed, yet Buddy's hands remained steady, guiding them through the chaos until he found a clear approach to a flat stretch of land nestled within the craggy terrain.

"Touchdown in three... two... one..." Buddy counted down, his voice barely rising above the tension thickening the cockpit. The ship landed with a soft but decisive thud, and a heavy stillness settled over them, taut as a drawn bowstring. The agents exchanged glances—eyes bright with adrenaline, pulses drumming in their ears—as they braced for the unknown.

A weighted silence followed; each agent caught in the gravity of what lay ahead. Tang activated their combat suits, the familiar weight grounding them against the encroaching dread. Bertie strode to the back of the ship, triggering the ramp. As it extended with a slow, mechanical hiss, he paused and glanced over at Kerra."

"Do you smell that?" he asked, closing his eyes and inhaling deeply. "It's like a blend of lavender and citrus."

"It's... oddly relaxing," Kerra murmured, raising an eyebrow.

"Perfect, considering we're heading straight into a warzone," Bertie quipped, striding down the ramp with a chuckle he couldn't quite suppress.

The rest of the team followed, stepping cautiously into the alien landscape. Jagged cliffs loomed above them, their razor-edged peaks casting long, menacing shadows.

"I spotted a Vark outpost on our way in," Micky said. "Roughly five miles from here."

With a shared nod, the Dream Agents activated their enhanced speed, launching forward like arrows. Tang, keeping a measured pace behind them, scanned the terrain, already mapping the best vantage point atop a nearby hill."

"Jagged cliffs loomed above, their razor-edged peaks casting long, menacing shadows. In the distance, crude, fortified Vark outposts emerged—harsh intrusions against the otherwise breathtaking lunar landscape, a stark reminder of the peril that lay ahead.

'Keep low. We don't know if any of the Vark are lurking around,' Micky advised, his voice steady as his sharp gaze swept the terrain. The weight of the mission pressed down on him, a constant reminder of the risks ahead.

Behind the agents, Tang pushed himself to quicken his pace, his narrowed eyes scanning the landscape. Memories of past encounters with the Vark surfaced—conflicts where reckless decisions had led to devastating consequences. A knot of unease tightened in his stomach as he raised his communicator."

"I'm right behind you," he said, his voice calm yet edged with urgency. "The element of surprise is critical; we can't afford a full-scale engagement. I'll be with you shortly."

As the Dream Agents reached the outpost, they swiftly concealed themselves within the dense underbrush of the surrounding jungle, their senses sharp as they assessed the situation ahead.

Micky caught Sumeet's gaze, detecting the flicker of anxiety in his friend's eyes—a silent testament to the weight of what lay before them. This was no longer just training or theoretical threats; for the first time, they were stepping into real, tangible danger, despite their advanced combat skills.

Just behind them, Bertie remained poised and vigilant, ready to act the moment the need arose. A small smile played on his lips as he glanced at Micky, unable to ignore the irony— how the same man now leading them had once been locked away in an asylum."

"Let's use our powers to scout," Micky suggested, snapping the group's focus back to their immediate surroundings. "Sumeet, can you whip up a small wind-based diversion to draw their attention?"

With silent nods, Sumeet summoned a powerful gust of wind that exploded into a sudden dust storm, sending debris swirling into the air in a chaotic spiral. The storm's intensity caught the two Vark sentinels off guard, forcing them to recoil as the biting grit filled the air around them. Seizing the opportunity, the Dream Agents moved swiftly and with purpose, their enhanced senses allowing them to melt seamlessly into the jungle's shifting shadows.

Silent as ghosts, they advanced toward the nearest entrance, the pounding rhythm of their mission thrumming in their chests. Each step was weighted with the looming threat ahead, laced with anticipation and an acute awareness of the danger lying in wait.

"Perfect. Now, let's move," Micky whispered, his voice taut with urgency as he signalled for the others to follow. He led the way, crouching low as they wove through the dense jungle, every movement measured and precise. The air crackled with tension. Glancing back, he caught the steely determination in his teammates' eyes, their resolve unwavering despite the silent spectre of fear trailing them. Together, they slipped between scattered rocks and patches of brittle earth, knowing that even the slightest noise could spell disaster.

As they neared the outpost's perimeter, tension coiled around them like a tightening noose. Kerra steadied herself, her pulse hammering as she scaled a nearby ledge, each movement deliberate yet laced with risk. Below, Bertie wrestled with a growing sense of dread, his mind dissecting the formidable structures looming ahead. With a sharp inhale, he visualised the outpost's internal layout, but unease gnawed at him. The closer they crept, the heavier the weight of unseen eyes pressing down on them—a stark reminder that a single misstep could spell disaster. Through the structure, he spotted several Vark gathered, their armoured forms looming in the shifting shadows.

"Four Vark inside," Micky murmured. "And there's a guard posted at the entrance."

"Time for a little teamwork," Micky said, glancing at the others. "I'll create a distraction while Sumeet and Buddy flank from the left. Bertie, Tang, and Kerra—you take the guard."

"Sounds good. Let's move," Buddy replied, adrenaline surging through him, sharpening his senses.

The plan unfolded with precise coordination. Sumeet summoned a surge of energy, triggering a rockslide that thundered behind the outpost, instantly drawing the Vark's attention. As the sentinels turned their heads, Micky and Buddy slipped into position while Bertie and Kerra crept toward the entrance.

The guard at the door, caught off guard, tightened his grip on his weapon, but before he could react, Kerra lunged, using her strength to disable him in one swift motion, slamming him against the wall with a resounding thud. Meanwhile, Sumeet and Tang swiftly dispatched the two perimeter guards.

"Inside!" Micky urged, and they filed into the dimly lit outpost. The air was thick with the acrid scent of oil and metal, a stark contrast to the vibrant aromas that had greeted them upon landing. The agents quickly assessed their surroundings, taking in the metallic crates and high-tech equipment scattered throughout the space.

"Look for anything that resembles the embryos—we need to know if they've breached the barrier," Bertie instructed, scanning the area alongside Buddy.

Buddy moved to one of the crates, prying it open to reveal rows of suspended containers, each pulsing with a soft glow. "These aren't the embryos—they're weapons."

"This place is heavily fortified," Tang murmured, glancing up at the armoured walls and the shadows clinging to the ceiling. "Even so, the presence of so few Vark guards suggests they weren't expecting us."

"The Vark have clearly established a stronghold here. If they've gone to such lengths to protect this area, they're not just guarding embryos—they might be hiding something else," Micky interjected.

"Exactly," Sumeet added, irritation creeping into his voice. "And it's not just about the embryos. There must be a strategic reason for their fortifications."

"If they have Tarek Its—the Rivaxian assigned to care for them—along with the embryos, he could be in serious danger, if not already dead," Tang said grimly.

Bertie shot them a stern look. "Hold on. We don't even know if they've broken through the forcefield, let alone all that rubble from the blast."

"Tarek Its is likely a key figure for them. If the Vark have broken through and captured him, they may be holding him hostage to use as leverage against Rivaxia, or they could be forcing him to reveal critical information about our world and its technology," Tang said.

"What if he's still alive?" Buddy posed, his voice barely above a whisper. "What if he's been caring for the embryos this whole time, hiding them from the Vark? We have to consider the possibility that he's still in Tanaxa V."

"Then it's even more vital that we move quickly and stealthily," Kerra said, her eyes flashing with steel. "We must locate Tarek Its and secure the embryos, but we need to be prepared for resistance."

"We can't just grab the embryos and run," Micky said as he examined the crate further, noticing what looked like a complex locking mechanism on the side. "If Tarek Its is alive, we need to formulate a plan to rescue him."

"We need to get to Tanaxa V as quickly as possible," Micky said.

Bertie nodded. "Agreed. We need to keep moving towards the main buildings, but first, open that last crate, Sumeet."

Without hesitation, Sumeet fired his weapon at the lock, pried the crate open, and peered inside.

"I think we have our answer," he said grimly. "They've broken through—there are two cylinders here containing frozen embryos."

"Then we need to move," Tang urged. "We have no idea when they breached the barrier, so every second counts."

"We can't just leave these embryos behind," Sumeet protested.

"We'll collect them on our way back to the ship. With any luck, it'll take some time before the Vark realise this outpost has fallen," Tang assured him.

As the darkness settled around them, they mapped out a route that would take them undetected to the outskirts of Taxana V. As darkness began to fall, they felt a slight chill in the air—their senses heightened, knowing they were nearing a critical juncture in their mission.

"Let's stick to the shadows and move out at first light," Micky suggested. "My enhanced vision will help us navigate through the terrain, even in low light."

"Perfect." Sumeet nodded, satisfied with the plan. " I take a walk along the lake shore, which will give me a better opportunity to assess their positions."

"I'll come with you," Said Tang.

"Stick to the rocks by that lake!" Micky urged, directing them closer to the landscape's natural defences.

As Sumeet and Tang walked along the lakeside, they heard the distinct, haunting song of the Haldriane echoing across the water. The eerie melody made their situation feel even more unsettling. With each cry, the trees around the lake pulsed with a deep purple glow—an indication that they were all connected in ways beyond human comprehension.

"What is that sound? It's mesmerising… and honestly scaring the crap out of me," Sumeet asked.

"It's the Haldriane," Tang replied, glancing across the shimmering lake. "They sense we're here, but they're harmless. They pose no threat."

As they took a break, they sat on the rocks by the water's edge.

"This truly is a wondrous world," Sumeet murmured, peering into the depths of the lake.

Suddenly, a Haldriane surfaced, locking eyes with him from just a few feet away.

Startled at first, Sumeet then felt an overwhelming sense of calm wash over him. The Haldriane reached out a slender hand, and as Sumeet touched it, swirls of turquoise and green flowed across his skin, shimmering with specks of silver—like stars scattered across the night sky. A connection sparked between them. Then, unexpectedly, the Haldriane spoke to him telepathically, its voice slow and melodic.

"Suuuuuumeeeeet…" it intoned, drawing out his name in a haunting melody that sent chills down his spine. "Daaaaaaanger…"

The word lingered in the air like a heavy fog, filling him with a sense of urgency that clashed with the serene beauty surrounding him.

Before he could fully process its meaning, the Haldriane slipped beneath the surface of the water, vanishing in a swirl of shimmering ripples. A quiet unease settled in the pit of his stomach.

Back at camp, Sumeet spotted Buddy sprawled on the ground, his hat tilted over his eyes. Excitement bubbled inside him as he rushed over.

"You'll never believe what happened out there!" Sumeet exclaimed, looking around at the group. "A Haldriane came out of the water and spoke to me!"

"Yeah? What did it say?" Kerra asked, raising an eyebrow.

"It said, 'Sumeet, danger!'"

Buddy let out a loud laugh. "No shit, mate, we're all in danger! We're about to take on the Vark!"

The group erupted in laughter at Buddy's perfect timing, though unease still lingered beneath the surface.

The night passed in a mix of restless anticipation and light-hearted conversation, each agent reflecting on what they had learned and the path that lay ahead.

As dawn broke, the first rays of sunlight cast a golden glow over the jagged peaks surrounding them. They gathered their equipment, double-checking their gear to ensure they were prepared for the challenges ahead. Suits were calibrated and primed for action. With one final check-in, they took their positions, ready to advance into Tanexa V.

"Let's go show those Vark what we're made of," Buddy said, cracking a grin, excitement buzzing in his veins.

"Remember, our main objective is to gather intel, secure the embryos, and locate Tarek Its," Micky reminded them. "Stay sharp, and we stick to the plan."

The agents moved stealthily through the rocky terrain, maintaining formation and staying vigilant. Micky led the way, his enhanced vision sweeping every angle, while Sumeet followed closely, prepared to create diversions if necessary. Bertie and Kerra flanked the group, poised to strike at a moment's notice, while Buddy and Tang trailed just behind, coordinating their movements.

As dusk settled over Tanexa V, the twin suns began their descent, casting a warm glow that softened the edges of the towering structures ahead. The fortified walls loomed before them, their imposing presence reinforced by the sight of armoured Vark warriors patrolling the perimeter, sending a shiver down their spines.

Their eyes traced the heavy metal plating, each section glinting under the fading sunlight—a silent testament to the stronghold's might. The air bristled with shouted commands and the ominous clatter of armour, tension thickening with every passing moment. They would wait a little longer, until full darkness cloaked the land, their hearts pounding in anticipation of what was to come.

"What's the plan, boss?" Buddy whispered; his gaze fixed on Micky.

"We need to wait for a guard shift or a moment when their attention wavers. Let's wait until it's dark, though—that way, we can move more easily," Micky said. "We'll slip in, find a vantage point, and gather intel on their operations—see if Tarek Its is here."

They fixed their gaze on the patrolling guards, each second stretching into eternity. The distant wail of a battle horn echoed through the air, a haunting contrast to the suffocating silence that gripped their small group.

"Now!" Micky hissed, his eyes narrowing as a guard turned away, momentarily distracted. With a swift motion, he conjured a gust of wind, sending loose stones skittering across the far end of the compound. The sharp clatter broke the uneasy stillness, drawing the attention of the Vark stationed nearby. Their heads snapped toward the disturbance.

"Move!" Micky ordered, his voice edged with urgency.

The team darted forward, melting into the encampment's shadows. Their heartbeats thundered in unison, adrenaline surging through their veins as they wove deeper into enemy territory.

They crouched behind a towering stack of crates; every sense honed to a razor's edge. The air was thick with tension as they strained to catch the Vark's conversation inside the command post. Each word drew them further into the tangled web of danger surrounding them.

"The embryos are nearly ready for transport. We cannot afford any mistakes," one of the Vark leaders growled, his voice reverberating through the enclosed space like a dark omen. "If the Rivaxians discover we have them, they'll do everything in their power to reclaim them."

Another Vark warrior spoke, his tone sharp.

"What about the caretaker? He's been unnervingly quiet since we captured him. I suspect he's hiding something. Perhaps it's time we applied a little more persuasion."

"If he doesn't open up by tomorrow, I'll hand him over to you and the 'Doctor' for… shall we say, alternative techniques," the leader said curtly, a glint of menace flashing in his eyes. "For now, keep a close watch on him. Let's hope he breaks soon and reveals their broader plans. Something feels off, and I don't like it."

With that, he strode towards the doorway, casting a wary glance back.

Micky met his teammates' eyes, dread settling in their chests as the grim reality of Tarek Its capture washed over them.

"We don't have much time," Sumeet whispered urgently, his voice barely audible over the rustling leaves. "We need to find Tarek Its and the embryos before they're taken back to the Vark world."

"Agreed," Micky said, urgency sharpening his resolve. "Let's split up. Buddy and I will check that corridor leading to the back of the structure and look for a way in—or at least a window to peek through. Sumeet and Bertie, scout the east side. Tang and Kerra, stay close and watch for any guards."

They swiftly reviewed the plan, each member mentally preparing for their role before melting into the shadows. The air thrummed with tension, the weight of their mission pressing down on them.

Micky and Buddy crept towards the dimly lit corridor entrance, where two Vark soldiers loomed—tall, menacing, and clad in heavy armour that glinted ominously in the low light.

"We need to find a way past them," Micky murmured, scanning for alternative routes. His eyes landed on a vent. "Look over there—let's climb up through that."

"Give me a moment," Buddy replied, focusing his energy. "I'll summon a gust of wind to kick up some dust and mask our approach." With that, he conjured a sudden storm, swirling dust through the air until the Vark could barely see a foot in front of them.

"Go—quickly! Get inside the building!" Micky ordered, urgency sharp in his voice.

"Let's do it! Follow me," he said, readying himself. Shifting into position for a perfect leap, Micky sprang upward in one fluid motion, gripping the vent's edge. With a controlled burst of telekinetic energy, he pushed the cover aside, creating just enough space for them to slip through.

"Give me your hand, Buddy!" Micky called, reaching down to pull his friend up.

Buddy grasped the edge of the vent, hauling himself through before lowering into the dark, narrow space. Micky followed closely behind. They crawled through the duct, the air thick with dust and the sharp tang of metal. Micky focused his energy, clearing debris as they moved, ensuring their path remained unobstructed.

Emerging into a storage room packed with ominously stacked crates and sleek, sophisticated technology, they paused, straining to listen. The muffled voices of Vark soldiers outside confirmed they had not yet been discovered.

"Look at this," Micky whispered, gesturing toward a series of crates against the wall. He pried one open, revealing an arsenal of advanced weaponry and gadgets—each piece making Earth's finest technology look archaic in comparison.

"Impressive," Buddy muttered, his heart hammering as he took in the sight. "These aren't just weapons—they look like they could disrupt our powers. We need to stay sharp. Tarek Its and the embryos could be in one of those adjacent rooms."

The guards outside shifted away. Micky peered through the door—clear. The corridor lay empty.

"Let's move," he said.

Keeping low, Buddy and Micky crept down the corridor, stopping outside a large room about fifty feet from the storeroom.

"Quick, inside—before we're seen!" Micky urged, glancing back down the hallway.

They slipped into the room, and Micky swiftly pulled out a listening device, pressing it against the wall, eager to decipher the conversation inside. The measured cadence of authoritative voices echoed through the barrier—someone was issuing commands. Micky exchanged a tense glance with Buddy.

"They're talking about Tarek Its, and it doesn't sound good," Micky whispered, the weight of their situation pressing down on him.

"Can you see through the wall?" he asked, urgency sharpening his tone.

Buddy closed his eyes, focusing on the barrier. Images flickered in his mind—Tarek Its sat bound to a chair, a Vark warrior towering over him, demanding answers. Fear and anger charged the air. Tarek Its face bore heavy bruises, his arm wrapped in a tight bandage.

"He's in there," Buddy said, his voice steady but tense. "Two guards nearby. He's being interrogated."

Micky clenched his jaw, shaking his head.

"We need a distraction," he whispered, scanning the room for anything useful. "Something to pull their attention away from Tarek Its—just long enough for us to make our move."

Buddy nodded, his mind racing.

"I can manipulate the environment. If I send a power surge, the lights will cut out. That should be enough of a distraction for me to hit the door hard and take them down. You get ready to free him."

"Let's do this," Micky urged, adrenaline surging through him.

"What's that?" one of the Vark guards barked, looking up as the lights flickered. "Go and investigate!"

"Now!" Buddy shouted. He and Micky charged through the door, closing the distance to Tarek Its in a heartbeat. The Vark warrior hesitated, momentarily stunned by the sudden blackout—just long enough for Micky to strike.

With a surge of speed, Micky shot the first Vark before tackling the second. Wrestling for control as chaos erupted around them, he drove his dagger into the alien's chest. Nearby, Buddy darted to Tarek Its side, swiftly untying the ropes binding him to the chair.

"We're here to help! Hang on!" Buddy said, urgency fuelling his movements.

"Thank you…" Tarek Its gasped, struggling to catch his breath. "I thought I was done for. Who are you? You're not Rivaxians."

"No, we're Dream Agents," Micky replied, his eyes sweeping the room for further threats.

Tarek Its exhaled sharply, looking up at Buddy. "Wow, we actually did it. The ships got through."

Meanwhile, on the other side of the facility, Bertie and Sumeet stepped into a large unit bathed in eerie blue light.

"Look here!" Sumeet exclaimed, excitement bubbling over. "These look like storage units for the embryos they showed us on Rivaxia."

"Yes, they are!" Bertie confirmed, urgency sharpening his tone. "Let's grab what we can and get out of here!"

They hastily secured as many cylinders as they could carry, stuffing them into their two backpacks.

"We'll have to leave most of them; we can't carry everything," Bertie said, his voice tight with urgency.

Sumeet peeked cautiously out the door, his heartbeat quickening as he spotted a Vark soldier standing nearby.

Without hesitation, he dashed forward, launching himself at the soldier with precision, knocking him to the ground—but the sudden movement triggered a piercing alarm that shattered the silence, echoing ominously through the facility. Red lights flared, bathing the corridors in a ghastly glow.

"Quick! Let's go!" Bertie shouted, adrenaline surging as they sprinted down the corridor, their footsteps hammering in sync with their racing hearts.

Back in the interrogation room, Micky pressed his back against the wall and peered through the door into the chaos outside. His breath hitched as soldiers stormed toward them, their shouts crashing like thunder.

"Now we've got trouble," Micky muttered, his chest tightening with anxiety as he glanced toward the main door. Alarms blared, and the pounding of boots grew louder.

"We can't stay here!" he urged, gripping Tarek Its arm and hauling him to his feet. "Can you walk?"

"Yes, I can walk out of here just fine!" Tarek Its declared, determination gleaming in his eyes despite the circumstances.

"Which way?" Buddy asked urgently, scanning for an escape route.

"Down this corridor," Tarek Its directed.

"No, backtracking is faster," Micky countered. "We need to regroup with the others—that's our best shot at getting out of here."

"Agreed." Tarek Its nodded. Together, they hurried down the corridor just as Sumeet and Bertie came racing toward them, their faces a mix of exhilaration and tension from their own scouting efforts.

"There you are!" Buddy gasped, relief flooding through him. "We got some of the embryos—not all—but we need to leave with what we have. We also uncovered key intel on the Vark's movements—"

"No time for that now! We have to move—now!" Micky cut in, urgency thrumming through him. "They're onto us."

"Follow us—we'll lead the way!" Micky commanded, surging forward as they braced themselves for the chaos ahead.

They sprinted down the corridor, the thunderous stomp of Vark boots reverberating behind them, shaking the floor with each step. Concern flashed across Tarek Its face as Buddy risked a glance back—two Vark warriors were closing in, weapons drawn, their guttural shouts slicing through the air.

"Don't look back!" Micky barked; his voice sharp with urgency. "Just focus on reaching the exit!"

With that, the Vark opened fire, bullets striking the walls and a trolley in the corridor.

Sweat poured down Tarek Its face as they tore through the winding passages, Sumeet harnessing his wind abilities to drive back their pursuers. Dust and debris billowed behind them, forming a chaotic veil that, with any luck, would slow the Vark down.

"Over there!" Tarek Its shouted, pointing towards an exit leading to a back alley—a potential route to safety.

Summoning every last ounce of strength, they charged forward, barrelling through the exit and into the sunlight. They spilled into a narrow space between the campus perimeter and the rugged terrain beyond. For a fleeting moment, the open air felt like hope—but the urgency of their escape remained palpable.

"Keep moving!" Micky called out, leading the charge, adrenaline surging as they burst into the open air. The harsh glare of the twin suns, now high in the sky, stung their eyes after the dim interior of Tanaxa V—but there was no time to adjust.

"Faster!" Buddy urged, pushing them forward as they closed the distance. In the courtyard, a battle raged—Kerra and Tang held the perimeter, gunfire echoing as they fought to hold their ground.

"Launch the mortars!" Tang shouted, unleashing a barrage.

As the Vark closed in, something massive thundered behind them—a towering Pyronyx in pursuit.

"What the hell is that?" Kerra yelled, breathless as they ran.

"It's a Pyronyx," Tang shouted back. "Don't stop, and don't look back!"

Micky shouted for them to pick up the pace as the Dream Agents activated their enhanced speed.

With that, he skidded to a stop, whirled around, and fired his disruptor at an approaching guard. The blast struck true, killing him instantly. The Pyronyx charged ahead, but Micky didn't follow.

"Keep going! I'll hold them off!" he shouted, pivoting sharply and sprinting back towards the encampment to intercept the approaching Vark patrols.

"No! We can't leave you!" Kerra protested, her voice filled with desperation.

"There's no time! Get Tarek Its and the others to safety!" Micky shot back; his tone resolute. "I'll do what I can to slow them down. Go!"

With a heavy heart, Kerra nodded, tears streaming down her face, but she knew every second counted. "Stay safe! I love you!" she called out as she and the others sprinted towards the ship.

Micky glanced back at her, blowing a kiss before turning to face the enemy. Behind them, the echoes of his battle rang through the air, each impact a reminder of the sacrifice he was making.

The Pyronyx, to their astonishment, rushed past Micky—completely ignoring him—and charged straight towards the Dream Agents.

Sumeet stumbled, falling hard against a large rock. His breath hitched as the massive creature loomed over him, its glistening fangs bared, saliva dripping onto the ground. Inches from his face, it let out a deep, guttural growl.

This is it for me, he thought, frozen in place.

But then, unexpectedly, the Pyronyx hesitated. Slowly, it stepped back... and then lowered itself onto the ground beside him.

The realisation struck—Micky had slain its master. And now, by some unexplainable bond, Sumeet was its new master.

Swallowing his fear, Sumeet pushed himself to his feet and took off running, his newfound protector racing alongside him.

Inside the ship, Buddy swiftly punched in the activation codes, the engines roaring to life with a deep, throaty growl. "Hurry!" he shouted, his gaze flicking anxiously toward the ramp as it lowered.

Sumeet and the Pyronyx sprinted up the ramp, following Tarek Its into the ship. Kerra and Bertie were ahead, carrying the precious embryos.

"Get in!" Tang urged, throwing a quick glance over his shoulder, his pulse pounding. A group of Vark soldiers was closing in fast, their weapons drawn, their eyes burning with fear and determination.

"Get us out of here!" Bertie shouted, shoving Tarek Its further inside. "We'll cover the rear!"

Buddy's fingers flew over the controls. "I'm on it! We need to lift off before they get too close!"

At the rear entrance, Bertie and Sumeet took defensive positions, weapons ready. The ship's systems hummed and flickered to life; the air thick with urgency as they prepared for take-off.

In the distance, they saw Micky stumble and fall, struck by enemy fire from the Vark.

"Micky's down!" Bertie shouted.

"We have to help him!" Kerra screamed, panic rising in her voice.

"We can't. We have to complete the mission—Micky knew that before we came here," Bertie replied, his voice tight with anguish.

Tang rushed to activate the ship's defensive protocols.

"Hold on, folks—this is going to get bumpy!" Buddy yelled over his shoulder.

With that, the ship lurched upwards, engines roaring as it took heavy fire from multiple angles below.

"Let's do this!" Sumeet shouted, releasing the wind barrier just as the door shuddered violently. He pushed with everything he had, reinforcing it—for now. But how long would it hold?

"Kerra, help me with the systems!" Bertie shouted, moving to Buddy's side. Kerra scrambled into the cockpit, hands flying over the controls as she prepared to assist.

"Engaging evasive manoeuvres," Tang chimed in, swiftly adjusting the navigational systems. "We need to gain altitude—fast!"

As they climbed higher into the atmosphere, the Vark sentries below scrambled, their smaller crafts launching into the sky.

"They'll be on us any second!" Buddy warned, adrenaline surging as he pulled sharp turns to evade incoming ground fire.

"Let me help!" Sumeet shouted, locking onto an approaching Vark craft. Summoning a fierce gust of wind, he channelled a crackling bolt of lightning, directing it toward the enemy ship. The energy struck mid-flight, sending the craft veering wildly off course before spiralling out of control.

"I think that bought us a moment!" Sumeet shouted, his heart pounding. "But we can't wait around—there'll be more!"

The team surged forward, weaving through the turbulent skies as the Vark stronghold shrank behind them. But Tang knew they weren't safe yet.

"Keep your eyes on the sensors! They'll have more ships in pursuit!" he warned, his voice calm despite the tension.

"Give me a damn minute, old chap, will you?" Bertie snapped; his eyes locked on the dashboard as his fingers flew over the controls. The readings flickered wildly—multiple ships closing in fast. "They've launched fighters! We need to boost speed and gain altitude—now!"

"Buddy, push the engines to max!" Bertie commanded, stepping up in Micky's absence. "We need to break free of the atmosphere—engage the cloak!"

"It's not working!" Tang shouted. "I'm on it—just give me a few moments!"

"Thrusters at full power!" Buddy responded; his voice tight with focus. With expert precision, he manoeuvred the ship, gripping the controls as the craft jolted forward, tearing through the clouds. Suddenly, a volley of laser fire erupted from behind, lighting up the sky as the Vark pilots unleashed their firepower. "Brace yourselves!" Buddy shouted, yanking hard on the controls to evade the incoming blasts.

"Hold on!" Sumeet exclaimed, focusing intently. He channelled his energy, sweeping his arms outward to summon a swirling wall of wind behind them. The turbulent air caught some of the energy blasts, deflecting them as they whizzed past the ship. But the momentary relief was cut short—the engine had taken a hit and was losing power. Bertie glanced back as they ascended, flashes of light flickering amidst the chaos. "Eyes ahead! We need a clear route to shelter!"

They climbed higher, bursting through the cloud cover into a brilliant blue sky streaked with wisps of white. The contrast was striking—though the danger still loomed behind them, the crisp air of freedom sent a surge of adrenaline through them all.

"Two hostiles incoming on radar!" Sumeet called out, his eyes fixed on the flashing alerts. "We need combat manoeuvrability—now!" "Let's go evasive!" Bertie yelled, adrenaline coursing through his body. "Buddy, keep us steady while Sumeet creates wind currents to shield us!"

Sumeet nodded, channelling his powers more intensely. With a deep breath, he conjured a swirling mass of air around the ship, creating a temporary bubble of protection. He felt the vibrations of the laser fire ricocheting off the makeshift shield.

"Firing back!" Buddy declared a "Evasive manoeuvres— now!" Bertie yelled, adrenaline surging through him. "Buddy, hold us steady while Sumeet reinforces the shield!"

"Here goes nothing!" He fired while weaving through the chaos, his shots striking true. Explosions erupted behind them, sending debris spiralling through the sky.

"Brilliant shot!" Bertie shouted, a surge of triumph coursing through him as the enemy ship wavered. They were gaining ground, but he knew the fight was far from over. "More Vark ships incoming!" Bertie shouted, his finger stabbing toward a fresh wave emerging through the clouds. "Looks like they've mobilised the whole fleet! We need a safe zone— somewhere to assess the engine damage and plan our next move. We can't outrun them forever!"

"Hold tight!" Buddy yelled, wrenching the controls as he sent the ship into a sharp turn, weaving through a narrow cloud corridor. The expert manoeuvre threw off the pursuing Vark, forcing them to scatter. Suddenly, Sumeet shouted, "Over there! An island! It's not far! If we can reach land, we might be able to shake them off!"

"Set a course!" Bertie ordered, urgency sharp in his voice. "Kera, can you plot a safe approach?"

"Already on it!" Kera replied, eyes locked on her screen. "It's rocky, but it should give us enough cover to hide."

With Buddy guiding the ship toward the island and Sumeet holding their shield against the incoming fire, they pushed ahead, the weight of danger pressing in from behind.

As they neared the island's coastline, a flicker of hope sparked—if they could make it to shelter, they might just have a chance. Night was falling, and darkness crept over them like a shroud.

"Almost there!" Bertie shouted, forcing himself to push past the fear and uncertainty that had gripped them since their clash with the Vark.

As they neared their destination, jagged cliffs and dense foliage emerged from the shadows. With a final burst of speed, they descended rapidly toward a secluded cove near the shore, aiming for a swift yet controlled landing.

"Look! An island!" Sumeet shouted, urgency sharpening his tone as he pointed through the cockpit window. "It's close! If we can reach land, we might just lose the Vark's!" "Touchdown!" Buddy exclaimed, releasing a breath he hadn't realised he was holding as the engines wound down to a low hum. An eerie silence settled over them, thick with tension and uncertainty.

"Tang, is the cloak working?" Bertie shouted.

"Yes! Activate it now," came the response.

With the cloak engaged, Sumeet scanned the screens frantically. "Let's give it a moment—make sure they've passed us by." "Good thinking," Bertie said, his eyes flicking between the control panels and the darkened shoreline. "We need to be careful. If they catch us now, it's over."

They monitored the ship's sensors, waiting for what felt like an eternity. As the minutes crawled by, the tension in the cockpit thickened. The small screen flickered, displaying movement above them—Vark ships slicing through the sky, searching.

"Come on... come on "...," Buddy muttered, tapping the console impatiently as they held their breaths, silently willing the ships to move on. At last, the final Vark ship vanished into the night, leaving only an eerie silence overhead.

"Now! Let's get to work!" Bertie commanded, adrenaline surging through him.

Deeming the area safe, they disembarked, hearts pounding as they slipped into the dense foliage for cover.

"Buddy, check the engines. I'll scout our options," Bertie ordered, his tone firm. "We need to intercept their communications—find out what the Vark are planning.".."

As they checked their equipment, the tension grew heavier. They worked swiftly, and after a few nerve-racking moments, their efforts paid off—they had successfully tapped into the Vark communication lines.

"Let me handle this—I've done it before," Tarek Its said, fingers flying across the console. A few rapid keystrokes later, he let out a triumphant shout. "I've got it!"

Then, just as they began deciphering the incoming messages, a chilling revelation hit them like a lightning bolt:

Micky was still alive.

He was wounded, captured, and set to be transported to the Vark home world—along with the remaining embryos.

Panic gripped them as the full weight of the situation crashed down.

"We need to get back to Rivaxia," Bertie said, his expression grim. He turned to Buddy. "What's the status of our engines?"

"They'll get us there. It's mostly external damage—thankfully, they didn't hit any essential systems," Buddy replied.

"Then we have no time to waste. Buddy, get us out of here—fast. "With that, the engines roared to life, propelling them straight back to Rivaxia."

CHAPTER 14

In the Grip of the Vark

I n the depths of NASA's command centre, tension hung thick in the air as the control room tracked the Dream Agents' progress on the massive screens. Alarms blared as Micky's vitals spiked off the charts, his heart rate climbing to dangerous levels.

"Quick!" a technician shouted, his voice slicing through the chaos. "Administer beta-blockers now—we need to stabilise him before he goes into cardiac arrest!" The team scrambled for the necessary equipment; their faces tight with concern as the numbers on the screen flickered ominously.

After a tense few moments, the technician successfully administered the beta-blockers. Slowly, Micky's heart rate began to stabilize. The frantic alarms in the control room faded as his vitals returned to safer levels. Sweat beaded on his brow, his body still rigid within the pod, lost in a deep, surreal dream state.

The medical team monitored the readings closely, a wave of relief washing over them as the numbers steadied. "His condition is stable," Dr. Swales reported to Rory, a mix of relief and concern in his voice as he scanned the monitors.

"Do not wake him as pulling him from this state could exacerbate the situation." Rory said as they exchanged anxious glances, knowing that waking him too soon could trigger further complications. "What is that on his arm" asked Rory pointing to a large burn near his shoulder.

"It looks like something shot him, but nothing like we have here on earth. It's not a bullet wound, it's a deep burn"

"Doctor, can you treat that please," instructed Rory. "Keep a close eye on him and brief me if anything changes. As I said though, do not wake him as we have no idea what that could do to him given the situation Rory turned and walked out, heading back to his office to consider his next move.

Back on Rivaxia, the leadership gathered on the landing platform, tension thick in the air as they awaited the Dream Agents' return. Suddenly, a ship broke through the clouds, its battered hull bearing the scars of a fierce battle. As it descended toward the landing pad, a wave of anxiety swept through the assembled leaders.

As the Dream Agents finally landed, a wave of relief swept through the crowd—quickly overshadowed by urgency. The ship's engines faded to a low hum as the agents disembarked, their steps heavy with the weight of their mission. Securing only 10% of the embryos had been a hard-fought victory, yet the harrowing news of Micky's capture loomed over them like a dark cloud, threatening their resolve.

Uneasy glances flickered between the Rivaxian leaders, tension rippling through the assembled ranks. The Dream Agents were determined to brief them on their findings and rally support for a rescue. Time was slipping away, and the stakes had never been higher.

As they made their way to the central command hub, the agents exchanged quiet remarks about the mission, their voices laced with exhaustion and determination. Key Rivaxian leaders, including Dr. Fem Dam, awaited their arrival, the atmosphere thick with anticipation.

The agents were ushered into the dimly lit chamber, where holographic displays flickered, casting an eerie glow on the faces of both human and Rivaxian onlookers. The weight of their journey hung in the air.

Tarek Its stepped forward, and before he could speak, Dr. Fem Dam rushed toward him, pulling him into a tight embrace. "Tarek Its, I can't believe you're here!" Dr. Fem Dam exclaimed, holding him tightly. "It's so good to see you—I didn't know if you were alive or dead."

"I'm okay," Tarek Its assured her, though his voice was heavy. "But Micky has been taken prisoner."

He quickly outlined their findings, his words measured but urgent. "We intercepted their communications—Micky is scheduled to be transported to the Vark world, along with the remaining embryos."

The room fell into a heavy silence. The revelation struck like a dagger, its weight pressing down on everyone present. Dr. Fem Dam's expression darkened, the full implications settling in. "We must act swiftly," Dr. Fem Dam said, her gaze sweeping over the Dream Agents. "If the Vark's intend to use Micky as leverage, it could spell disaster for us all."

Tarek Its nodded; his expression grim. "We need intel on their transport schedule—how and when they plan to move him. If we can pinpoint their route, we might have a chance to intercept them."

Murmurs of concern rippled through the Rivaxians. The Vark's had grown more formidable with each encounter, their power escalating at an alarming rate.

"If Micky is valuable enough for them to capture," one of the Rivaxian leaders warned, "then we need to be prepared for anything. As discussions intensified, the stakes of the mission became even clearer.

"My people," said the Cha, his voice steady. "Remember, we need the embryos, and of course, we need Micky. We must keep our heads cool and devise a proper strategy. I will leave you to deliberate and expect your plan in two days."

With that, he turned and exited, leaving the others gathered around an enormous table to begin their discussion.

"Their defences will be even tighter now," Kerra said, anxiety creeping into her voice. "We must get Micky—he was shot and is likely in critical condition."

"Whatever their original plans were, they've probably changed since our last encounter. My guess is that Micky and the embryos are already on the Vark world," Bertie said, scanning the faces around the table.

Meanwhile, in the cold, shadowed confines of a heavily armoured Vark transport ship, Micky stirred, groggy and bound. The ship thrummed ominously as it tore through space, bound for a world unlike Sankat 3 or Rivaxia. His pulse pounded as he strained against the restraints, his mind scrambling to make sense of his surroundings. Then, the brutal truth struck—he was a prisoner of the very beings they had fought so hard to resist. The thought sent an icy dread coursing through his veins.

As the transport neared the Vark world, Micky glimpsed a stark, frozen wasteland through the porthole—so unlike the warm, vibrant beauty of Sankat 3 or Rivaxia. The planet's surface was a merciless expanse of ice, scarred with jagged formations and sheer, towering cliffs. A blizzard raged, the wind howling as it whipped snow and ice into a relentless storm, sculpting an inhospitable world as cold and unforgiving as the Vark civilisation itself. When the transport's ramp lowered and an icy gust rushed in, Micky shivered—not just from the cold, but from the unshakable dread curling in his gut. This was a world where mercy did not exist.

Rough Vark soldiers yanked him from his seat, their metallic exoskeletons glinting ominously in the dim light of the ship's interior. Micky's pulse pounded as they marched him into a vast Vark compound, where steel and ice fused into imposing, unyielding structures. The air hung thick with dread, the acrid stench of despair seeping into every corner, intensifying the weight of his predicament.

He was thrust into a dimly lit chamber, the oppressive gloom fractured by the hollow echoes of distant cries. As his eyes adjusted, his breath hitched at the sight of the other prisoners—gaunt, hollow-eyed souls from an array of species, all crammed into a single, squalid dungeon. Panic flared in his chest until his gaze landed on a hunched figure against the far wall, their posture radiating utter defeat. Desperation surged through him as he lunged forward.

"Who are you?" Micky asked, kneeling beside the figure, studying the older man's face, partially obscured by shadow.

The stranger slowly lifted his head, revealing a weathered face etched with pain. "I'm Zuk Nall," he rasped, his voice hoarse from years of suffering. "I'm Rivaxian. I was in charge of Tanexa V, but I was captured when the facility fell to the Varks."

Micky's eyes widened as he processed the revelation. "Zuk Nall? I've heard rumours about you... The Rivaxian world believes you're dead. They have no idea you're a prisoner. You were the one trying to save our race from extinction."

Zuk Nall managed a faint smile, though desperation clung to him like a shadow. "That was a long time ago. I've been here far too long... tortured far too much. I don't even know what I might have told them." He winced, shifting slightly to get a better look at Micky. "What about you? How did they catch you?"

Micky's heart pounded as he recounted his harrowing capture, reliving the moments that led to his imprisonment. "We were on a mission to recover embryos when we were ambushed. I thought I'd gotten away..." His voice faltered, the weight of his reality pressing down on him. "I'm a Dream Agent."

Zuk Nall gave a knowing nod, a weary smile ghosting his lips.

"It's a miracle… we did it," he said, his voice weak but laced with relief, a faint smile forming.

Suddenly, an unspoken understanding passed between them—a connection forged in shared suffering.

"They've been extracting information from me for years. I'm surprised to see a human—the Varks must be escalating their plans." His tone darkened. "You need to stay strong. It's the only way to survive this hell."

Before Micky could respond, the heavy door groaned open. A Vark guard stepped inside, his head concealed beneath a helmet, thick armour gleaming in the dim light. A sinister grin spread across his face beneath his mask. "Welcome to your new home, human. We have much to discuss," he sneered, a chilling laugh slithering from his lips.

Micky's stomach churned as he was dragged down the corridor and shoved into a cold, metallic room at the end. A brutal shove forced him into a chair, his arms bound tight. The interrogation chamber was stark and unforgiving, the harsh glare of overhead lights stripping away any sense of refuge. Across from him, Zuk Nall was yanked forward, grimacing as the guards restrained him.

"Why do we never see their faces? What are they going to do to us?" Micky whispered, his pulse pounding with fear.

Zuk Nall's expression hardened, his resolve unwavering despite the despair. "They will try to break you, just as they did with me. But don't give them what they want. We have to resist, no matter the torment they inflict."

The lead officer—a towering Vark clad in intricately marked armour—began to circle Micky like a predator sizing up its prey. Leaning in, he let his voice drop to a menacing growl. "We know you're associated with the ones they call Dream Agents. Tell us everything about their operations and the embryos."

Micky clenched his jaw, refusing to yield. "What are Dream Agents? I won't tell you anything," he spat defiantly, his thoughts fixed on his friends back in Rivaxia.

The Vark officer let out a brief, amused laugh, momentarily surprised by Micky's audacity. "Very well," he sneered, signalling to the guards. Without hesitation, they advanced—and the pain began.

Hours dragged on as Micky endured the brutal interrogation, drawing what strength he could from Zuk Nall's steady presence. Zuk Nall watched him with a mix of concern and quiet admiration. Together, they clung to the fragile hope of escape, even as the suffocating darkness of the Vark world threatened to consume them.

The cold metal of the chair pressed unforgivingly against Micky's back as he stared down the officer, fear coiling in his chest. The interrogation room was stark and unrelenting, mirroring the oppressive weight of the world beyond its walls. The harsh overhead lights seemed almost purposeful in their cruelty, each glare intensifying the bleakness of his predicament.

The Vark officer seized Micky's arm, twisting it cruelly, his breath thick with sulphur and contempt. "You can't hide forever, human. We know the Dream Agents are planning a counterstrike, and your silence won't save you. Tell us about their operations, or the pain will only worsen."

Micky remained silent, refusing to let fear dictate his response. The officer's patience thinned, and with a sharp gesture, he summoned the doctor. The physician stepped forward, instruments in hand, his expression devoid of warmth or mercy. "Then let's begin."

"Don't let them break you!" Zuk Nall shouted, his voice raw with urgency. "You're stronger than you think!"

Micky nodded subtly, bracing himself for the torment ahead. The metallic instruments gleamed menacingly under the harsh lights, each glint sharpening the fear coiled within him. He steeled himself, resolute in his duty to protect the secrets he carried and the lives of his friends.

As the doctor approached, Micky's thoughts flickered to Kerra, Buddy, Sumeet, and Bertie—he pictured them working tirelessly to save him. He saw their faces, heard their laughter, felt their unwavering determination. The memory fuelled the fire inside him. He would not betray them. Not now. Not ever.

The first instrument scraped across the table, sending a chill down Micky's spine as the doctor readied it. He loosened one of Micky's arm restraints, his intent chillingly clear—to sever his hand.

Before the Varks could strike, a blaring alarm shattered the tension, echoing through the chamber. The lights flickered erratically, casting jagged shadows as the walls trembled with the sudden upheaval.

"What's happening?" the Vark officer barked, frustration tightening his expression. "Secure the prisoners!"

The guards hesitated, exchanging uneasy glances as the siren wailed on, disrupting the interrogation. Seizing the moment, adrenaline surged through Micky—this was his chance. Across the room, Zuk Nall met his gaze, a faint spark of hope flickering in his weary eyes.

"Now!" Micky urged in a hushed but urgent tone. The chaos was their chance.

He swiftly freed his other arm and sprang from the chair, catching the guards off guard. Using the confusion to his advantage, he shoved the nearest one, knocking him off balance. A weapon clattered from the Vark's grasp, and Micky seized it. It was heavier than he expected, but he gripped it with steely determination.

"Zuk Nall, we have to move—now!" he shouted, scanning the room for an escape route. Zuk Nall nodded, his spirit rekindled by the disorder unfolding around them.

Together, they charged toward the door, quickly taking down the last two guards who were still scrambling to regain control. Seizing their moment, they surged through the opening and into the cold hallway beyond.

The blaring alarms echoed around them, a deafening cacophony that consumed their fear. Micky's heart raced as they sprinted down the corridor. The compound pulsed with tension—every second counted. They had to escape before the Varks could regroup.

"Over there!" Zuk Nall shouted, pointing to a staircase that led to an upper level. "It might give us access to the roof. We'll find a way out from there!"

They bolted for the stairs, urgency propelling them upward. As they climbed, a flicker of hope ignited in Micky's chest. They had a chance—if they could break free, they could warn the Dream Agents before it was too late.

When they reached the summit, a small door swung open, revealing the frigid expanse of Vark World—a stark contrast to the warmth they had left behind. Stepping into the blizzard, they were immediately assaulted by icy winds that lashed at their faces. Micky narrowed his eyes against the swirling snow, struggling to find his bearings.

"Look!" Zuk Nall shouted, pointing towards a nearby ridge. "If we can reach it, we might find shelter and reassess our situation."

Micky gave a determined nod and forced his way through the biting wind. Every ache and ounce of exhaustion melted away as adrenaline surged through him. "We just need to stay focused," he called over the howling gusts. "We'll find a way back to Rivaxia!"

With determination fuelling their steps, they pushed forward, leaving the shadows of captivity behind. Yet, as they ventured deeper into the frozen wasteland, the harsh reality of their surroundings pressed in. The biting wind clawed at their skin, seeping through layers of clothing, while the relentless snowfall blurred their vision, making it nearly impossible to identify any landmarks. A creeping sense of isolation settled over Micky as he trudged through the knee-deep snow, each step a stark reminder of their perilous escape.

"This way!" Zuk Nall shouted, jolting Micky from his thoughts as he pointed towards a cluster of jagged rocks jutting from the icy ground. "We can use those for cover!"

They forced their way towards the rocky outcrop, seeking shelter from the punishing wind. As they crouched behind the stones, Micky's breath came in quick, misting bursts in the freezing air. He took a moment to steady himself, his gaze sweeping the desolate landscape for any sign of Vark patrols.

"What now?" Zuk Nall asked, his weary face lined with worry. "The Varks will notice we're missing soon. We need a plan."

Micky nodded, his mind racing. "We have to find a way to contact Rivaxia. There must be a monitoring station nearby. If we can send a signal, Bertie and the others might be able to track us."

Zuk Nall grimaced, shivering against the biting cold. "The nearest Vark facility is a few clicks east. It's risky, but if we can get there unnoticed, we might have a chance."

"Then we move—now. We won't last much longer in this cold. Otherwise, the Varks will only find two frozen corpses."

They moved cautiously, keeping to the cover of the rocks as they pressed eastward, their breaths misting in the frigid air.

Micky scanned the swirling snow, his gaze fixed on the shadows, ready to react to any lurking threat. The crushing isolation of Vark world bore down on him; every rustle, every muffled sound sent fresh waves of unease prickling through his spine.

"We're almost there," Zuk Nall said, his voice barely carrying over the wind. After what felt like hours of navigating the treacherous terrain, Micky glimpsed a faint glow in the distance—shrouded by the storm, nestled between towering ice cliffs. "That must be it! We can't afford to waste any time."

They pressed forward, moving as swiftly as the brutal conditions allowed. The glow intensified, revealing a small, fortified structure encased by towering walls of ice. It looked as though it might house communication equipment—their best hope of reaching Rivaxia.

"We need to get inside," Micky urged as they neared the entrance, his voice low and measured. The building was heavily guarded; Vark sentries patrolled the perimeter, their menacing silhouettes barely discernible against the swirling snow.

"Do you see a way in?" Zuk Nall whispered, shifting his position behind the rocks.

Micky, using his vision skills to see through walls, scanned the area, his mind racing as he searched for gaps in the guards' rotations.

"There!" He pointed to a back door, nearly concealed beneath overhanging ice. "If we can reach it without being seen, we might be able to slip inside."

As they waited for a gap in the guard patrol, Micky felt the cold seeping into his bones. They needed to move—now. The stakes grew higher with each passing moment. "Just be ready to go," he warned Zuk Nall, who nodded, his expression grim.

The moment came. Micky and Zuk Nall sprinted across the snow, their hearts pounding in sync. As they reached the door, Micky's hands trembled, fumbling with the handle. He pushed it open just as the guards turned their backs.

They slipped inside and shut the door behind them, sealing out the frigid winds. The lights flickered overhead, casting an eerie glow over a room filled with equipment that looked both advanced and primitive.

Micky's gaze locked onto a central control panel. Without hesitation, he rushed over, Zuk Nall close behind.

"Let me try to access their systems," Micky said, kneeling before the array of buttons and screens. His fingers flew over the controls, working to bypass whatever security the Varks had in place. "If I can get this to work, we might be able to send a signal back to Rivaxia."

"Be quick!" Zuk Nall urged, his eyes darting to the door. "We don't have much time."

As Micky tapped into the system, the pressure mounted. His eyes flicked between the flashing lights and the door, each second stretching unbearably.

"Come on, come on—damn it!" he muttered under his breath, willing the machine to cooperate.

The screen flickered to life—just as a blaring alarm shattered the silence, echoing through the building. Micky's heart lurched as the lights pulsed wildly.

"They know we're here!" he shouted, panic surging through him.

"Get that message sent!" Zuk Nall urged, his eyes locked on the door. "I'll cover you!"

Forcing himself to focus, Micky's fingers flew over the console, feverishly typing in commands.

"I need to say this before the Vark arrive—just in case I don't make it. Before all this," Zuk Nall began, his voice steady despite the chaos surrounding them, "we were working on something big—an advanced time machine. If we succeed, this nightmare we're trapped in will never have happened."

Micky glanced up, surprise flickering across his face. "A time machines? Is that even possible?"

Zuk Nall nodded, determination burning in his weary expression.

"We believed so. It was a project towards the end of my work with the Dream Agents—a way to either prevent traumatic events or escape them entirely. If I can re-establish contact with my team, we might still have a chance. But towards the end, I started to worry... What if we weren't building something to undo disaster, but rather, to create one?"

Micky's mind spun with possibilities.

"What do you mean by 'more sinister'?"

"It's nothing. I think I've been here too long… and we don't have time to talk about it now. Just ignore me. Get that message sent!"

"Okay, I understand. I was held for years—it plays tricks on your mind. But right now, we need to focus. If we can warn Rivaxia and halt the Varks' plans, we might create an opportunity to finish what you started."

"Yes!" Zuk Nall urged, his eyes brightening with hope. "You just need to get that signal through. Without our data, they'll make mistakes. They won't anticipate the danger if they don't know we're coming."

Zuk Nall's expression hardened with resolve as he moved toward the door, assuming a protective stance. "Get that message sent! I'll hold them off as long as I can," he urged. "We can't let them capture us again."

Taking a deep breath, Micky turned his attention back to the console, his fingers flying over the illuminated keypad as he accessed the encrypted communications. "Just a few more seconds," he murmured.

Zuk Nall peered through the small window in the door, watching shadows shift beyond, listening intently for the enemy's approach. If all goes well, we'll rewrite this moment, he thought.

Suddenly, the screen flickered ominously before stabilising—a successful connection. Micky's heart pounded as the signal came through. "I've got it!" he shouted, relief flooding him.

With a final keystroke, Micky sent out the urgent message, detailing the Varks' plans to experiment on the embryos here on their homeworld, along with their own dire situation and coordinates. He held his breath as the transmission bar filled—then exhaled in relief when confirmation flickered into view.

"Now, let's get out of here!" he urged, his pulse quickening at the thought of escape.

The alarms blared louder, reverberating through the walls. Zuk Nall nodded, his expression wary yet determined.

"Quickly! We need to find a way out before they close in. Keep moving if we want to survive."

Micky and Zuk Nall sprinted through the dimly lit corridors of the Vark stronghold, their footsteps echoing against the steel floors, blending with the distant sounds of gunfire and chaos. They ducked into a side passage, weaving through the shadows, their hearts pounding—not just from exertion, but from the looming threat that felt dangerously close.

Suddenly, a deafening explosion rocked the corridor, sending debris flying. Micky glanced back to see Zuk Nall standing his ground, eyes fierce with determination.

"Go, Micky! I'll hold them off!" Zuk Nall shouted, his voice cutting through the chaos.

"No! We can't split up!" Micky protested, but Zuk Nall had already taken position, his stance unwavering as the dark forms of Vark soldiers rounded the corner.

With a heavy heart, Micky forced himself to press on, knowing Zuk Nall was about to face the oncoming storm.

Shots rang out behind him, spurring him forward. Adrenaline surged through his veins as he rounded another corner, lungs burning from exertion. For a fleeting moment, he thought he had escaped—until the harsh voices of Vark soldiers drew closer. The ground trembled beneath his feet as another explosion shook the stronghold.

Moments later, a piercing shout rang out behind him. Micky froze, his heart plummeting. He spun around just in time to see Zuk Nall stagger, a grimace twisting his face as a shot struck him. The sight ripped through Micky; his friend had fought with everything he had.

Summoning his last reserves of strength, Zuk Nall raised his weapon and took down two soldiers before his body finally gave out. He collapsed, the fight draining from him.

"Zuk Nall!" Micky cried, panic surging through him. He lurched forward, desperate to reach his fallen friend—but it was too late. The chaos around him seemed to fade, drowned out by the pounding in his chest, until the soldiers surged forward.

Outnumbered but defiant, Micky fought with everything he had. But the enemy closed in, overwhelming him. Hours later, he was tossed into a dimly lit cell, the heavy door slamming shut behind him.

Time felt warped as he waited in despair. The faint sound of footsteps echoed through the corridor, growing louder until a familiar figure emerged—the Vark General, his expression unreadable.

"I'm glad the message got through to Rivaxia," the General said, a low laugh rumbling beneath his mask. "Our plan worked flawlessly. You swallowed every bit of misinformation we fed you, and now they believe exactly what we wanted them to."

Micky's heart pounded as the implications of the General's words sank in. "What are you planning?" he demanded, his defiance unmistakable.

The General leaned in, his voice a chilling whisper. "While your forces scramble to reach the Vark world, we are already poised to invade Rivaxia. It will be ours before they even realise what's happening. And you? You'll find out your fate soon enough."

As the General strode away, leaving Micky alone in the shadows, the weight of despair pressed down harder. Yet deep within him, a glimmer of hope flickered to life. Zuk Nall's sacrifice would not be in vain. If Rivaxia was to be warned, Micky would find a way to escape again—to turn the tide before it was too late. The chains of his prison only strengthened his resolve. He would fight back—for Zuk Nall, for Rivaxia, and for their shared dream of freedom from the darkness of the Vark world.

CHAPTER 15

Echoes of Hope

Back in Rivaxia, the Dream Agents reconvened, the air thick with urgency. They needed to strategise—and fast.

"We're running out of time," Bertie pressed, his determination unwavering. "We have to find a way to infiltrate the Vark world. We can't abandon Micky or the embryos—they're both far too important."

As the discussion unfolded, Tarek Its mind raced with the implications of Micky's capture. "We need to gather resources, contacts—anyone who might assist us. If we want this rescue mission to succeed, we must plan with absolute precision."

Just as the tension in the room reached its peak, the door swung open. Jax burst in, his face alight with exhilaration and disbelief. "You won't believe it! We've received a message from Micky—straight from the Vark world!"

The room erupted in murmurs of hope and disbelief.

"How is that possible? What did he say? Is he okay?" Bertie's voice trembled with anticipation.

Jax took a deep breath, struggling to contain his excitement. "He couldn't have been clearer—Micky's alive! He sent precise details about the Vark stronghold. And there's more—Zuk Nall is alive too!"

A wave of joy surged through the Rivaxians. Dr. Fem Dam, usually poised and composed, let out an uncharacteristic cry of triumph.

"This is incredible! Zuk Nall is alive! It's a blessing from the Nur gods!" she exclaimed. The others quickly joined in the celebration, their spirits soaring with renewed hope.

"Wait a second—who is Zuk Nall?" Bertie asked, cutting through the celebration.

"He was the head scientist at Tanaxa V—our greatest mind! We thought he was lost forever. This is nothing short of a miracle," Dr. Fem Dam replied, her voice thick with emotion.

Jax stepped forward. "There's more. Micky's message warns that the Vark are about to begin gene enhancement experiments on the embryos. We need to act now."

Bertie straightened, regaining focus. "Alright, everyone, stay calm—we have to move fast. With both Zuk Nall and Micky alive, we have a real chance to pull this off. They know more about the Vark than anyone. We must get them—and the embryos—out before the Vark put their plan into motion."

Sumeet scanned the faces of his comrades. "What's our next move?" he asked, eager for direction.

Dr. Fem Dam stepped forward; her earlier excitement now replaced with a sense of urgency. "Micky identified a weakness in the Vark's security system. If we exploit it, we can create a diversion to cover our entry. I also have black-market contacts who can smuggle us in—provided we offer the right incentives."

"Good thinking," Tarek Its said with a nod. "Let's map out a route, secure supplies, and gather more intel. We also need to see how many Rivaxians are willing to join us. If we're going to breach the Vark stronghold, we'll need every ally we can get."

As they began to strategise, the relentless ticking of the clock weighed heavily on them. The road ahead would not be easy, but the thought of rescuing Micky and Zuk Nall—along with the embryos—fuelled their resolve, igniting a fire that could not be extinguished. Every heartbeat echoed their shared conviction: they would not leave their friends behind. As the meeting progressed, ideas flowed, plans took shape, and hope continued to blossom.

Strategies and tactics flew across the table as the Dream Agents pooled their resources and skills. Dr. Fem Dam leaned in closer, her voice steady yet passionate.

Tarek Its added, "I'll coordinate with the scouts. We need to chart a safe route that avoids the main patrols. If we can get close enough before the invasion begins, we can strike fast and hard."

The flickering lights of hope illuminated their faces as they delved deeper into their strategy. Knowing that Micky and Zuk Nall still drew breath rekindled their spirits, fuelling the urgency of their mission.

Time moved swiftly, and as preparations escalated, the agents were more focused than ever. They had to find their friend. The risks were great, but so was their resolve. The possibility of a successful rescue now lay within their grasp.

As they finalised their plan, Tarek Its glanced up. "We are ready. We will bring them back. Everyone, be ready to leave in three hours." With that, the Dream Agents and the Rivaxians left the room.

Dr. Fem Dam walked down the corridor and into a secure room, glancing over her shoulder to ensure no one had followed her.

CHAPTER 16

Chronicles of Time

The door to the laboratory slid open with a hiss, revealing a vast room filled with arcane machinery and glowing screens pulsing with data. Dr. Fem Dam stepped inside, flanked by two skilled technicians, Lira and Jax. This was no ordinary laboratory; it was the heart of their ground-breaking project—the Temporal Chrono Spectra Modulator (TCSM).

"Alright," Dr. Fem Dam said, her voice steady but laced with excitement. "Where are the results from the latest tests?"

"I've reviewed them, Dr. Fem Dam, and they indicate we're 98.7% ready," Jax replied, meeting her gaze.

"Let's run the final checks and retest," she instructed.

"Systems are online," Lira reported, her fingers flying over the control panel as she analysed multiple readouts. "Power levels are stabilising, and phase variance is within acceptable limits."

"Ensure the temporal calibrations are precise," Jax added, scanning another console. "We can't afford any anomalies, especially given what we're about to attempt."

At that moment, the electronic door slid open with a soft, mechanical hum, and Cha strode in, exuding authority. Four armed bodyguards flanked him, their presence adding to the gravity of the moment. The technicians instinctively straightened. Dr. Fem Dam acknowledged him with a nod. "Welcome, Ruler Cha."

"Dr. Fem Dam, is the TCSM ready for testing?" Cha asked, his calm yet commanding voice tinged with curiosity.

"Yes, Ruler Cha," she replied, suppressing her eagerness. "We previously reached 98.7%. I'm hopeful this trial will push us closer to full readiness. We're prepared to proceed with both the initial test and the live trial. Safeguards are in place to ensure a smooth operation."

Cha studied the machine, nodding as he circled it. "This technology could alter the course of our history—for better or worse. Are you certain you grasp the full implications of what you wield? Have you followed Zuk Nall's plans precisely?"

"Exactly as he laid them out—with some enhanced modifications," Dr. Fem Dam assured him, her tone sincere. "We've run extensive simulations and theoretical assessments since the last test. I'm confident we can navigate time safely without compromising our reality, but we won't know for certain until we test it. We're almost there—98.7% ready!"

Cha studied her for a long moment before nodding. "Proceed, but I expect a comprehensive report after each testing phase. You're venturing into uncharted territory now."

"Understood," Dr. Fem Dam affirmed, turning back to the technicians. "Let's initiate the test run. Lira, activate the projection chamber."

Lira took her position, her fingers deftly gliding over the controls. The room thrummed with energy as the time machine's core pulsed, vibrant lights cascading across the chamber. "Commencing test sequence in three... two... one."

A blinding flash engulfed the machine as it roared to life. At the heart of the chamber, a holographic projection materialised—an intricate tapestry of moments flowing through time. Dr. Fem Dam watched intently, her heart pounding with a mix of hope and apprehension.

"All readings are positive," Jax announced, his eyes widening with wonder. "The temporal field is stable!"

Cha observed intently; arms crossed. "What happens next, Dr. Fem Dam?"

"We will now proceed to the second phase," Dr. Fem Dam explained. "First, we'll send a controlled object through the temporal field. If successful, we'll advance to a live subject—a Rivaxian volunteer."

"Ensure all proper protocols are followed," Cha warned sharply. "This is a risky endeavour. We are so close."

With the first phase complete and confidence mounting, Dr. Fem Dam prepared for the next step. She summoned one of the volunteers, a palpable energy crackling in the air. "Vela Sornyx, you are one of the bravest Rivaxians in our history. Are you ready?"

"Vela Sornyx, your people stand with you through every step of this test. You will be remembered for eternity," Cha said, bowing his head.

"I am ready, Almighty Cha," Vela Sornyx replied, stepping forward with determination. "I trust the science, Dr. Fem Dam."

"Let's do this," Dr. Fem Dam said, guiding her to the machine's platform. "Remember, stay aware of your surroundings and remain calm. You'll be back in an instant—I promise."

As the sequence initiated once more, the chamber flooded with brilliant light. The machine whirred and pulsed, sending vibrations through the air as Vela Sornyx stepped into the heart of the temporal field. In an instant, she vanished from sight, leaving the room in heavy silence.

Seconds stretched into eternity until the machine hummed, pulling her back. Vela Sornyx reappeared, breathless but unharmed, exhilaration lighting up her face.

"It worked! I was there... and back!" she exclaimed, her voice brimming with wonder. "I saw time flowing like a river—it was incredible!"

The room erupted with excitement as Dr. Fem Dam turned to her team, then to Cha.

"This is just the beginning. We'll refine the technology and ensure it is wielded responsibly. With this machine, we can reshape history, safeguard our future, and defend Rivaxia from threats before they even emerge."

Suddenly, Vela Sornyx let out a piercing scream, her body convulsing before she collapsed. By the time her head struck the floor, she was dead—her face withering before their very eyes.

Dr. Fem Dam lifted her gaze to Cha, her voice strained. "I'm sorry, sir. We clearly need to conduct further tests."

Cha's expression darkened. "There's no time. We need this to work—especially with what the Vark are planning with the embryos. I will not accept failure. Do you hear me, Dr. Fem Dam?"

The atmosphere in the laboratory thickened with grief and tension. Dim lights flickered weakly, casting eerie shadows over the grim scene. Vela Sornyx, once a hopeful volunteer, now lay lifeless—a casualty of their relentless ambition. At the centre of the room, Dr. Fem Dam stood motionless, concern etched deep into her features as she scanned her team. Shock, fear, and grim determination mirrored in every face around her.

"We can't let this tragedy deter our mission. You heard Cha—we must succeed," Dr. Fem Dam said, her voice steady despite the turmoil within her. "We need to analyse the results of the last test thoroughly. We must understand what went wrong before attempting another run."

Jax, the lead technician, nodded gravely as he pulled up the data on the screen. "I'll review the readouts immediately. We need to identify any anomalies that may have caused the failure."

Lira joined him; her eyes filled with concern. "And we must ensure every safety measure is reassessed. We can't risk another life."

Dr. Fem Dam tapped a slender finger against the console, her voice crisp. "Let's begin with the power fluctuations and phase variances. They remained within limits, but every parameter requires scrutiny. No detail is too small." The weight of her words settled over the room.

As Dr. Fem Dam and her team pored over the data, a shadow moved silently beyond the reinforced walls. Sumeet, still trying to clear his head after Sankat 3, had lost his bearings while wandering the facility's gardens. He stumbled upon a seldom-used entrance, hoping for a shortcut back inside.

He wandered the echoing corridors, unease settling over him like a creeping shadow, until he found himself peering through a frosted window—no larger than a postage stamp—into a brightly lit laboratory. Inside, Dr. Fem Dam and her team clustered around glowing screens, their faces lit with intensity. But on the floor lay Vela Sorynx—lifeless.

Snippets of conversation drifted through the air, murmurs of timelines and the manipulation of fate, each word sending a chilling wave of dread through him. Something was profoundly wrong.

Suddenly, an alarm blared. Dr. Fem Dam's head snapped up. Through the glass, she spotted Sumeet lingering too long by the doorway, his attention fixed where it shouldn't be. Without hesitation, she strode to the door and pulled it open.

"Sumeet! Come in," she said, motioning for him to enter, though an undercurrent of tension coloured her tone.

Surprised by the invitation, Sumeet hesitated before stepping across the threshold. The door slid shut behind him with a faint hiss, sealing him within the charged atmosphere of innovation and unspoken intentions.

"Dr. Fem Dam, this looks... interesting. What exactly is going on here?" Sumeet asked, his voice steady but laced with concern. "I heard something about a Temporal Chronos Spectra Modulator, or a time machine as Jax called it. Why haven't you informed the Dream Agents about this? And what happened to her?" He pointed at Vela Sorynx, his gaze fixed on her face, horror creeping into his expression.

Dr. Fem Dam's demeanour shifted slightly as she gestured for Sumeet to join the discussion at the central table. "What are you talking about? There is no time machine. That would be impossible to develop!" she said, almost laughing at him.

"Maybe I was mistaken then. No problem. I should go and rejoin the other Dream Agents," he said, rising to his feet.

"Hang on, Sumeet. Relax. Let me show you what we're really working on," Dr. Fem Dam said, her tone measured. "It's a project to extend our lifespan. As you know, we are dying, and the embryos are our only hope. Sadly, our first test on Vela Sorynx failed—she aged instead of growing younger."

"Yes! Can you imagine?" Lira interjected passionately. "If we could extend life, we would be willing to share this with humans."

Suddenly, the Cha stepped back into the lab, his gaze icy as he registered the presence of a Dream Agent. "We must protect Rivaxia at all costs, Sumeet. To do that, we need to take decisive action. Can you imagine what this breakthrough would mean for our dear and close friends— the human race?"

Just then, Sumeet sensed that something was deeply wrong.

"Wait, I'm sorry, but I'm not buying this. The whole issue isn't really about the Vark and saving Rivaxia, is it? Why do all these panels have times and dates? You're trying to create a time machine!" he said urgently. "Did the Vark really attack Rivaxia, or was it something you did?" His heart pounded in his chest.

A stunned silence enveloped the room. Dr. Fem Dam's eyes darkened at the implications of Sumeet's words. If news of their plan spread, everything they had worked for could unravel.

In that moment, Sumeet knew he was in danger.

"I need to alert the other Dream Agents about this project. They deserve to know the truth!" he declared, stepping back, ready to flee.

"No!" Cha intervened, his voice a low snarl. "I will not allow you to disrupt our efforts."

"You're wrong, Cha. This will lead to disaster!" Sumeet fired back, his indignation igniting the room.

"Disaster for whom?" Dr. Fem Dam retorted sharply, her eyes glinting with a dangerous light. "For the Vark, or for the future we envision? You are nothing but a pathetic race of feeble creatures—we only used you to get to the Vark!"

Before Sumeet could react, a guard stepped forward, weapon drawn. Panic surged through him as the true depth of their intentions sank in.

"No! You can't—" he began, but before he could finish, a deafening shot rang out, echoing through the chamber. His eyes widened in shock as he collapsed to the ground, lifeless, blood pooling around him.

Dr. Fem Dam and her technicians remained unfazed, merely exchanging glances that betrayed their shared resolve. The price of his discovery had just been paid—in the most final way.

"Clean this up. I want that machine working," Cha commanded.

CHAPTER 17

Shadows of Deception

In the main chamber, anticipation hung thick in the air as the Dream Agents awaited their final briefing before the mission to Vark. Dr. Fem Dam entered with authority, her expression resolute and uncompromising.

"We need to discuss Sumeet," she announced, her voice commanding. "He will not be joining you on this mission. He's remaining behind to work on a critical project—one that is vital to our future."

Lira stepped forward, her eyes glinting with support. "The Doctor is right. Sumeet's technical skills are crucial for this project," she stated confidently. "His expertise in technology and strategy could significantly enhance our ability to combat the Vark and strengthen our defences."

Jax nodded in agreement, his tone earnest. "Exactly. Each of us has a role to play in this mission, and Sumeet's focus on this project is imperative. If he can refine our tech and improve our systems, it'll give us a stronger foothold when we engage."

Bertie glanced at Buddy, his brow furrowed in confusion. "But surely we need him with us? Our numbers are so few," he said, turning back to Dr. Fem Dam.

She smiled at Bertie, her tone measured. "This isn't merely about individual contributions; it's about the success of the entire mission. We must leverage each of our strengths effectively. While you head to Vark world, as we've said, Sumeet will be working on integrating new technologies that could ultimately shift the balance in our favour."

Dr. Fem Dam's voice remained firm as she continued, "Utilising our best resources for specific tasks is vital. Sumeet's technical acumen will allow him to develop innovative solutions that the Dream Agents in the field will need. It's about synergy, and every role is crucial."

The agents listened, still confused, yet placing their trust in the Rivaxians. Under Dr. Fem Dam's leadership, every decision she made—though veiled in strategic brilliance—was ultimately about maintaining control, steering Rivaxia towards its goals, and ensuring the darker truths remained hidden from view.

As the tension in the chamber began to ease, Dr. Fem Dam felt the weight of their loyalty, yet she was acutely aware of the fragile web of deception she was weaving. Just then, Bertie spoke.

"Dr. Fem Dam," he began, his voice firm with authority, "is there any chance we could see Sumeet before we head out on the mission? It would help us feel more connected to the operation he's overseeing. We've already been through so much, and with Micky missing, it would be good to wish him luck."

A flicker of irritation crossed Dr. Fem Dam's expression, but she quickly masked it with a practised smile. "Bertie, I understand your desire to see him," she replied, her tone smooth yet dismissive. "However, Sumeet has already left the planet to work from the far moon, where he can focus without distraction alongside our team of experts. It's for the best, truly. We need him fully concentrated on developing the innovations we rely on."

The Dream Agents exchanged glances. Though they nodded in acceptance of her words, uncertainty still lingered in their eyes.

"But…" Bertie pressed, his face etched with concern. "What if we need specific insights from him? Wouldn't it be helpful to have direct communication lines open before we leave?"

Dr. Fem Dam shifted slightly, exuding an air of feigned authority. "In his current location, Sumeet can operate with greater security and fewer interruptions," she explained, her tone unwavering. "He's already contributing remotely, and I assure you, he will provide regular updates and support. His work is critical, and we must respect the parameters he's set for himself in this endeavour."

Jax leaned in, reinforcing Dr. Fem Dam's statement. "She's right, Bertie. Sumeet needs space to concentrate—it's essential for the mission's success. Besides, we can't risk the Vark discovering his location. He's capable, and we can trust him to keep us informed," he said, though doubt flickered in his eyes.

Dr. Fem Dam still sensed the unspoken questions hanging in the air, the simmering doubts among the agents, but she pressed on. "Focus on your roles here and trust that Sumeet is where he needs to be," she continued, her tone firm yet smooth, as she sought to dispel any lingering uncertainty.

Although the agents accepted her words, a lingering unease remained. They wanted to trust in the plan, yet an undercurrent of scepticism murmured among them. As Bertie nodded, still visibly hesitant, Dr. Fem Dam felt a flicker of satisfaction at the brief silence she had imposed. The truth of Sumeet's fate lay buried beneath her composed exterior, concealed by the weight of her formidable presence. She knew that every layer of deception woven now was vital to the mission's success, and she was resolute in maintaining control over the narrative that would propel the Dream Agents into the unknown.

As the Dream Agents prepared to depart, the changes to their plans and mission loomed over them, shadowed by uncertainty. Bertie and Kerra walked side by side towards the weapons chamber, their conversation animated yet edged with concern.

"I still can't shake the feeling that it's odd Sumeet is gone—without a word to anyone," Bertie said, glancing sideways at

Kerra. "He's always played such a critical role in our missions. Why send him away now?"

Kerra nodded. "I know what you mean. It's unsettling not having him here. What if we run into unexpected challenges? His expertise on the ground would have been invaluable." She hesitated, then added, "And Dr. Fem Dam's explanation just doesn't sit right with me. Why the far moon?"

Bertie sighed, his unease mirroring hers. "It feels like there's more to it, doesn't it? Like they're keeping something from us? First Micky, and now Sumeet? Makes you wonder what's really going on behind the scenes."

Dr. Fem Dam walked back into the lab, where the Cha was still waiting.

"How did it go?" he asked, a note of urgency in his voice.

"I think we're in the clear for now, but what about Earth? They'll know by now that Sumeet is dead," Dr. Fem Dam said, looking at the Cha.

"I'll transmit a message. I'll say he was killed in combat or something similar. I'll go now." With that, the Cha walked out of the lab.

Meanwhile, back on Earth, alarms blared ominously within Sumeet's chamber. Red lights pulsed across the stark walls, casting the room in an urgent, flickering glow. Technicians scrambled; their faces tight with panic as they fought to assess the situation.

Sumeet lay motionless in his pod, his body marred with burns—evidence of a catastrophic event.

"Get the medics in here!" a technician shouted, fingers flying over the control panel as he tracked Sumeet's plummeting vitals. "We need to stabilize him—now!"

The air was thick with urgency. A medic pressed two fingers to Sumeet's wrist, their expression darkening. "His vitals are flatlining!" they cried, their voice rising above the blaring alarms.

Rory burst into the chamber; eyes wide with alarm. "What's happening?!" he demanded, his heart hammering as he took in the chaos. "First Micky vanishes, and now Sumeet? We can't afford this!"

"Stand back!" a technician barked, lunging for the defibrillator. They worked swiftly, charging it for a life-saving shock. "We have to bring him back!"

As they battled against time, Rory paced, anxiety clawing at his chest. "What's wrong with him? How could this happen?" The weight of unfolding disasters pressed down on him, and every second stretched into eternity.

They pressed the defibrillator to Sumeet's chest, electricity surging through him in a desperate bid to restart his heart. Medics shouted updates, their voices taut with urgency, eyes locked on the erratic readouts. But the longer they fought, the clearer it became—time was slipping away.

"Come on, come on!" one medic urged, desperation bleeding into their voice as they pressed the button again, sending another jolt into Sumeet's motionless form. The monitors stuttered, a brief flicker of life—then the flatline returned, a cruel confirmation of the stakes at hand.

A wave of nausea crashed over Rory. "Is he stable? What's happening?" he demanded, panic lacing his voice. His gaze darted from one technician to another, searching for answers that refused to come.

"The neural stabiliser isn't responding!" a medic cried, hands trembling as they fought to stay composed. "We're losing him!"

Each second stretched into eternity, Rory's pulse hammering in his ears. "No, no, this can't be happening!" he shouted, his mind spiralling back to earlier conversations with Sumeet—plans, hopes, and dreams now slipping through his fingers. "We can't lose him!"

The lead technician's expression was grim as they worked feverishly to stabilise Sumeet. "Increase power to the defibrillators!" they commanded. "We're trying again!"

Moving with desperate precision, the medics readied themselves. "Clear!" one of them shouted, adrenaline surging as the team instinctively stepped back. The current jolted through Sumeet's body—his chest convulsed, a flicker of life—then nothing.

"Vitals are flat! He's crashing!" a voice rang out above the chaos, the weight of the words hitting the room like a physical blow.

Rory felt a lump rise in his throat as he watched the chaos unfold, helpless against the relentless march of time. "Sumeet! Come on!" he shouted, as if sheer willpower could pull his friend back. The thought of losing another agent— another friend—so soon was unbearable.

The medic's voice wavered with urgency. "Prepare for CPR! We need to keep his blood flowing!" They pressed down on Sumeet's chest with steady, rhythmic force, their determination unwavering even as hope dimmed.

The room pulsed with frantic movement, yet a crushing sense of despair thickened the air. Rory's pulse pounded as he pleaded, his voice raw. "Don't do this to us! Fight, Sumeet! Fight!"

The monitor emitted a long, unyielding beep—a sound that sliced through the room like a blade, signalling the one truth they had all dreaded.

"We've lost him," the lead technician murmured, their voice hollow. With those words, the air in the chamber thickened, heavy with insurmountable sorrow. Eyes brimming with disbelief met one another as the weight of their losses pressed down, too vast to grasp.

"I'm calling it," the chief physician said quietly. "Time of death: 12:43."

The realization settled like a shadow, creeping over them, making the moment feel unreal. They had risked everything to carve a path forward—only to watch it unravel before their very eyes.

"Rory," one of the medics said gently but firmly, "we did everything we could. His body simply couldn't withstand what happened to him on Rivaxia."

Rory strode to the wall-mounted phone and called for Lewis, knowing the Chief needed to be informed immediately. The moment Lewis stepped into the laboratory; the weight of their grim reality settled over the room like a suffocating fog.

"Lewis," Rory said, his voice tight with emotion, "we need to talk about Sumeet. You have to understand what's happened."

Lewis's expression grew serious as he took a seat across from Rory. "What news, Rory? Has something happened to him? I take it this isn't just a routine update."

Rory drew in a deep breath, the weight of the moment pressing down on him. "Sumeet is dead. The incident in his chamber... it was catastrophic. He was vital to our operations, and now we're at a significant disadvantage."

Lewis's eyes widened in disbelief. "This is… devastating. Sumeet had his finger on the pulse of our tech advancements." He exhaled sharply, running a hand over his face. "What have we done? We put these people in danger."

The weight of Sumeet's demise lingered in the laboratory, thick and suffocating. Rory and Lewis stepped away from the chaotic scene, retreating to a quieter corner of the facility. Though grief pressed down on them, the urgency of their situation demanded immediate action.

"We need to figure out our next steps," Rory murmured, his voice barely above a whisper. "With Sumeet gone…"

"Agreed," Lewis said, pressing a hand to his forehead in deep thought, his teeth worrying his lower lip. "But what does that mean for our operations? Do we continue with the mission? Is anyone else in danger?"

Before Rory could respond, a message notification buzzed on his device. He hastily opened it.

"Quick, people—there's a signal coming in from Rivaxia," Rory told the waiting team. At that moment, the Cha appeared on the big screen, his hands clasped together, head bowed slightly.

"By now, you will know that Sumeet has been sadly lost. He fought a courageous battle on Sankat 3 and was fatally wounded. As you now understand, this resulted in his body on Earth also perishing. The other Dream Agents are pressing forward and have requested that you do not wake them. They are fully aware of the risks and remain committed to assisting us. I will provide further updates in due course. I am deeply sorry for the loss of Sumeet; it is with great sorrow that I speak to you today."

Rory and Lewis exchanged a glance, momentarily lost for words.

"Keep an eye on the other agents, and call me immediately if anything changes," Rory said as he walked out of the door with Lewis, heading into the conference room.

Lewis leaned back in his chair, contemplating the implications. "I appreciate what the Dream Agents and the Cha are saying, but we need to consider their safety."

"But waking them now would expose them to unnecessary anxiety and stress—it could be a real danger," Rory replied, taking a sip of coffee. "I wouldn't recommend it without a controlled re-entry."

Lewis studied him in silence.

"Are we not risking more lives by leaving them there? We can't afford that kind of gamble, surely."

"As I said, I think it's more dangerous to pull them out too quickly," Rory replied.

"Let's run with it for now, but I need you and the team to be ready to extract them immediately if the situation worsens," Lewis said. "Regardless of what that means."

"Got it. We will. I'll update you every hour on what's happening," Rory said.

With that, the two left the conference room—Rory heading back into the lab, while Lewis made his way outside.

CHAPTER 18

Loyal Bonds

B ack on Rivaxia, the suns hung high in the sky, bathing the hangar in golden light as an electric sense of anticipation crackled in the air. The team moved with steady purpose, making final preparations to board the spacecraft. Overhead, bright lights flooded the vast launch area, their glow reflecting off the sleek hull of the vessel. Each crew member carried the weight of the mission ahead, their movements precise and deliberate.

Bertie walked in step with the others, his mind a storm of thoughts about Micky and Sumeet—the gaping absence of his friends pressing down on him. A sudden brush against his leg pulled him from his thoughts. To his surprise, a Pyronyx had taken to following him closely. The creature, a mesmerising fusion of vibrant colours, padded alongside him in perfect sync.

"Tang," Bertie called, glancing over his shoulder at the familiar silhouette of the Pyronyx ambling at his side. "Is this normal behaviour for them?"

Tang chuckled softly, observing the creature's comforting demeanour. "They tend to bond closely with those they deem worthy. Looks like you've got a new friend, Bertie."

As they neared the spacecraft, Kerra joined them, her laughter light and teasing as she took in the scene.

"Oh, that's adorable. He's your friend now, is he? I thought Sumeet was its master. Have to say, not really my choice of a pet, though!" she teased.

With a wave toward the creature, Bertie grinned. "Seems like it!"

Once onboard, Buddy, the spacecraft's ace pilot, sprang into action, swiftly initiating his extensive pre-flight protocols:

1. Powering Up Systems: Buddy pressed a sequence of buttons, igniting the ship's core systems. Displays flickered to life, flooding the cockpit with crucial data for take-off.

2. Flight Control Calibration: He fine-tuned the flight control surfaces, ensuring they responded precisely to his commands, and verified the thrust vectoring for optimal stability.

3. Fuel Level Check: A quick glance at the digital readout confirmed their fuel reserves were well above the required threshold for the journey ahead.

4. Navigation System Update: Buddy keyed in the mission coordinates, scanning for anomalies or unexpected shifts in the surrounding space since their last check.

5. Engaging Defensive Shields: With a flick of a switch, he powered up the defensive systems, readying the ship for any potential threats along the way.

6. Inertial Dampeners Online: He engaged the inertial dampeners, ensuring the crew wouldn't feel the brunt of turbulence during ascent.

7. External Communication Checks: Activating the communication systems, he established a steady link with Rivaxia, transmitting and receiving updates as needed.

8. Life Support Systems: A swift diagnostic confirmed stable oxygen levels and fully operational life support, ensuring a safe environment for the crew.

9. Cabin Pressure Adjustment: He fine-tuned the cabin pressure to match the atmospheric conditions of the launch site, guaranteeing a smooth transition for everyone onboard.

10. Final System Checks: A last sweep through all critical systems flashed green across the board—everything was ready for launch.

After completing his extensive pre-flight checklist and confirming the ship's readiness, Buddy leaned back in his chair for a moment. This is the best part of the job, he mused, and no one ever gets to see it. With a satisfied smirk, he turned his attention back to the ascent preparations.

Across the cabin, Kerra glanced over at Bertie, who remained seated beside his new Pyronyx companion.

"This is strange," she murmured, narrowing her eyes. "Really strange, given what we've been told about these creatures. It's far too attached to you—that's not normal." Rising from her seat, she motioned for Bertie to follow her to the back of the cockpit.

Bertie followed, his expression shifting as he considered the implications. "Yeah, I was thinking the same thing. A

Pyronyx stays loyal to its master until one of them dies," he said, his voice lowering to a more serious tone. "And this one looks like it's chosen me as its new master… So what does that mean for Sumeet?"

Kerra glanced back at him, concern flickering across her face. "Are you saying this creature is now bonded to you because Sumeet isn't here?"

"Exactly," Bertie replied, his gaze dropping to the floor. "Sumeet was its master. I don't think we're getting the whole truth here, my dear. If you ask me, something bad has happened to Sumeet, no matter what they're telling us." The uncertainty gnawed at him. "I just can't shake the feeling that there's more to this than meets the eye. Feels like they fed us a weak story to explain his absence. We need to stay alert and figure out what really happened."

Kerra sighed, concern for their friend mixing with doubt about the Rivaxians' story.

"I get what you're saying. We might need to be ready for things to be more complicated than we've been led to believe."

"Let's go back to our seats and figure out our next move," Bertie suggested. "Stay sharp."

Bertie and Kerra made their way back through the cabin, their minds racing with unanswered questions. The Pyronyx trailed closely behind, its colourful scales shimmering under the overhead lights as it remained faithfully by Bertie's side.

Once they settled in, Bertie turned his attention to Buddy, who was busy at the control panel, guiding the ship through space toward the Vark world.

"Hey, Buddy," Bertie called out. "How long until we enter Vark space?"

Buddy glanced up from the console, focused yet unruffled. "According to the maps, we'll cross into Vark space in three days. We'll approach the fourth planet along the way and land on its moon."

"Do we know anything about the moon?" Kerra asked, her curiosity sparking.

Buddy nodded, scrolling through the data on his screens.

"Yeah, it's mostly uncharted, but rumour has it there are some resources. We might find useful intel—or at the very least, a safe place to regroup while we figure out our next steps."

Bertie leaned back in his seat, crossing his arms as he processed Buddy's words. "Let's hope it's not crawling with Vark. We need to stay focused and avoid unnecessary conflict if possible."

"That's the plan," Kerra agreed, striving to maintain an upbeat tone despite the unease creeping in. "I'll check our gear and go over the intel we have. If we're heading into potential danger, we need to be ready for anything."

As the ship finalized its pre-flight preparations and the crew settled into their routines, the atmosphere hummed with a mix of anticipation and doubt. As they ascended into the vastness of space, thoughts of Sumeet and Micky weighed heavily on their minds. They didn't know Sumeet's fate for certain, but the explanation they had been given felt lacking—leaving them questioning what truly lay ahead.

"With each passing moment, their resolve grew stronger. They were no longer just agents on a mission; they were guardians of a legacy, determined to uncover the truth about Sumeet and the hidden world awaiting them in Vark space."

CHAPTER 19

Fractured Alliances

I ce crystals clung to the bars, mocking warmth. The low hum of the facility vibrated through Micky's bones—a constant, chilling reminder of his isolation and despair. Then, the door hissed open, releasing a pneumatic sigh into the frozen air. A guard, clad in black armour that shimmered under the dim lights, stepped inside, his expression a mask of cold indifference. 'Micky, our leader wants to see you.'"

"His muscles screamed in protest as he forced himself to his feet, the stiffness a stark reminder of his prolonged confinement. He followed the guard through the labyrinthine corridors, past glowing panels flashing incomprehensible data, while the whirring machinery created a disorienting symphony of purpose. Each echoing footstep in the frigid corridor heightened the tension, tightening the knot of unease in his stomach. The door ahead slid open, revealing an interior far more comfortable than his cell. The guard gestured curtly. 'Wait here.'

The contrast between the stark cell and this opulent room was unsettling, fuelling Micky's apprehension. This wasn't an interrogation—it was far too comfortable."

"He sank into the plush chair, the softness a jarring contrast to the cold, metallic floor. The walls were lined with screens displaying swirling galaxies and intricate star maps—mesmerizing in their complexity, their beauty a cruel mockery of his predicament. He scanned the room, searching for potential exits, each detail a possible lifeline in this suffocating luxurious prison.

Then, the door hissed open again. A towering figure entered, draped in heavy robes, their face obscured by a fully enclosed helmet. The leader moved with a predatory calm, exuding an aura of unnerving authority that sent a chill down Micky's spine.

The game had begun."

"How are you?" he inquired; his voice smooth but edged with menace.

"Fine," Micky replied defiantly, squaring his shoulders. Determination burned in his eyes. "You won't break me."

The leader tilted his head slightly. "No, you are tough," he admitted, a reluctant note of respect in his tone. A flicker of intrigue sparked behind his visor.

"You killed Zuk Nall," Micky accused, his voice rising. "He was a true warrior—unlike you."

"Ah, that 'terrible Rivaxian,'" the leader chuckled, dismissing Micky's words with a wave of his hand. Turning, he ran a gloved hand over a gleaming console beside him. "You should consider yourself fortunate."

"My name is Velthorian. I lead the Vark army, and I've been waiting to meet you for some time." He paused, then added casually, "Would you like some pizza?"

Micky blinked. "Pizza?" Confusion flickered across his face. "How do you even know what pizza is?"

Velthorian chuckled, the sound rolling through the room like distant thunder. "You'd be surprised. Even in a world of war, we appreciate a variety of culinary experiences."

Micky smirked, seizing the chance to prod. "Is that why you lot always wear those masks? To hide your ugliness?"

"Velthorian held Micky's gaze as he handed him a plate with a steaming slice of pepperoni pizza and a sparkling drink, its tiny bubbles fizzing to the surface. He sank into the chair opposite, the room thrumming with low, pulsing energy.

'Let's talk,' he said, his voice measured and controlled. 'I'm about to tell you the real story—not the fantasy the Rivaxians want you to believe. For countless generations, we were their slaves. We shattered our chains on Moon Elara, and this war between Vark and Rivaxia? It's the final reckoning of that fight for freedom.'"

"Micky leaned forward, amusement flickering in his eyes. 'And you expect me to believe this fairy tale?'

Velthorian regarded him in silence, inhaling deeply before speaking. 'I understand this is a lot to take in, and that you're weak and exhausted. I'm not finished with you yet, but you need rest before we continue. You're not going back to your cell—you've seen enough of that place. I'm going to show you something of the Vark world, our way of life. But before I take you outside...' His hand moved to his helmet, the gesture slow and deliberate, his expression carefully unreadable."

"The metallic hiss of the locking mechanism disengaging was the only sound in the room as Velthorian lifted his hands to his helmet. His movements were slow, methodical— almost ritualistic—imbuing the moment with a quiet sense of foreboding. The tension thickened with each measured motion. Then, with a sharp, decisive shift, the helmet retracted, revealing a face that left Micky speechless.

It was human.

Only then did Velthorian finally meet Micky's gaze. 'Yes, Micky, I'm human—just like you.'"

"Before Micky could respond, the door hissed open, and guards stepped inside, their armour gleaming under the dim light. Velthorian gestured towards them. 'They're taking you to a different room. Trust me—you can shower. You need it. We'll continue our conversation tomorrow.'

Micky's eyes darted between Velthorian and the guards. Had he imagined what he saw? Could the Vark really be human, or was this just another trick to confuse him?"

"As they ushered him out, the promise of warmth and cleanliness mingled with his confusion, tangled with the tension of the impending confrontation between Vark and

Rivaxia, leaving Micky caught in a whirlwind of intrigue and survival.

As he struggled to steady his racing thoughts, he was led into a room that smelled faintly of antiseptic and lilacs—an oddly soothing combination for a place like this. The guards stepped back as the door slid open, revealing a nurse of a different species. She wasn't Vark."

"They were known as the Lythari, distinguished by their luminous skin that shimmered in shades of turquoise and silver. Renowned for their healing abilities and compassionate demeanour, they stood in stark contrast to the oppressive environment surrounding him.

"Hello, I'm Myra," she said, her voice soothing as she approached Micky. "I'm here to attend to your injuries. But first, get into the shower."

"After discarding his torn clothes, he made his way to a small shower cubicle in the corner. Water cascaded over him in refreshing streams, washing away the grime and exhaustion of days in captivity. As he stood under the warm spray, Micky's mind raced. The Vark were human. The Rivaxians were the enemy. Processing it all was anything but easy."

"Once out of the shower, Myra approached with quiet grace, her gaze scanning his wounds with practiced precision. Her delicate hands moved methodically, applying a soothing balm to his cuts before carefully wrapping his wrists, raw from the relentless bite of the cuffs.

"Your kind has suffered for too long," she murmured, her voice barely above a whisper. "I can help you—but you must trust me."

Micky exhaled sharply, his pulse still hammering with the remnants of adrenaline and fear. "I appreciate it," he said, his voice edged with exhaustion. "I just... want to get out of here."

"Once she finished tending to his wounds, Myra gestured towards a wardrobe nearby. "You can change into these when you're ready. But first, I want you to lie down. I'll help you sleep."

Without warning, she ran a hand across Micky's forehead, and the world vanished into darkness.

He woke to an eerie stillness, the soft glow of the room oddly subdued after the facility's constant hum. He'd slept—or rather, had been forced into sleep—for what felt like a week, though it had only been six hours. Time, he realised, had lost all meaning. His body ached, weak and sluggish, his mind clouded with lingering exhaustion."

"He opened the wardrobe to find an array of garments—soft, lightweight, and breathable. They shimmered subtly under the dim light, their unfamiliar textures both intriguing and unsettling. He selected fitted tunic and loose trousers. The fabric felt strange, almost ethereal against his skin—a stark contrast to the roughness of captivity. Yet, the comfort was a small mercy, a fleeting relief in a world of shifting uncertainties.

Just as Micky was sinking into his thoughts, an electronic chime echoed through the room. A holographic display flickered to life on the wall, and a mechanical voice intoned, "Attention. Dinner will be served at 8 PM. Please step outside the door to be escorted."

"Micky took a moment to steady himself, smoothing down the fitted tunic and adjusting the loose trousers, which now felt strangely liberating. As he pulled his damp hair back, his reflection caught his eye in the polished wall. He barely recognised the gaunt figure staring back—dark circles under his eyes, a hardened expression betraying the turmoil within.

Before he could fully brace himself for what lay ahead, the door slid open with a soft hiss. The guard reappeared, signalling that it was time. Micky followed him through a labyrinth of corridors, the sterile lighting casting elongated shadows across the metallic walls. Each footstep rang against the cold surfaces—a stark reminder of his captivity."

"At last, they arrived at a grand hall, its imposing entryway framed by intricate designs that rippled like liquid metal. Micky stepped inside, his breath hitching as he took in the vast expanse before him. A long table stretched out like a river of polished ebony, adorned with gleaming cutlery and elaborately arranged dishes that hinted at an extravagant feast.

At its head sat Velthorian, his presence a seamless blend of authority and intimidation. "Welcome, Micky. I trust you had a good rest," he said smoothly. "Please, take a seat," he added, gesturing to the empty chair opposite him."

"A ripple of unease coursed through Micky as he neared the table, his instincts screaming that he was walking straight into a trap. Still, he sat, jaw set, determined to hold his ground.

Before he could steady his breath, the heavy doors swung open once more, revealing the imposing silhouette of the Vark leader. Clad in ornate armour, he had removed his helmet, and for the first time, Micky saw that he, too, was human. He strode forward, flanked by two towering bodyguards, their expressions concealed behind impenetrable visors."

"Greetings, Micky," the leader said, his voice rolling through the hall like a thunderclap. "I am Lord Thraxon, High Ruler of the Vark Empire."

Micky's pulse quickened at the weight of the title, the very sound of it thickening the air with tension.

Thraxon paused, regarding Micky as one might assess a piece of art, his gaze both calculating and unreadable. "We know about the Dream Agents and the Rivaxian plans," he continued, his voice unnaturally calm yet laced with an unmistakable edge. "I imagine you're still trying to comprehend how you've found yourself in a distant galaxy, sitting in a room with two humans?"

Micky met the High Ruler's gaze, the weight of scrutiny pressing down on him. "Yes, you could say it's not every day something like this happens."

"We are more alike than you can possibly imagine," Thraxon said, his piercing stare locking onto Micky. "We look the same, but we share far more than mere appearance—except, of course, we are not Dream Agents."

"I could never be like the Vark," Micky snarled, defiance burning through his words. The air between them crackled with tension as he refused to yield to Thraxon's imposing presence.

"I am human, like you," Thraxon declared, his voice reverberating through the chamber. "But I chose to unite my people—to rise and forge an empire from the ashes. You and I share the same blood, the same capacity for hope and anger. It's time you understood that the lines between us are not as clear as you believe."

He exhaled, his expression softening. "Micky, I am truly sorry for what we put you through these past days. We had to be certain you weren't a fake Dream Agent—just another trick from the Rivaxians. And there was also the possibility that Zuk Nall might confide in you."

Micky stared in shock, struggling to process everything. How could we have got this so wrong? This was not just the leader of an alien race—he was a brother in struggle, a testament to humanity's unyielding spirit across the stars.

His mind raced back to what Zuk Nall had told him about the Temporal Chrono Spectra Modulator. Should he reveal it? Not yet, he decided. I must be sure.

The atmosphere shifted. The grand hall now pulsed with the unspoken tension of alliances yet to be forged and enmities still unresolved. Micky faced a reality that would challenge everything he thought he knew—about the world, and about himself.

"Micky, Velthorian will show you the real Vark world. You will see how we live, what we fight for, and why we hope you will join our cause against the Rivaxians."

Thraxon leaned forward, his expression earnest. "For centuries, the Rivaxians have crossed the cosmos to Earth, taking people as slaves. They exploited a wormhole—a gateway that allows them to traverse vast distances in the blink of an eye. Anyone who dared to stand in their way was met with brutal force."

Micky's mind reeled as he processed Thraxon's words. "Are you saying that legends about the Bermuda Triangle, ancient disappearances, and sailors' myths were all true? That they weren't just stories to frighten children?"

"Yes," Thraxon confirmed, his voice steady. "Those tales were remnants of real encounters with the Rivaxians. Ships vanished; people disappeared—all swept away through that wormhole. It was a source of power; one we were fortunate to nearly destroy."

"Wait." Micky shook his head in disbelief. "This can't be true. There is no wormhole. It's a micro-wormhole—something far too small for ships to pass through!"

Thraxon nodded slowly, recognizing Micky's confusion. "Yes, what you refer to as a micro-wormhole is a genuine phenomenon, but it was once much larger, capable of accommodating vast ships. We attacked and destroyed those significant wormholes, and now only micro-wormholes remain. However, don't underestimate their potential. While their size may limit direct travel, the Rivaxians have mastered the art of manipulating even the smallest rifts in space. You are evidence that they can still reach you." Micky frowned, grappling with the weight of this revelation. "But you said they were dying—that their species was on the brink of extinction."

"Yes," Thraxon replied, his gaze piercing into Micky's. "And here is where the truth cuts deeper. You may think we attacked their world out of malice, but it was an act of necessity. They set off a bomb designed to destroy our people, but by their own miscalculation, it annihilated their ability to reproduce. It was only by sheer fortune that they triggered it themselves—a day of reckoning brought on by their own ambition, their own machinations."

Micky's reality wavered as he absorbed Thraxon's revelation, the implications crashing over him like a tidal wave. "So, you're telling me the Rivaxians are dying because of their own actions—not because of you?"

"Exactly," Thraxon said, a thread of sorrow weaving through his voice. "Though we bear the scars of our battles, the Rivaxians doomed themselves. Their reckless ambition, their insatiable thirst for power—these were the poisons that tainted their world and sealed their fate. They sought conquest, but in their greed, they engineered their own destruction."

Micky sat back, the weight of Thraxon's words pressing down on him. It was difficult to reconcile the narrative he had always believed—that the Vark were the enemy—with the reality unfolding before him. Perhaps the line between right and wrong was far more blurred than he had ever imagined.

Thraxon studied Micky's expression, his gaze sharp and searching. "Understand this: the struggle for survival is universal. We all carry the capacity for both hope and destruction. The real question is—what will you choose? But for now, go. See our world for yourself, and then we will speak again."

Velthorian stood and gestured for Micky to follow. They walked down a corridor until they reached a solid wall of ice. He placed his hand against it, and the ice vanished, revealing a vast cavern bathed in sunlight. Waterfalls cascaded, sleek modern buildings rose in the distance, and the air was filled with the sounds of laughter. As they wandered through the bustling scene, Micky noticed a mix of species—many of them human.

Suddenly, a child tugged at Micky's jacket.

"Are you a human?" the child asked.

"I am," Micky replied.

"This is amazing. I'm really struggling to grasp everything that's happened here," Micky said. He took a deep breath, the weight of the conversation shifting his perspective. "We were led to believe that the Vark were the monsters, the aggressors—killing everything in their path. But now, you've shown me a world I never imagined existed—a world where many species live in harmony. We may have even killed our own people, believing you were the enemy."

"It's a price we've all had to pay on our journey to the truth," Velthorian said. "We have to live with that."

In that moment, an understanding flickered in Micky's mind, illuminating a path forward—one that transcended species, animosities, and fear. This conversation wasn't just about survival; it was about the possibility of change—and perhaps unity amidst the chaos.

Suddenly, Thraxon appeared, striding towards Micky, a bit smile on his face. "Well Micky, you have seen the real Vark world, we are not the enemy. We need you—and the other Dream Agents. You all possess unique knowledge of the Rivaxians. We stand on the precipice of our final push against their empire, and your insights could make all the difference.

"Imagine this: a coordinated strike, where Vark warriors and Dream Agents unite, combining our strengths to face the Rivaxians head-on. This could be our chance to reclaim our freedom and ensure they never threaten another world again."

Micky could almost envision it—soldiers clad in advanced armour, their battle cries echoing through the cosmos as they stormed the Rivaxian stronghold. The final confrontation painted a vivid image in his mind: ships soaring through starlit skies, a fleet of Vark vessels, empowering a diverse coalition ready to topple their common enemy.

The rush of excitement was tempered by the weight of responsibility. Micky knew he had allies back home—fellow Dream Agents who are still fighting under the Rivaxian influence. "I need to warn my fellow Dream Agents," he stated fiercely, determination coursing through him. "They need to know what's coming. They have to be ready to fight alongside us."

Thraxon, looking at him with a nod of understanding. "I appreciate your loyalty to your people, but we must act strategically. First, let's solidify our forces here. We're leaving for Rivaxia tomorrow to finish this once and for all. You'll have time to relay your message, but rest first. You need to clear your mind and prepare."

Micky felt the weight of uncertainty lifting slightly. He realized this was his moment—not just to fight but to lead. If he could connect with the Dream Agents, they could amplify the Vark's efforts and strengthen their army against the looming Rivaxian threat.

"Very well," Micky conceded. "I'll gather my thoughts tonight. But once we set out for Rivaxia, I won't hesitate to reach out to my allies."

"Good," Thraxon said, a flicker of approval in his gaze. "We have a monumental battle ahead. Rest well tonight. At dawn, we gather our forces for the final assault."

As Micky turned to leave the grand hall, anticipation and anxiety coiled within him. This was the turning point—not just for the Vark or Rivaxia, but for every world under the Rivaxian grip.

Days of captivity would give way to days of liberation. The prospect of uniting against a common enemy filled Micky with a renewed sense of purpose. He would not only fight for his own freedom but for the countless others who had fallen under the Rivaxians' oppressive shadow.

In the stillness of the night, as he prepared for what lay ahead, Micky realised he wasn't just stepping into a battle— he was stepping into a legacy of hope, resilience, and the shared strength of all who dared to defy tyranny.

At first light, Micky, Velthorian, and Thraxon boarded the lead ship. The Vark armada surged forward, bound for Rivaxia and the final showdown.

CHAPTER 20

Veils of a Liars Game

Back on the moon, the Dream Agents and a small contingent of Rivaxians gathered in the cramped quarters of their vessel, preparing for the imminent assault on the Vark homeland to retrieve Micky and the last of the embryos. The atmosphere crackled with tension; each member acutely aware that this mission could shift the balance of their struggle against oppression.

Bertie, the tech-savvy agent, hunched over his console, methodically running final checks. Just as he secured the last of the systems, a blaring alarm pierced the air, signalling an incoming message on a secure channel.

"I'll take this in my room," Bertie announced, his voice steady despite the sudden disruption.

"I'll come with you," Tang offered, eager to assist.

"Wait, Tang," Bertie interrupted, shaking his head. "This is from Rivaxia—specifically for Dream Agents only. It's direct from Cha. You finish the modifications to the sensors."

Tang sighed but nodded in understanding, stepping back as Bertie turned towards the rear of the ship. Buddy and Kerra exchanged glances before following him into the small, dimly lit room that served as a makeshift communication hub.

"Okay," Bertie exhaled, activating the console, determination hardening his features. "Let's see what this is."

The screen flickered to life, and Sumeet's face appeared, urgency and caution flashing across his expression. "Guys, I'm sending this over a secure channel. I hope you're alone."

A knot of unease tightened in Bertie's stomach. There was something deeply unsettling about Sumeet's demeanour.

"This is a recording," Sumeet continued, his voice steady but laced with underlying tension. "I need to warn you—I don't think we're being told the truth about what's happening here."

The Dream Agents leaned in, their focus sharpening.

"There's a highly secured room here—one I've never been inside," Sumeet went on. "I've overheard conversations, and they keep mentioning something called a Temporal Chrono Spectra Modulator - a time machine. I don't know what it is, but it sounds important."

Buddy frowned, casting a glance at Bertie and Kerra, both of whom were tense, absorbing the implications of Sumeet's words.

"I'm going to investigate further. I'll update you when we meet," Sumeet concluded, his image flickering uncertainly.

Then the screen went dark, leaving the Dream Agents in heavy silence, each grappling with the weight of Sumeet's revelation.

"What do you think he means by a time machine?" Kerra asked, her expression tightening with concern. "Could it have something to do with the assault plans?"

Bertie crossed his arms, deep in thought. "If the Rivaxians are developing something as powerful as a time machine—

or if they already have one—it changes everything. We need to be ready for whatever they're hiding."

"I'm more worried about Sumeet right now. He clearly hasn't gone on a mission with the Rivaxians. I fear something's happened to him—something bad. And with the Pyronyx acting strangely, I don't like where this is heading."

Silence settled over the room as they exchanged anxious glances. The urgency of their mission now felt overshadowed by the uncertainties lurking in the shadows.

"Okay," Bertie finally said, breaking the tension. "Let's focus on the assault plan first—we still need to get Micky out. Keep your eyes open for anything unusual. And watch Tang closely. We don't know what he knows... or if he's really on our side."

After a heated debate, the Dream Agents made their choice, steeling themselves for the mission ahead. They returned to the cockpit, finalising preparations to extract Micky from the Vark's grasp. With a renewed sense of determination to find the truth, they set course for the Vark world.

As their ship roared through the void of space, they remained unaware that the Vark armada—hundreds of ships strong—had already begun its journey toward Rivaxia.

By the time the Dream Agents arrived, the Vark world was eerily silent—a ghost town devoid of life. They landed their ship with practiced stealth and slipped through the empty, metallic corridors of the facility. Every room, every shadowed corner yielded nothing. The absence of Micky and the embryos sank like a stone in the pit of their stomachs.

"This place is empty," Kerra whispered, dread creeping into her voice. "Where's Micky? Where are the embryos?"

"It's like we've walked into a trap... a dead end," Tang muttered, his disbelief evident. "What does this mean for us?"

With no further answers to be found, they returned to their ship, a heavy sense of defeat hanging over them. Anxiety morphed into a need for answers, a search for clarity in a world turned upside down. Ignorant to the fact that the Vark world really hid deep beneath the surface where thousands are safe and hidden from the Rivaxians. Only feet from where the Dream Agents were standing.

Bertie knew they needed to contact Cha and Dr. Fem Dam. "I need to reach out to them; something isn't right."

Once aboard their vessel, Bertie activated the communication console. The screen flickered to life, revealing Cha and Dr. Fem Dam, their expressions icy and calculating.

"Hello, Dream Agents, was your mission successful?" Cha inquired. "Did you secure the embryos, and Micky, of course?"

"We reached the Vark world," Bertie reported, his voice unwavering. "There was nothing there—no sign of Micky or the embryos. It was completely deserted."

Dr. Fem Dam's eyes narrowed, confusion etched across her features. "This makes no sense. What do you mean there was no one there? You were meant to retrieve the embryos—you are our eyes and ears, yet you fail to deliver on even the simplest of expectations."

"Now, wait just a minute! I don't like your tone, and I certainly don't like what you're implying," Bertie snapped, his glare locked onto Dr. Fem Dam. "What I can tell you is that we found maps and plans—and the entire Vark armada is heading to Rivaxia right now, while we're stuck here."

Cha's expression hardened as he spoke, his tone dripping with contempt.

"You Dream Agents have proven to be weak and incompetent. I knew relying on humans would be a mistake. We enslaved your kind thousands of years ago. You let fear cloud your judgment and missed a crucial opportunity. Do you truly believe the feeble Vark stand a chance against us? Nothing will halt the rise of the Rivaxian Empire—least of all your ineptitude."

Bertie glanced at Kerra and Buddy, confusion and anger balanced evenly in his gaze. Betrayal surged through the Dream Agents, a cold, bitter weight settling in their chests. They had believed their efforts would make a difference, that their contributions might tip the scales in their favour. Instead, they found themselves cast aside—insignificant and scorned.

Bertie demanded, "What have you really done with Sumeet? Where is he?"

"He's dead. And soon, you will be too," Cha sneered, his voice laced with disdain. "You are nothing but a burden. We were foolish to believe humans could be of use to us. Our strategies have shifted—you have all become liabilities, and we can no longer allow you to interfere. Cut the communication. I refuse to waste another second on these pathetic creatures," he spat.

With that, the connection was severed, leaving the Dream Agents in stunned silence. The grim reality of Sumeet's murder hit them like a crushing blow. The weight of Cha and Dr. Fem Dam's contempt hung in the air, tightening around them like shackles. Betrayed and discarded in their moment of need, they now faced an uncertain future—one that made them question their very purpose.

"What now?" Kerra asked.

"We head back to Rivaxia. From what we know, that's our only way back to Earth," Bertie said. "Tang, are you with us?"

Tang stood in silence for a moment, digesting the conversation. Then, with quiet resolve, he nodded. "I've been lied to just as much as you have. Of course, I'm with you."

CHAPTER 21

The Tides of Time

As the Vark armada surged towards the outer reaches of Rivaxia's solar system, tensions ran high in the TCSM laboratory. The air crackled with both fear and determination as Dr Fem Dam and her team of scientists worked feverishly, each heartbeat echoing the impending fate of their universe.

Jax dashed through the bustling lab, adrenaline coursing through his veins as he approached Dr Fem Dam, her face a mask of concentration.

"Dr Fem Dam!" Jax called out, breathless. "After multiple tests, we're ready for another systems assessment."

Dr Fem Dam turned sharply, her expression a blend of relief and focus. "What about the handheld Temporal Recalibrators ? Are they operational? Each Rivaxian must be able to reset the time machine once we arrive at our destination—especially if the system is damaged."

"They're ready as well," Jax confirmed, a hint of pride colouring his tone. "I'll be the test pilot—we don't have time to select anyone else." With that, he stepped onto the platform.

Meanwhile, above the planet, the Vark fleet closed in on its target. Cha rushed into the lab, urgency dripping from his every word. "Dr Fem Dam! The Vark are about to invade. Is the time machine ready?"

"Yes, it is ready, Almighty One," she replied, steel in her voice.

As the Vark prepared for their invasion, a crushing sense of failure and fear filled the cockpit of the Dream Agents' ship as they arrived at Rivaxia space. The screen flickered, revealing a single, terrifying image: the Vark armada—an endless sea of warships blotting out the suns as it closed in on Rivaxia. No longer a scattered force, they had become a unified juggernaut, an unstoppable tide poised to annihilate everything in its path. The scale of it was staggering—a cosmic horror unfolding before their eyes. Hope felt like a fragile thing, barely clinging to existence in the face of such overwhelming power.

The swirling stars outside flickered ominously, a stark reminder of the peril ahead. Kerra's face was ghostly pale, her features contorted in horror as she stared out the viewport at the terrifying sight before them. "Oh my God," she breathed, her voice trembling with disbelief. "We're finished! Look at that armada—there must be a hundreds, if not thousand of ships out there!"

The Vark fleet loomed vast and unyielding, its warships lined up with ruthless precision against the endless void, weapons primed for annihilation. The absence of Micky and Sumeet weighed heavy in the air—Micky was supposed to lead them. Instead, they faced nothing but certain doom.

A frantic shout shattered the tension. "We're receiving a message from the Vark lead ship!" Buddy exclaimed, his fingers flying across the console as he activated the communication feed.

"They must be demanding our surrender—if we're lucky," Bertie muttered, his voice heavy with dread and resignation.

But as the screen flickered to life, the last thing they expected appeared. Micky's familiar face filled the display, raw determination carved into his features.

"Micky!" Kerra gasped, a wave of relief crashing over her as tears spilled down her cheeks. "You're alive! Thank God!"

"Listen," Micky urged, his voice firm despite the chaos raging around him. "What I'm about to tell you might sound unbelievable, but you have to trust me—the Vark are not our enemies. They're made up of many species, including thousands of humans. They're just like us."

"So, we knew the Rivaxians were the bad guys; we just didn't realise the Vark were the good ones," Bertie said, frustration sharp in his voice. "I'm sorry to tell you this, Micky, but the Rivaxians have murdered Sumeet."

"Oh my God, I'm so sorry about Sumeet," Micky said, grief flashing in his eyes. "He was one of the good ones—I'll miss him. But we don't have time to grieve now. We need to focus on the mission and make those murdering monsters pay."

"We've all been deceived. The Rivaxians twisted the truth to serve their own ends. We weren't just fighting against the Vark; we were fighting to uphold the Rivaxians' control. The embryos we've been hearing about aren't Rivaxian—they belong to the Vark. The Rivaxians intended to manipulate their DNA to ensure their own survival."

"Why would they lie to us?" Kerra's voice wavered with confusion.

"Because the Vark were once like us—enslaved by the Rivaxians. Their struggle isn't against us; it's for their freedom. This invasion is a desperate attempt to reclaim their home and put an end to the Rivaxians' lies and destruction."

"I can explain everything later—there's so much to tell!"

"If we stand with the Vark, we can break free from the Rivaxians' grip. But first, you must let go of the past and see the truth for what it really is."

The screen flickered, sending a ripple of unease through the room. But Micky's expression remained steady, unwavering as he locked eyes with his friends. "You must take that leap of faith. It could be our only chance."

As the Dream Agents absorbed his words, uncertainty clashed with hope. They stood at a crossroads—a pivotal moment that could alter the course of their fates.

"Wait," Tang interjected, shaking off his disbelief. "I need to speak to Cha. I want to hear it from him. He is my leader, no matter what Micky says."

Tang stepped up to the console and contacted the laboratory, his heart hammering as the screen flickered to life. Cha's image appeared, framed by the sterile walls of the lab, his expression hard and unreadable.

"My Almighty Cha," Tang began, his voice steady yet edged with anxiety. "I know we have failed you, but I must ask you something important."

Cha's brow arched, disbelief flickering across his face at Tang's audacity. "You have pushed too far, Tang, but I will allow you one question."

"Have you lied to me and the Dream Agents? Are the Vark truly our enemies, or is there more to this story?" Tang pressed, desperation creeping into his voice.

Before he could finish, Dr. Fem Dam, who had been observing in silence, suddenly erupted in frustration. "I've had enough of this nonsense!" she shouted, her voice slicing through the cockpit like a blade. She stormed to a nearby cabinet, wrenched it open, and seized a Pulsar rifle, her fury radiating from every movement.

"I have had enough of the Dream Agents—and enough of your questioning!" she screamed.

Panic surged as she levelled the weapon at the Dream Agents' transport system. "Dr. Fem Dam, no!" Tang shouted, realising too late the gravity of the situation.

She pulled the trigger. A blinding flash of energy erupted, striking the transport system dead centre. Sparks exploded as the machinery convulsed, a violent surge of power rippling through the ship—then chaos descended.

"Kerra!" Tang cried out in horror as her image flickered, twisted, and then disappeared before his eyes, her screams swallowed by the void. Buddy lunged forward, but in an instant, he too was consumed, disappearing without a trace.

"Tang!" Bertie's voice pierced through the chaos just as his image began to fade, his hand reaching out desperately. "No! Stay with us!"

Then—silence. The cockpit lay still, the console emitting nothing but the distant echoes of what once was. The weight of loss settled over Tang like a shroud. Yet, amid the void, a new disturbance shattered the stillness.

A Rivaxian ship materialised without warning, its weapons locking onto the Vark lead ship. A relentless barrage of fire erupted, each blast ripping through the darkness with devastating precision.

Inside the Vark ship, screens exploded, and consoles flickered wildly amid the chaos. Thraxon, caught off guard, was struck by debris and collapsed, slumped and wounded.

"Micky!" he gasped as Micky rushed to his side, cradling his head in his hands.

"Micky," Thraxon wheezed, his voice barely a whisper. "There is something more I need to tell you."

"This can wait—I need a medic over here now!" Micky shouted.

"Listen to me," Thraxon insisted, his voice laced with urgency. "We had an agent on Sankat 3… they infused my DNA into yours. My time is over, but you must lead the Vark to victory."

His eyes grew still as life slipped away.

As Micky laid the leader's head gently on the floor, a strange sensation washed over him. He stared at his hands and arms in disbelief as they began to fade into thin air, mirroring the leader's final moments. Before he could grasp the implications, an invisible force wrenched him away— pulling him back to Earth.

As he vanished, he made one last desperate command to Velthorian. "Send in the invasion force—we must take Rivaxia!" he shouted.

CHAPTER 22

Through the Rift

Back at NASA, alarms blared through the facility—relentless and jarring—punctuating the atmosphere with urgency and panic. Red lights flashed overhead, casting an eerie glow over the chaos unfolding within. The acrid scent of burning wires thickened the air. Technicians scrambled to stabilise malfunctioning systems, their faces a mixture of fear and determination, as they dashed about with fire extinguishers, battling the flames.

"What the hell is happening here, people?" Rory shouted, his voice cutting through the cacophony as he pushed through the frenzied crowd. His heart pounded, adrenaline coursing through his veins—he knew something monumental had just occurred.

Amidst the turmoil, a sudden hiss sliced through the clamour—the sharp release of pressurised systems. Kerra's pod illuminated from within. With a soft whir, the glass canopy retracted, and she jolted upright, gasping for air, her expression clouded with confusion.

"Kerra!" Rory exclaimed, rushing to her side. He barely had time to process her emergence when Bertie's pod hissed open nearby, followed swiftly by Buddy's. Bertie stepped out, his face mirroring Kerra's shock.

"What the hell is going on?" Rory demanded, his eyes darting between them, searching for answers.

"We've been betrayed!" Kerra cried, her voice quivering with urgency. "The Rivaxians have lied to us—they're the real danger, not the Vark!"

A stunned silence settled over the group as they struggled to process her words.

"What?" Rory stammered, glancing at Bertie and Buddy for confirmation. "That can't be true—they've been attacking us!"

Buddy sat in his pod, his head bowed, sweat rolling down his face.

"The Vark are human, Rory. They're damn humans, just like us," he said, tears streaming down his face.

"What happened out there?" Lewis asked, reaching out to Bertie. "What did they tell you?"

"It was Micky. He was on the Vark lead ship and made contact. He told us the Vark are not the enemy," Bertie explained, his voice steadying slightly as he recalled the chaos. "The Vark were once enslaved by the Rivaxians— kidnapped from Earth over thousands of years, along with countless other species across the galaxy. They fought for their freedom, and we've been drawn into their conflict without fully understanding.

"Dr. Fem Dam destroyed the transporter—that's why we were instantly sent back to Earth."

Rory's expression hardened. "How could we have been so wrong? We've been fighting against the wrong side all this time."

A wave of tension rippled through them as the weight of betrayal settled in.

"Because the Rivaxians have controlled everything," Kerra said, her frustration surfacing. "They've manipulated the narrative, concealing their true motives."

With that, Rory stepped toward Bertie and Buddy. "Are you two okay? Where is Micky?

"I'm afraid Micky's ship was hit by the Rivaxians—it took heavy damage."

"No! I can't lose him twice!" Kerra cried out.

Suddenly, Micky's pod opened, and he climbed out. Kerra ran over to him, hugging him and kissing his cheeks. "Thank God you're okay," she said.

"I'm fine," he said, looking back at her and holding her tightly, brushing her hair back. "No need to worry."

"Shit, we've been misled and missed every damn thing around us. When the hell did all this happen?" Buddy said, glancing at Bertie with a grin.

Back in the NASA lab, Micky and the Dream Agents gathered in a conference room, the air thick with urgency. Rory and Lewis, exhausted yet focused, sat at the table, their expressions grave as they awaited Micky's account of the unfolding calamity.

"Micky," Rory began, his voice steady but laced with urgency. "We need to know everything. What happened out there?"

Taking a deep breath, Micky gathered himself, the weight of his revelations pressing down on him like a heavy mantle. "The embryos we sought to protect were stolen from countless species," he explained. "The Rivaxians were using them to manipulate DNA, trying to create a super race of Rivaxians. They've been conducting experiments for centuries, taking individuals from various dimensions, including those here on Earth."

"I bet those suckers used the damn Bermuda Triangle to take people," Buddy interjected.

"Carry on, Micky," Lewis said, shaking his head at Buddy.

"The Vark were among those captured, imprisoned for generations, and used for their dark purposes."

Stunned silence fell over the room as the implications of Micky's words sank in. Lewis exchanged a troubled glance with Rory, realising the depth of the manipulation they had all suffered.

"But there's more," Micky continued, his voice growing sombre. "My DNA was further manipulated by a Vark agent on Sankat 3. I'm not just any human, or any dream agent—I am the direct descendant of the Vark leaders. When Thraxon died in my arms, as I held his head, a part of him became a part of me. My people need me. I must find a way back to them."

Rory looked at Micky, a mix of disbelief and concern flooding his expression. "That's not possible," he stated firmly. "The Rivaxians have destroyed the portal on their side. There's no clear way for us to get back to the Vark. We can't simply walk through. Besides, are we really ready for all this?"

Lewis turned to Rory. "We've come this far—there's no point stopping now."

Micky nodded, determination burning in his eyes. "My people will find a way to rebuild it on the other side. If they've managed to survive against all odds, they can do it again. I have to reach them—we have to reach them!"

"I understand the risks," Micky said, his voice steady. "But we're fighting for more than just survival. This is about truth—freeing not just the Vark, but everyone the Rivaxians have deceived. We have to rally the allies we have left, no matter the cost."

"Then we need a plan," Rory said, leaning forward, his voice firm with determination. "If we're going to help you get back, we must gather every piece of information on the remaining portals and the Vark's current status. It's time to mobilize."

"First, we review the data and gather intel," Rory instructed, his focus sharpening. "If any trace of the Rivaxians' technology or portal data remains, we'll find it. We can't let their actions dictate our fate any longer."

Micky smiled, a flicker of hope reigniting in his chest as he looked around at his friends and allies. Together, they would stand against those who had sought to divide them, ready to take control of their own destiny.

Back on Rivaxia, the atmosphere was thick with electric tension as the Vark began their invasion. Thousands of Vark warriors descended from the skies, their warships touched down with thunderous force around the main building, turning the once-peaceful landscape into a war zone. The earth quaked under the sheer force of their arrival, and the air pulsed with the weight of impending battle.

Deep within the central command, Dr. Fem Dam stood beside the Cha, her face an unreadable mask as chaos raged beyond the fortress walls. They had endured countless storms together, but this was different—this was the moment their twisted journey had been leading to.

"Come, Almighty One," she urged, her voice steady under pressure. "We need to send our team into the Xenotransference Portal. We can't appear in our current state once we arrive in the new time period, and we must blend seamlessly into our surroundings. Our mission's success depends on it."

The Cha looked back at Dr. Fem Dam, nodding in agreement as he weighed her words. "Do you truly believe this will work?"

"It worked with Jax, and we have no other choice," Dr. Fem Dam insisted, urgency colouring her tone. "If we fail to blend in, they will see us as enemies, and we will face immediate hostility. This era on their planet is infamous for its violence. We cannot afford to jeopardise the mission. The Xenotransference Portal is our best chance to spread confusion and infiltrate their ranks."

"And if it fails?" Cha pressed, crossing his arms tightly. "What happens then?"

"Then we will have wasted our final moments in a futile struggle," Dr. Fem Dam replied frankly. "But if we succeed, we will tip the balance of power entirely."

Cha hesitated for a moment, weighing their options amid the chaos of war raging outside. At last, he nodded, a steely determination setting in his eyes. "Prepare the Xenotransference Portal and ready the team for the jump. Ensure the perimeter is secured!" a general shouted.

As alarms blared and commands echoed throughout the command centre, Dr. Fem Dam caught sight of the Vark forces massing outside, steeling herself for the journey ahead. The Vark were driven by the hope of reclaiming their freedom, and the Rivaxians were about to face a long-overdue reckoning.

With the Xenotransference Portal primed, Dr. Fem Dam and Cha stepped into position, the device thrumming with energy around them. As the familiar hum enveloped them, they surrendered their identities, embracing the unknown. In mere moments, they would emerge into the chaos outside—hidden in plain sight, yet poised to shape the course of destiny.

"Let us be the shadows unseen," Cha declared, his voice firm as the transformation began. "We will be the architects of our fate—the architects of this victory."

As their forms shimmered and shifted, Dr. Fem Dam felt the tension coil within her. They stood on the precipice of a defining moment—one that would either cement their dominion over galaxies for generations or bring about their ultimate downfall.

"Now, we move forward," Cha commanded, determination radiating from him as the transformation completed, their identities hidden beneath layers of deception.

"Follow me, Cha. Step onto the platform—we're ready to jump. Hold this device; it will allow you to jump again once we reach our destination."

As they leapt, Dr. Fem Dam cast one last glance at the door just as the Vark burst in.

"Where are they?" a Vark general shouted.

In the background, a countdown echoed. Five... four... three... two... one.

With that, the lab erupted in a fiery explosion, obliterating everything inside.

Suddenly, the Rivaxians materialized at their destination— Earth, 1972. Miami.

The Cha, slipping on a pair of Ray-Ban Wayfarers, gazed up at the towering building before them, his expression puzzled.

"What do we think happens here?" he asked, turning to the other Rivaxians. His eyes landed on the sign.

"Miami Jai-Alai Fronton," he read aloud, the unfamiliar words rolling off his tongue. A flicker of uncertainty crossed his face.

"I wonder... is this where they execute people? A very strange and weak race, these humans," said the Cha, glancing around.

"We need to get a car and head over to the Miami Beach Convention Centre. And while we're at it, let's decide on our human names," Dr Fem Dam said.

"I'm on it. I'll be back with transport," said Jax.

The Rivaxians moved with practised efficiency, slipping into a waiting van. As they neared the Convention Centre, the overwhelming security presence created a suffocating atmosphere of dread. The arrival of a convoy of black cars only intensified the ominous feeling. High-ranking figures emerged, their faces alight with excitement—this was their moment.

The Cha stared at them; his expression unreadable. A faint smile played on his lips. "Excellent," he whispered, the word chilling in its implication. "He is here."

Back on Rivaxia, Velthorian strode into the main lab. Fixing his gaze on one of the Vark, he commanded, "Get that communications console working—now."

He moved to another console, its screen frozen on Earth, 1972—Miami.

"Sir, communications are ready," a soldier reported, his voice tight.

The screen in the NASA building flickered, revealing a battle-scarred Velthorian. His image shimmered, unstable. "The Rivaxians," he rasped, "have used their time machine. They're in Miami, 1972. This link… it may not hold."

Lewis's face hardened. He looked at Rory and the Dream Agents. "This is bad. This is critically bad."

Velthorian's image flickered as it faded from the screen.

"The Rivaxians wouldn't have chosen this location randomly. Investigate the events taking place at the Miami Beach Convention Centre—this is a deliberate attempt to rewrite history," he said, just as the transmission cut out.

Panic seized Micky. "Get him back! Get him back!" he shouted; his voice raw. "I need to be on Rivaxia. Now. My people need me. We have to stop them before it's too late!"